PRELUDE TO MAYHEM

MAYHEM WAVE SERIES #1

FROM THE BESTSELLING AUTHOR OF ∪NHAPPENINGS

EDWARD AUBRY

Prelude to Mayhem
Mayhem Wave Book 1

CONTENTS

FOREWORD

Welcome to the Mayhem Wave. Or perhaps welcome back. If this is your first trip into that world, you might want to skip this preamble (and the minor spoilers herein), and dive right into the tale.

This story first found life in a book called *Static Mayhem*. That novel spun an ambitious yarn of a world upturned by an apocalypse-level magical event, and the story of how it ended up in its final form is probably as long as the book itself. It picked up some attention on TheNextBigWriter.com, a workshop website, where it reached #1 on the ranking system there after hundreds of critiques trickled in over the course of a year. It won the "Strongest Start" contest on that same site for best opening chapters, granting me a cash prize and professional editing of the manuscript. A truncated version of the story advanced to semi-finalist in Amazon's first "Breakthrough Novel Award" contest. A screenwriter contacted me about the possibility of pitching the book to studios, which we discussed over expensive hamburgers on his tab in a Hollywood restaurant. At the time, I congratulated myself for the book having earned me a free lunch, surely more than most aspiring authors ever achieve.

In 2010, WorldMaker Media, the publishing arm of TheNextBigWriter, picked up *Static Mayhem* as one of their first titles when they launched. It sold respectably well for a first book from an unknown author, and accumulated some decidedly positive feedback on Amazon and Goodreads.

That original version of *Static Mayhem* was a long book. It told two stories, closely related, but distinct. The first section presents Harrison's quest to find other survivors, and serves as a sort of slow burn reveal of where his world stands. The second section tells a more significant story, as those survivors work together against an adversary who wants to end everything they have preserved and rebuilt.

If you read the first published version of *Static Mayhem*, you will recognize *Prelude to Mayhem* as a greatly expanded and fresh take on that first section. More than half of this book is new content, and what I did take from *Static Mayhem* has been reworked to give it more polish and more depth.

If you read that earlier book, you might also recognize the character of Dorothy O'Neill. While her appearances there amounted to a handful of cameos, an older version of that character is the central figure in *Mayhem's Children*, the sequel to *Static Mayhem*. Her back story is newly revealed in *Prelude to Mayhem*, and revisiting her first meeting with Harrison provided an opportunity to more fully develop the father-daughter relationship between them described in the other books.

A revised version of *Static Mayhem* is also on its way (minus the section that became this novel), including some new material, and reworked throughout. All of this leads up to the release of the brand new *Mayhem's Children* next year.

So, for those of you returning to my sandbox, I'm very happy to have you back. I think you will find I made it worth your while to start over from the beginning.

[PART 1]
INTERSUBSTANTIAL

[1]

HARRISON

Around the time his car reached ninety miles an hour, Harrison closed his eyes. The road curved in front of him, and he steered from memory. Late on a weekday afternoon, I-91 might once have been crowded with traffic, but other cars no longer posed a hazard. He pushed in the clutch and waited for the car to coast to a stop. The sense of motion diminished. By the time the speedometer dropped to zero, he had opened his eyes to survey the scraps of twisted iron and concrete rubble composing the ruins of the Holyoke Mall parking garage.

The car had come to rest on the shoulder of an exit ramp overgrown with sunflowers, a half-mile shy of the mall. Behind the parking garage, the mall remained intact, at least on the outside. Inside, though, previous expeditions revealed things had fallen into chaos. No shops, no merchandise, no restaurants—all now empty lot after empty lot. Up near the skylights, local flora ran rampant.

Trekking over the embankment and around the bend in the mall parking lot driveway, Harrison headed for his destination in one of the satellite buildings, the Barnes & Noble. On his last visit, he had picked up a copy of *The Great Gatsby*, for which he had left a ten-dollar bill on the counter to maintain the illusion of normality. He planned to leave more money today, in exchange for a copy of *Tom Sawyer*.

As he made his way to the empty parking lot, he glanced over at the vast field of sunflowers a hundred yards away. Some of the enormous blossoms had risen from their natural droopy state, and tracked his movement. The first time, the entire field, an easy fifty thousand, silently scrutinized his behavior. Now fewer than fifty tracked him, evidence of his predictability.

"Nothing to see here!" he shouted in their direction.

Several flopped back down. The rest continued to watch.

Harrison stood six feet tall, and in the time since he had lost all concern about his personal appearance, his dark brown hair had grown long and unkempt. The luxury of a good shave cycled back once every two weeks, and he was due. Clad in a short-sleeve plaid shirt unbuttoned over a Pink Floyd T-shirt and a pair of cut-off jeans, he took an odd satisfaction in the scruffy look, a badge of his having walked away from his day job forever.

At the edge of the parking lot, he stopped, his breath catching in his throat. A broad, dark lump lay in the dirt before him. "Damn. Another one," he whispered. Closer to it, he could make out the pebbly skin and the beginnings of that god-awful smell. Including this one, he had found six dead dinosaurs in ten weeks. While he had yet to see a live one, he felt neither surprise nor disappointment on that count. It made sense these displaced creatures would not live long in such a random environment. If the dinosaurs had all come into the world at the same time, when everything else changed, they must have been dying off.

He reached into his breast pocket and removed a small plastic clamshell case containing a pair of sleek, dark glasses. When he put them on, the lenses darkened in response to the sun, although no more than an hour remained until dusk. Harrison tapped the edge of the glasses. A three-dimensional display appeared in front of his face. It provided him with the date, time, temperature, relative humidity, mean barometric pressure, and wind speed. It also included a readout for wind direction, but for reasons unknown, it had only ever given him error messages. He tapped them twice more and cycled through two categories of data, until the word "infrared" appeared.

The fallen beast showed no deviation from the ambient temperature. That might mean a corpse, or it might mark it a cold-blooded animal. He tapped twice more to bring up a passive sonar display overlaid against the natural background. Birds, small rodents, and insects showed faint blips as they pinged away in their native tongues. The dinosaur showed nothing. Dead for certain, then. A live animal, and a large one at that, would give a visible heartbeat.

He removed the glasses and moved closer. From his angle, he could see only the dinosaur's back, notable for its lack of adornment. Of the ones he had seen so far, all were equipped with armor or horns, except for

4

the gigantic sauropod, which smelled too horrible for close inspection. None had been species he recognized from his boyhood dinosaur phase. As he closed in on this one, its distinguishing features became clearer. Blood drained from his face as he took them in. The powerful hind legs and short forelegs, the huge head, even the claws he observed with some degree of detachment. But, oh, God, the teeth. Like bone knives.

A predator.

Five minutes later, he sped down the road at ninety miles an hour, his eyes wide open.

[2]

DOROTHY

Engrossed in an ACT practice test, Dorothy had no sense of the coming rain until she heard the thunder. It both startled her and called her to action.

"Oh!" She looked up and out the wall of glass beside her. The parking lot in front of the Hallmark store she called home showed no signs of moisture, but the overcast sky had grown darker than it should be for this early in the evening. She took a moment to pause her timer, and climbed down from the stool she had set up behind the sales counter. Donning a yellow raincoat from a coat tree near the front door, she made her way to the stock room and out the back door, taking care to prop it open behind her.

A milk crate sat on the pavement next to the dumpster. She stepped onto it to give herself enough height to flip the lid up and over without straining. It crashed down with a satisfying *bang*. The cardboard recycling bin had sliding side doors, and she pulled those closed as well. As the second one clanged shut, the first drop hit her nose. She pulled her rain hood over her head before dashing back inside.

Dorothy washed her hands at the bathroom sink. Handling garbage can lids still felt icky. The warm water flowed over her skin, providing a sense of comfort and security. She shut off the tap before pulling a comb through her straight blonde hair, still tidy, but starting to get long enough she would normally have it cut. She took a moment to remove and polish her thick eyeglasses with a handkerchief hanging from a hook on the bathroom wall, and headed back to her test.

After pulling up her stool, she picked up the timer, which had less than two minutes left. She sighed, cleared it and set it down. A flash of lightning momentarily lit up the room, and the pit-pat of raindrops hitting the roof kicked in. A few seconds later, the rumble of thunder followed. Dorothy congratulated herself on getting the trash bins sealed in time, although she had no way of knowing if her strategy of keeping the garbage dry would truly reduce the smell, nor how long that would be effective even if it did. In truth, she managed everything in her environment by guesswork. She had only turned fourteen a month before the world as she knew it came to an abrupt halt, with herself the lone apparent survivor. Dorothy had never once gone camping before, let alone acquired any survivalist skills. And yet, here she was.

She flipped to the answer key in her ACT prep book, and began scoring the test. As an intellectual exercise, it moderately satisfied her, but it would never replace school. She needed to find a proper bookstore. The ACT book had been a lucky find in the Hallmark store break room. Some college-bound employee hoping for his or her best shot at a good school had brought it in to work on the day he or she had disappeared without warning, educational goals unfulfilled. Though sincerely grateful for the accidental gift, Dorothy would cheerfully have traded it in for a copy of *Wuthering Heights*, or a chemistry textbook. As if to drive that point home for her, she finished scoring the practice test, with a composite score of 35. One point below the absolute maximum, and better than 99.7% of students who took the test. Her third practice test, and her third 35. With only a ninth-grade education under her belt, she was measurably college ready. If only there were still colleges, she would be all set.

A packet of beef jerky sat on the counter next to her book, and she absent-mindedly dipped her hand into it, pulling out the last morsel and a silica gel pack. She tossed the silica gel and the empty packet in the trash, and popped the final scrap of jerky in her mouth, where she drew the salty, savory experience out as long as she could. The end of the jerky brought her back from fantasies of higher education into her current reality. She still had food, but provisions were running low.

Tomorrow would have to be another supply run.

The hike to Dorothy's supply station took roughly ninety minutes. She got an early start to beat the heat, but found the ground still moist from the previous night's rain, and as the sun climbed, that translated into uncomfortable humidity. She pulled one of two water bottles from her knapsack and downed the last swallow, less than halfway to her goal.

Four ribbons, each a different color, hung from a tree in front of her. She paused to inspect them. Though she could still distinguish them from each other, the sun had done a good job of bleaching them over the past month. Soon they would all fade to white, and she would need to replace them before that happened. This was the last tree to harbor all four colors. Blue and green diverged from here, splitting off in separate directions leading to clothing and medicine. Red and yellow continued along together until they split up to follow trails leading to food and, the least visited area, bowling.

Of the four locations, the one with food was, unfortunately, entirely unsuitable for human occupancy. It was a small neighborhood grocery store, with a huge section of outer wall missing, exposing it to the elements. The inside provided adequate shelter from rain, but she needed better protection from the cold, and from whatever predators might roam the Earth. Of the other three locations, Dorothy chose to settle into the Hallmark store as her home base not only for its creature comforts, but also its proximity to a hardware store in the same strip mall. Several appliances once for sale there remained connected and functional, and the decision came down to laundry. Much easier to spend the day hiking to fill a knapsack with supplies than to drag a duffle bag of dirty clothes four miles each way.

Toward the end of her journey, red and yellow parted as well. The final two-color tree landmark put her about ten minutes out from her destination. She followed the red—rapidly becoming pink—ribbons, visible every twenty yards or so, though in truth she had essentially memorized the route. The ribbons would stay however, and she would replace them with ones easier to spot. As much as she didn't need them now, at some point, the Wisconsin winter would come, and these woods would look unfamiliar under a blanket of snow.

Her quarry at last came into view. The shop stood alone in a small clearing, its outer walls ragged, as if wrenched away from whatever larger urban structure it had been part of. Dorothy approached cautiously, mindful of scavengers. On her first visit to this store, she had pulled all the fresh meats and deli foods—too spoiled for her to eat—and thrown them into the woods for any animals who took an interest. Evidently, the locals had gratefully received her gift, as none of it remained when she returned for her second supply run. She never saw whatever ate it, and without the benefit of a thank you note, she had no way of knowing what sorts of critters she had made happy, or encouraged to return for more. Seeing no animals outside, she ventured in.

Here, she did find fauna. The rainbow rats had returned, scurrying about with varying degrees of purpose. At least three dozen meandered about her, each one a different, bright and solid color, for all the world like a giant, comical box of rodent-shaped crayons.

"Git!" she shouted, waving her arms. "Go on, shoo!"

Most looked up at the noise, and then all of them bolted gracelessly into various hidey holes among the shelves of canned goods, chittering and squeaking. A lavender rat zipped right past her feet, and as she leapt backward reflexively to avoid it, it fled though a gnawed-out hole in the bottom of the office door. It took a second for the significance of that to register.

"Oh, no. No, no, no!" She scrambled to the door and threw it open, realizing a fraction of a second too late a likely sight behind it could be a multi-colored army of rats prepared to defend their base.

What greeted her was actually worse.

Dozens of boxes of breakfast cereal Dorothy had painstakingly moved and organized into this room lay strewn about the floor, covered in paper flakes that had been gnawed out of them. She picked up the closest box and shook it. A handful of loose Cheerios rattled, some exiting through a chewed hole. Boxes of pasta, bags of rice and assorted other dry goods had been similarly violated. A quick spot check confirmed a few containers had survived, but only a small fraction of what she thought until now she had safely squirreled away.

Tears rolled down her cheeks, as one by one, she pulled boxes from their resting places on the desk, the utility shelves, and in most cases, the floor. She summarily inspected each, and either threw them on the heap in the center of the room, or stacked them in the miniscule, salvageable pile.

Several packets of jerky had survived the rats' rampage, though not for their lack of effort. Bite marks scarred the still sealed packages, indicating the rats had simply chosen the path of least resistance in their gathering. She stuffed these packets into her knapsack, taking a moment to tear one open in a weak attempt to distract herself with food. As soon as she started chewing, the sobs came. She gave in to them, curling up in a ball on the floor.

[3]

CLAUDIA

On his way north, Harrison fumbled through a box of cassettes in the passenger seat. Mozart's clarinet concerto trickled from the speakers, in a manner altogether too relaxing for his frame of mind. He settled on a tape by a band named the Treadles and popped it into the deck. He had never heard of the Treadles, which stood to reason since none of the members had been born yet. In all likelihood, they never would be.

The cassette showed a copyright notice from 2031, which put it twenty-seven years into the future. The fact cassettes, already long obsolete by 2004, had somehow managed to survive as viable commercial products implied the Treadles might not even be from Harrison's future. Maybe they came from some other parallel one. In either case, a future no longer likely to happen.

In the three months since everyone Harrison had ever known and every trace of civilization flashed out of existence, he had not come across any other survivors. Random but devastatingly comprehensive destruction left behind fragments of building and roads.

Harrison initially assumed the world had come to an end. Perhaps a doomsday weapon had finally been put to use. But discoveries like future music, dinosaurs, and sentient sunflowers complicated that model. It wasn't an ending; it was a bizarre, colossal shuffling, and Harrison's life went on.

An enormous sign on the side of the road offered the irrelevant sentiment: *Welcome to Vermont*. The landmark meant he had about forty miles to go before I-91 came to an end at the bottom of a steep, tall rock. Some days, he would drive right up to the base of that cliff, stop, turn around, and head back.

With little else to keep him occupied, driving the length of I-91 had become a favorite outing as of late. Not much of it remained. It stretched from the cliff face in Vermont to a point a half mile north of where New Haven, Connecticut, used to be, where the road plunged into the ground, overgrown with brush. All the exit ramps still pulled away from the highway under helpful signs, although most of them now led to nothing, or roads that went no more than two miles in any direction, terminating in dead ends and more forest. He did luck into the occasional gas station and the music store where he acquired the Mozart and the Treadles. His greatest find, a motel with a single intact room, became his residence. Otherwise, the highway offered many exits to nowhere.

The Treadles tape did not improve his mood. He hit eject and caught the intro to "Here Comes the Sun" by the Beatles.

"Perfect." As he put the rejected tape back into its case, he began to sing along.

Thoughts of his next move troubled and eluded him. He often considered how it would feel to drive right into that Vermont rock at top speed. His newfound fear of carnivorous dinosaurs provided a point in favor of that choice. Better that than being eaten, though better eaten than not quite killed in a terrible wreck, with no hope of rescue, in a world without hospitals.

In the middle of his morbid line of thought, the song entered its bridge. He sang along at top volume, when it finally registered he should have heard nothing.

The song came from the radio.

He stopped singing. It would have been difficult to continue over the din of his heartbeat, anyway. Aware of safety concerns for the first time in a long while, he focused on the drive. A radio station existed and transmitted. Logically then, that station had an operator.

Another person had survived.

Despite what he had already seen, there must have been something left of Springfield, or maybe Hartford, that included a radio tower. The trip across the Vermont border ruled out Hartford as too far away for adequate reception. That left Springfield, which he could reach in about an hour if he turned around and hightailed it. If he decided he wanted to. Halfway through his attempt to concoct a search plan, the song ended.

"Hi," said a female voice on the radio.

He turned it up, hand trembling. "Hi." His throat tightened. Moisture nagged at the outer edges of his eyes.

"You're still listening to Claudia. That was 'Here Comes the Sun' by the Beatles. I'd like to take a moment to repeat my message for anyone listening who hasn't heard it yet. This is an open invitation for any survivors to meet me here in Chicago."

Harrison missed the next sentence, drowned out by the scream of his tires against the pavement. The seatbelt locked and bit into his chest.

"... further instructions. I'll be broadcasting until midnight, Eastern Daylight Time, for those of you still keeping track. Remember, come to Chicago. Tell your friends."

The initial chords of a Fleetwood Mac song whose title Harrison could not recall followed. He sat motionless, absorbing both the music and the new, life-changing information.

"Chicago," he said, "is a thousand miles away."

It took him about half an hour to get to the motel near the former location of Northampton, Massachusetts. The whole way there, he listened to Claudia. She presented a selection of pop songs from the sixties and seventies to which he sang along. A song still on his lips, he pulled into the motel parking lot.

Harrison killed the engine, his hand lingering on the ignition. After a brief pause, he continued the motion one click back to start the radio again. He sat there for four more songs before yielding to the desire for the comforts of home.

He emerged from his car as a plume of teal light shot straight up from a pine tree ten feet from the building. It left a vertical trail that extended several hundred feet. After a few seconds, the trail dissipated into tiny sparks that bounced around at random and fizzled out to nothing.

"Good one!" Harrison said to the tree. This light show presented itself almost every day, and the color varied.

He let himself into his motel room, chained the door, and sat on the bed. For the first time since he had moved in, he turned on the television. Finding snow on every channel, he turned it off again. "So much for that hunch." The alarm clock radio did not work, a detail he had noticed his first day, but never missed before now. For a moment, he entertained the idea of a whole night spent in his car. Then he thought about dinosaurs, and opted for the bed.

He had a beer.

He tried to sleep.

About two in the morning he rolled out of bed and turned on the light, covering his eyes against the sudden brightness. He groaned and sighed, having reached a state of paradox: too anxious to sleep, too depressed to stay awake.

And so, he planned his journey.

Using a piece of the motel stationery, he sketched a map of the continental United States. Even in his crude rendering, the distance looked imposing. One thousand miles. With the only road of any length yet discovered being the north-south I-91, he would likely conduct most of this journey on foot. The trek might be dangerous, but there was no way he would sit on his hands in a comfy motel room while whatever was left of humanity congregated in Chicago.

Preparations took the form of a bulleted list. First item: travel time. Given optimum walking conditions, he should be able to maintain a speed of four miles per hour. He budgeted himself ten walking hours per day, giving him an advancement rate of forty miles per day. Twenty-five days would add up to one thousand miles. If he left the next day, he would be there in under a month.

His crude map showed an empty swath of land where he would spend that month. Unexplored territory, everything frontier again. In an area roughly analogous to New York state, he scrawled *Here Be Dragons*.

Next bullet point: food. He had been surviving on snack foods and canned products. A month's provisions under current conditions could well amount to seventy-five cans of Spaghetti-O's and a spoon. Not doable, but he felt he could reasonably expect to continue to find ruins of stores as he explored westward.

Somewhere in there, the task of organizing finally brought his anxiety level down to the point where his exhaustion took over. His last thought before the stress of the day overtook his desire to stay awake involved gratitude no one could see how little he knew what he was doing.

JOHN

The salvageable dry goods almost all fit into fourteen plastic grocery bags. Dorothy double-bagged each one, then threaded more bags through the handles to tie them together into bundles of seven, each light enough to carry with one hand, but voluminous enough to be absurdly cumbersome.

The journey back home took several hours. Dorothy needed frequent rest stops to clear the strain on her hands. The awkward burden of carrying the bundles through the woods resulted in a few stumbles, and at one point, one of the bags tore open requiring some time to re-secure the food. In addition to those challenges, she also carried a backpack laden with canned meat, vegetables, and soups, as she did not want to make a second trip the next day to round up protein and vitamins to go with her plethora of carbohydrates. She managed the pack well enough at first, but as she forged on, it felt heavier and heavier.

By the time she finally made it to the Hallmark store, every part of her body ached. She held open the front door long enough to heave both bundles inside, then dropped the knapsack with a loud tinny rattle of cans probably being dented. After pushing the sack into the store with her foot, she stepped over it and collapsed onto the carpet. She reveled in the modest comfort of the scratchy fibers, a huge improvement over the dirt and rocks she had used for rest on the way back. After a few minutes of letting her breathing return to normal, she sat up.

Covered in sweat, she ruled sorting of groceries a lower priority than bathing and changing her clothes. She stood and made her way to a far corner of the store, where her entire wardrobe lay neatly folded and organized in plastic storage tubs. She untied and removed her hiking shoes, then pulled off her socks, and threw them in a laundry hamper. The cool air on her toes brought immediate relief from the heat of the long walk. From the tubs, she selected a T-shirt, shorts, underwear, a bra and two fresh towels, all of which she loaded into a duffel. After slipping her feet into a pair of flip-flops, she set out the front door for the hardware store.

Although proper showers were no longer an option, a functional bathtub sat on display in the plumbing department, its only drawback a lack of connection to actual plumbing, easily solved with a garden hose. Unfortunately, draining it meant pulling the plug and letting the water run out onto the floor, but given the bare concrete had at least one built-in drain, that problem was more aesthetic than pragmatic.

Focused on thoughts of warm bathwater and sweet-smelling bubble bath, she nearly missed the sight of a man sitting against the wall, past the entrance to the hardware store, slouched over, and possibly asleep.

Dorothy stopped moving. The discovery of another human being did not take her completely by surprise—she assumed others must have survived whatever wiped out almost everything and reset the world to wilderness punctuated by occasional ruins of civilization—but this did not match any of her intuitive predictions of how that would come about, and she found herself quite unprepared. Without even the benefit of a facial expression, nothing provided her with any sense of this man's intent. Dorothy's many talents did not include threat assessment.

Given the gray in his scraggly beard and his thinning hair, she estimated his age to be forty. Exactly as old as her father, though not having seen that man since he walked out six years earlier, she had no exact frame of reference for what forty looked like. His clothing looked to be in adequate repair, though as disheveled as his hair. He wore a simple plaid shirt and blue jeans, too warm for the July sun, which now beat directly onto him from its low, late-afternoon angle. As she resolved to risk an introduction, he beat her to it.

The man looked up, with a bleariness that matched his overall appearance. "Hey."

"Hello," said Dorothy.

For a few seconds they looked at each other, and then he put his head back down.

Dorothy frowned. After setting her duffle down gently on the walk, she cautiously approached him. As she grew closer, the tangy scent of body odor became more evident. He had worn out sneakers on his feet, one sole dangling down to expose a sockless toe.

"What are you doing?" she asked.

It took him a second to respond, which he did by raising his head and squinting at her. "What?"

"I said what are you doing."

"I..." he said, then apparently ran out of words. His eyes, brown and ordinary enough, opened a little wider. "What do you mean?"

Dorothy sighed. "You're obviously not carrying any food or water, you look terrible, and you couldn't even find a place to sit in the shade." She pointed to the store entrance, a few feet from where he sat. "The A/C inside there is still working, there are snacks at the register and running water, and you're napping out here trying to get a sunburn on your scalp. What," she asked again, forcing patience into her tone, "are you doing?"

He rubbed his face. Pushing himself up from the sidewalk, he nearly toppled, but managed to right himself and stand up. At his full height, he stood about half a foot taller than Dorothy's five foot five, and appeared quite a bit heavier than he looked sitting down. "There's snacks?"

"Yes." Dorothy closed her eyes and silently counted to five. "There are snacks. Candy, pop, chips, nuts. Not much, but if you're hungry, you should have something. I have more food next door."

He looked at the door, without the expected enthusiasm.

"Are you drunk?" asked Dorothy. "Or on drugs?"

He shook his head. "Just tired."

"Then why don't you come inside and sit in a real chair while I get you something to eat."

Dorothy fed her new guest a can of chili, served on a patio table in the seasonal department. He ate it without any particular urgency or enthusiasm. Whatever his story, he wasn't starving.

Dorothy sat across from him, sipping a Coke. The perspiration covering her body had dried, but with a lingering tackiness she found difficult to ignore. "You weren't surprised to see me."

He looked up at her for a moment with an unreadable expression. "Nope." He returned to his food.

"I wasn't surprised to see you either," she said. "I knew there had to be other survivors. Is that why you weren't surprised? Did you think that too?"

He nodded. "Seen one already. Maybe two." He presented this casual observation with no change of inflection.

Dorothy's heartbeat accelerated. "Maybe two?"

"Don't really want to talk about it," he said.

"Are they nearby?"

He put the spoon down on the table, and looked at Dorothy with his full attention for the first time. "What's your name?"

Dorothy considered withholding that information or lying about it. The longer she knew this person, the harder she found him to read. However, under the circumstances, she probably had nothing to lose. "Dorothy O'Neill."

"I'm John," said John. "Roth. Thank you for the food, Dorothy. You seem like a good kid, and it was real nice of you to help me out. I'm sorry I ain't too talkative, but I had a real bad week, and I just need to shake it off, okay? Soon as I finish up here and hit the can, I'll get out of your hair." He shoveled more chili into his mouth.

Dorothy's chest tightened. She stood, too quickly, hit with a momentary dizziness she forced herself to overcome while grabbing the edge of the table with both hands. "That's not how this works! You can't just leave me here alone!"

John gave no indication of being fazed by this outburst. "You seem to be all right on your own."

"That's not the point!"

He scraped the last of the chili from his bowl, and spoke through a full mouth of it. "I ain't your father. Whatever you need, seems to me you already got. Don't know what you think I have to offer, but I ain't that guy."

"And where exactly are you going when you leave?" asked Dorothy.

John swallowed. He stared at her for a moment, then wiped his mouth on his shirt sleeve and looked away.

"You don't even know, do you?" she said. "Why don't you stay for a while? At least until you have a plan."

He sat back in his chair. "Yeah. Okay. Maybe a day or two. That oughta give you enough time to figure out you don't want me around. What do you need me for anyway? You got stuff that needs fixed? I'll tell you right now, I got no desire to repopulate the species if that's where this is going."

"It's not," said Dorothy icily. "Though thank you for that reassurance."

He pushed back his chair and stood. "I'm gonna take a leak."

As he headed to the back of the store to find (she hoped) the men's room, Dorothy picked up his dirty dishes and took them to one of the functioning sinks to wash. John's desire to abandon her here was the last

17

thing she expected. She had bought herself a day, perhaps two, to convince him otherwise. But what case could she make with a person for whom it was not already intuitively obvious why he should stay?

How could she convince him it was reasonable not to want to be alone?

5

GLIMMER

Harrison slept until almost eleven o'clock the next morning.

"Dammit, dammit, dammit!" he said to his clock.

The notes he had made in the middle of the night lay scattered on the floor, but he did not move to pick them up. The crude map of his origin and destination looked back, mocking him. No way could he do this. It went right in the trash. Then he took the basket straight out to the dumpster.

With no pickups anymore, the stench from his waste disposal system had gotten unbearable. He had to hold his breath to get near it, let alone lift the dumpster's lid. Like many things about living here, that smell would get worse, and it forced him to accept his next step. Bad plan or no plan, he was Chicago bound.

Inside, he served himself a breakfast of Coke and cold chicken noodle soup, then took a shower. By noon, he set out to hit the shops. He got in his car, and as he pulled out of the motel parking lot, he turned on the radio.

Nothing.

He nudged the tuning in both directions. Faint static, but no more. Further adjustments made no difference.

"All right," he said. "That doesn't mean anything. There are plenty of reasons she could be off the air right now." The training from his brief and insignificant experience as a college DJ had been a joke, and offered him no clue as to why a station could be up one day and down the next.

Maybe she was alone. Maybe a fuse had blown. A drop of perspiration tickled his temple. He turned the radio off. Conjecture would serve no purpose. He would try again later. If Claudia never came back on, he would have to get himself to Chicago and find out what had gone wrong.

It took twenty minutes to reach the nearest working gas station with a convenience store. After filling his tank for the last time, he went inside to stock up. He grabbed one of every map available, two flashlights, and an entire display box of Slim Jims.

Harrison sat in his car for a while, eating Cheetos and counting rivers on the maps. If he could get himself across the Hudson, he wouldn't run into serious trouble until he got to the Ohio, by which time, with any luck, he would have traveling companions with brilliant ideas and resources.

"I need a compass!" He grinned in congratulation of his own ingenuity for a few seconds before the smile wilted. "Dumb shit. Of course I need a compass. I should have thought of that before I thought of food."

Back in the store, he found a dashboard compass in the automotive aisle, consisting of a ball suspended in water in a spherical container. The back of the blister pack showed how to attach the compass to a dashboard with a small square of double-sided foam tape, included. Retail value, $2.97. The peg held two, so he took them both.

Once outside, he held one of the compasses upright, and turned it left and right. The ball inside remained stationary while the container rotated around it. He rotated his body until the N faced him, and looked up. The front door of the convenience store lay directly ahead.

The early afternoon sun beat down on him, projecting his shadow ahead of him, and slightly to his left. He frowned. "That's not north. That's east." He shook the compass, turned it upside-down, and spun himself in a complete circle. None of these actions affected the instrument's resolve to describe the storefront as north. "Crap. I admire your loyalty, little guy, but I need something more objective."

Testing the second compass yielded the same results.

Harrison growled and rubbed his eyes. "Okay, I now have two piece-of-crap compasses. Can I, in any way, count them as assets?" He considered this for a few moments. "Let's try this on for size: both compasses point east. Maybe they're not broken. Maybe it's a design flaw. Maybe the factory screwed up and printed both globes in the exact same incorrect way. Maybe they work perfectly, but they're offset ninety degrees. This could still work."

He picked up both compasses, and with no better ideas for how to experiment with them, started walking.

Both interior globes rotated as he moved. Subtly at first, it became more obvious the farther he went. They continued to point parallel, though. He walked across the front of the building almost to the edge of the lot.

Both compasses still pointed to the door as their north.

Running back to the door, he inspected it for magnets. Nothing. He took one compass the whole way around the building. The ball performed a slow and graceful complete rotation. A repetition with the other compass produced the same effect. He walked away from the building and shielded himself behind the gas pump. No change.

"This makes no sense!" He shook the compass. "You make no sense! What are you doing?" He sighed. "This is no good. I need to find a real compass."

"That won't work," came a reply from behind him.

Startled, he spun around. Before him hovered a prehistoric insect, about the size of a pigeon, less than a foot from his face.

He screamed, and ran.

"Shitshitshitshitshit. Shit!" He threw himself behind his car. His heart pounding, he crouched next to the rear wheel on the passenger side. In his struggle to reconstruct his brief glimpse into a usable image, to identify what horror bug waited for him on the other side of the car, all that stood out were the giant wings. Huge, translucent, purple (maybe), in two parts like a butterfly (that can't be right) or a dragonfly. Yes. A dragonfly. A big, big dragonfly. That might be all right. They didn't bite (he thought), and they didn't have stingers (he was pretty sure). When nothing happened for a full minute, he gathered his courage and peered over the top of the trunk.

Right where the bug patiently hovered.

He screamed again. This time he didn't stop until he had gone around the back of the building and thrown himself flat against the dumpster. He scanned the yard for a big stick, but found nothing. He had gotten a better look at the bug this time, but not much. Definitely not a dragonfly, though. It didn't have the long tail, and its wings were much wider. Much more, in fact, like a butterfly, although it didn't move like one. And it wore a lab coat.

A white lab coat. In a valiant battle against every sane, reasonable thing he knew about what an insect should look like, that image managed to work its way to the surface. Once he got a grip on it, it anchored him. The image he tried to assemble in his mind's eye resolved itself. He walked around the dumpster, prepared for what he would see.

"Are you done yet?" the bug asked in a feminine voice.

21

He did not respond. The question had been posed by a woman with wide, translucent purple butterfly wings, about the size of a pigeon, wearing a white lab coat.

"Yeah. This... This is too much... right now." He shook his head. "I just... Can you...? I have to figure out this compass thing." He turned his back on her. Dead dinosaurs, sentient flowers and time-traveling cassettes were all everyday occurrences now, with weirder things surely yet to come. But at that moment, Harrison simply didn't consider himself ready for tiny butterfly scientists.

In the parking lot, he found the compass he had dropped and took it back into the store. The compass did not point to the door from inside. This complicated the problem. He wandered around the aisles until the sphere wobbled, then he walked in the direction it indicated as north. Near the refrigerators, he stopped at a spot where the sphere spun inside its housing. He backed off, and the pointer stabilized. No matter where he stood, this spot always registered as north. He returned to it and the ball resumed spinning. It continued to do so for the better part of a minute, and the compass grew warm in his hand. One step back again, and it halted. He inspected the spot on the floor where the compass went haywire, but found nothing remarkable about it. On his way back out the door, he collected two magnets he found stuck to one of the cash registers.

When he got outside, the small woman still hovered there. He nodded politely to her and went to his car, where he resumed his experiment with the compasses, this time using the magnets to try to drag the pointer off center.

"That won't work, either," she said.

Harrison hummed as he worked.

She flitted over to his car and landed on the hood. "Aren't you at all curious why it won't work?" She offered him a provocative shrug, and sat down cross legged.

"Obviously I am curious why it won't work." He rubbed his face, his façade of control cracking. "What are you even supposed to be? The Apocalypse Fairy?"

She gasped, threw her hands over her face, and rocked for a moment. Standing up, she shouted, "Fuck you!" Then she shot away. A thick trail of red sparks remained behind her. After a few seconds it faded and vanished.

Harrison stood still, frozen in his confusion. "Well... I didn't expect *that.*"

Harrison stowed all the supplies he foraged from the store in his car, and stayed for half an hour to study the maps. Despite this stalling, she did not return.

Tired of waiting, he got out to stretch his legs and went for a walk around the building. He found her perched on the dumpster, sulking.

"Why won't it work?" he asked.

She didn't look up. "Leave me alone."

"What's the matter?"

"You are!" she cried. "Ugh! I can't believe you called me that!"

"I was joking," he said.

She leapt up, and zipped straight to his face, hovering inches from his nose. A slight tingle emanated from her, like the static buildup on a TV screen. She threw her arms out, as if to give him a good view.

"Pick!" she shouted.

He blinked.

"See?" she asked.

He shrugged. "No?"

"Aaauugh!" she screamed, and flew off.

This time, he did not wait. He walked the rest of the way around the building. She paced about the hood of his car, and when he got there, she stopped, facing him, arms crossed.

"Pick. See," she said.

He shrugged again and shook his head.

"Ugh! I'm a pixie, you asshole!"

"Oh. I can see that."

"You called me a faerie." She renewed her sulking.

"There's a difference?"

She beckoned him closer. "Faeries…" She forced a calm voice. "Are. Ugly."

"Ah," he said. "And pixies are…?"

She opened her arms again and gave a slight curtsey. "Beautiful?" She waited a beat. "See?"

"Indeed." Now that he accepted the reality of her, he did find her striking. Her features were soft, and her eyes large, relatively speaking, and inviting. Her silver hair, which at first he had taken to be blonde, changed color subtly as she moved, like a tiger's eye stone or polished wood. "I have questions."

"Fire away!" She sat on the hood of his car.

"What's with the lab coat?"

"Oh!" She jumped back up. "Doctor Barbie! Do you like it?" She walked up his hood in her bare feet toward the windshield like a model on a runway, then turned around and strutted back down to the edge. "Check this out!" She pulled a pink plastic stethoscope from under the coat and made a show of plugging it into her ears and listening to her own chest. She inhaled with a loud hiss, then blew.

"Where did you get it?" he asked.

"There's a K-Mart back, um…" She pointed over Harrison's shoulder. "That way. Maybe fifty miles from here. It's underground, mostly, but the toy department's easy enough to get to." She sat again. "I figured I should put together a wardrobe before I introduced myself. Didn't want to make a bad first impression."

"What do you normally wear?"

She feigned an exaggerated look of embarrassment.

"Oh. Right. Um…" His awkwardness was not feigned.

"Don't worry about it." She smiled again.

"Why won't it work?"

"Aaaah. Now we return to the point." She leaned forward. An air of conspiracy filled her voice, as though she were inviting him to the inner circle and everything would now be different. "It won't work, because compasses don't point north anymore."

"They point to this convenience store?" he asked, still not quite there.

She shook her head, and her face took on a shadowy quality. "They point…" Her tone darkened, almost a whisper. "…to civilization."

He frowned. "Why?"

"Don't know." She grinned again. "Maybe they miss it." She hopped up and fluttered to eye level. "I'm coming."

"Coming?"

"To Chicago, silly. I want to see it. Not to mention that you'll never make it all by yourself. Don't take this the wrong way, Harry, you're plucky and all, but we both know you're already lost."

"I am not lost. I know exactly where I'm going."

She put her hands on her hips and stared down her tiny nose at him.

"Okay, I know approximately where I'm going. Wait a minute. You called me Harry."

"Are you not a Harry?"

"How do you know who I am?"

"I've been stalking you," she said

"How long?" he asked, somewhere between nervous and outraged.

"The whole time." She giggled. "And you are definitely lost."

Harrison shook his head. "What do I call you?"

"Glimmer!"

He laughed. "Is Glimmer your name? Or is it a job title?"

She rolled her eyes and spoke as if to a child. "It's a pixie name, doofus."

[6]

PROJECT

With the tub out in the open leaving privacy out of the question, Dorothy skipped her bath. While John explored the hardware store, possibly looking for useful tools to take with him, and possibly to keep himself busy while he bided his time before leaving her, she retreated to the bathroom in the back of the Hallmark store, and did the best she could with a washcloth and warm water from the sink. If she could persuade him to stay, it might be possible to build a modesty screen around the bathtub area. He might even have sufficient handyman skills to hook up proper plumbing to allow for real showers. Dorothy had no idea how complicated the task, nor whether an average man could perform it. One thing at a time.

Satisfied her skin and hair were at least adequately clean, she dried off and dressed in the fresh clothes she had picked out. She emerged from the bathroom with a towel wrapped around her head and carried the other towel and dirty clothes out to the hamper.

When she came into the sales floor from the back room, she found John at the greeting card display, flipping through them. She allowed herself a quick, hopeful smile. After dropping her wad of clothes into the hamper by her storage tubs, she strolled over to him. "Can I help you find something?"

"Oh." He faced her. "Hey." For a moment, she thought another man had wandered into the store. The long scraggly beard he had worn earlier had been shorn down to stubble. Uneven, but certainly tidier.

"You cut your beard off," she said.

"Yeah."

"It... looks nice."

"Oh. Thanks. Yeah, I wanted to shave it, but I couldn't find a razor." He held up a pair of scissors.

"I have razors in the back," said Dorothy. "Would you like me to get you one?"

He frowned. "That's... I don't want to use a girl razor."

"It's a blade on a stick. You won't know the difference."

"Yeah... I don't..."

Dorothy sighed and shook her head. "There's a pharmacy about an hour's hike from here." She glanced out the front window. The descending sun indicated far less than two hours of daylight left. "We can head out there tomorrow if you want to get some boy razors."

He hesitated. "Yeah, maybe."

Dorothy gave him a moment to follow up on that thought. He did nothing apart from looking at the scissors again.

"So," she prompted, "did you find anything good over there?"

"Yeah. Lots of stuff. Um..." He paused again.

"Yes?"

"Um, can I ask you to do something for me?"

An unexpected window of opportunity to win him over, to be sure. She jumped through it. "Sure. What is it?"

"I wanna... I don't like having this much hair. I was gonna try to cut it myself, but I'm afraid I'll screw it up. Is that something you can do? Cut hair?"

She smiled. "I think I can probably do that. Couldn't be any worse than you trying to do it yourself."

He frowned. "If it's too much trouble..."

"No, it's fine." She held out her hand for the scissors. "I haven't done this before if that's what you're asking, but I will do my best. Turn around. Let me see."

As he slowly spun in a circle, she took in what she had to work with. Mostly bald on top, he did have some hair in back, thick, curly, and obviously matted from weeks of no care.

"How short do you want it?" she asked.

"I don't know," he said. "Shorter than it is."

Dorothy nodded. "All right. Don't take this the wrong way, but I think we should wash it before we cut it."

"Don't take it the wrong way? You're saying it's dirty. What other way can I take it?"

"I'm just trying to be polite," she said. "Come on."

27

She led him back to the hardware store, where she instructed him to grab a plastic patio chair and bring it to the bathtub. She pushed the back of the chair up to the tub.

"Sit," she said. He did. "Don't move. I'll be right back."

A green garden hose lay draped over the edge of the tub. She followed it all the way to the back room where it connected to the spigot of a utility sink. She turned both the hot and cold taps to positions she knew from experience yielded comfortably warm water, and watched the hose writhe as it filled. Water splashed out of the hose and into the basin. Once she caught up to it, she held her hand under it for about half a minute until she ruled it acceptable.

"Lean back."

He tipped his head backward, and she ran water over it. His hair went from being clumpy to clumpy and wet. When she finished soaking, she set aside the hose and picked up a bottle of shampoo from the floor. She squirted a generous amount into her hand and went to work. As the eldest of three daughters growing up in a single-parent household, this was not her first time washing someone's hair. Massaging the shampoo into John's scalp, she encountered coarse grit. She did her best to balance the pressure; too light and he wouldn't get clean, too heavy and she would scratch him like sandpaper.

She managed to avoid making eye contact while she worked, and he did not move or make any sounds, so she could not gauge his reaction. For Dorothy's part, her awareness of John as the first other human being she had physically touched in nearly two months was keen. She tried not to think about it too much, but part of her found the contact refreshing. It would have been nice to do this with someone her age, preferably cute, but even with John she found it rewarding to slip into the role of big sister again. She missed taking care of people.

She hosed the shampoo out of his hair. Light brown water ran off his head into the tub. Dorothy reapplied shampoo without explanation, and the second time he rinsed clean. She then applied a generous amount of conditioner, which she painstakingly distributed with a pink detangler comb. Knots abounded, but she would cut them off soon enough anyway.

Finally, after letting it sit for the requisite three minutes, she rinsed out the conditioner, rubbed John's head down with a towel, and went to turn the spigot off. When she came back, she found him scrubbing the towel vigorously over his hair, no doubt retangling some of the knots she had worked so delicately to remove. While she tried to decide whether to scold him, he asked a question.

"Do you use this tub? Take baths?"

"Yes," she said. "You may have noticed I am mostly clean."

"How do you drain it?" He looked over the area around her bath setup. The boxy outer surface of the tub rested flush with the floor, impossible to see beneath.

"I pull the plug and run," she said. "When we're done here, I'll show you."

He gave her a quizzical look. "You just dump it on the floor?"

"It's not like I have a choice."

He shook his head. "That's no good. We need to hook this up to a pipe. I might not be able to connect it to a sewer, but I can probably rig it so it runs out the back door."

She shrugged, holding back a smile. "If you think you can do it, that would be great."

"Maybe," he said. "I'll have to get in there and see what it looks like. Never done any major plumbing before, but I fixed a kitchen sink once."

"Maybe that's the same," said Dorothy.

John frowned. "Maybe."

"Let's do your hair." Dorothy beckoned him away from the tub and had him bring the chair. She stood behind him as he sat, and teased sections of hair up with a comb to snip them off, making up the process as she went along. "So, who were the other people you met?"

After a slight pause, John said, "I met a guy named Rob a couple days after the thing happened. We didn't get along."

Dorothy carefully teased up some more hair and snipped. "What happened to him?"

"Don't know. Don't care. Didn't kill him if that's what you're asking."

"It's not." It was. Accepting that weak reassurance, she pressed on. "What about the other one? You said there were two."

This time he left a more profound pause. "I don't think she was a person."

Dorothy waited a beat for elaboration, and got none. "What do you mean?"

"Have you seen anything weird lately? I mean, you know, apart from the big thing. You find any weird gadgets that shouldn't exist, or stuff that doesn't seem natural?"

Too many ways to answer that question. Dorothy went with her best guess as to his intent with it. "There are these rats. They look like normal rats, except every single one of them has been dyed a different color. But I don't think anyone actually dyed them. I think that's just how they are. Is that what you mean?"

"Yeah," said John. "Something like that."

They both let that exchange sit for a bit.

"Why don't you think she was a person?" Dorothy finally asked.

"She turned into a wolf."

Dorothy finished the haircut in silence.

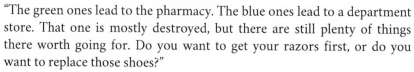

"The green ones lead to the pharmacy. The blue ones lead to a department store. That one is mostly destroyed, but there are still plenty of things there worth going for. Do you want to get your razors first, or do you want to replace those shoes?"

John brushed the colored ribbons on the first tree with his fingers. "Where does red go?"

"That's food. Maybe a thousand cans of it. I've been bringing it back here a few at a time."

"What about yellow?" he asked.

"That's a bowling alley. I've only been there twice. I don't think it has anything we need, but maybe you can help me check it more closely."

He directed his gaze off into the woods. "How far are the drug store and the clothing store from each other?"

"I'm not really sure. Everything is marked back to this place, not to each other. The clothing store is the closest to here, but we'll have to come almost the whole way back here first if you want to find the pharmacy too. I've done it in one day before. It's a lot of walking."

John rubbed his face. "Let's do razors first."

Dorothy responded with a blank stare.

"It's itchy," he said.

Dorothy walked over to a young sapling and pulled down on one of the lower branches. She folded it against the tree, splitting the bark, then worked at it until she could peel the green stick away from the trunk. She walked over to John, picking leaves off it. Then, looking him straight in the eye, she poked the stick into the hole in his sneaker.

"Ow! Jesus!" He bent down and massaged his toe through the hole. "What the hell?"

"So," said Dorothy with a cheerful lilt. "Do you want to get your razors first, or do you want to replace those shoes?"

"Shoes! I get it! You could have just said so in the first place!"

"I wanted it to be your idea." She set out along the blue ribbon trail.

They reached the department store in a little more than an hour. The roof had caved in, but Dorothy led John through the tunnel she had found and partially excavated. Even in its demolished state, the store had

30

enough functioning lights to make shopping manageable. John found a pair of hiking boots his size, changed into a new set of clothes in the dressing room, and filled two huge bags with fresh shirts, pants, briefs and socks.

From there, they backtracked to the four-color tree, left John's loot at its foot, and set out for the pharmacy. In addition to his razors, John loaded up on other supplies, including—thankfully—deodorant and toothpaste.

They returned at midafternoon. Dorothy put together a late lunch of tuna salad while John went to the bathroom to shave. It took longer than she expected. He finally emerged, with a face smooth and pale, if a little patchy in places, and bleeding in others. In the new clothes, and with some of the smell covered up, he was definitely coming along. Without the beard to hide his face, his double chin presented itself as considerably more pronounced. The overall effect was pudgy and boyish.

He pulled up a seat at the patio table and dug into his bowl of tuna. "I wanna take a look at that tub today. See what I can rig up for you."

"That would be great," said Dorothy.

This was working out nicely.

7

DEPARTURE

R ise and shine!"
Harrison woke to the pokey sensation of tiny feet on his chest. He opened his eyes.

Glimmer smiled at him. She looked different. In place of the lab coat, a military dress uniform gave her an unexpected air of authority. After several sleepy blinks, Harrison downgraded his initial assessment to pseudo-military. She wore a blue jacket whose wide collar contrasted her narrow skirt. A short, cylindrical hat and a pair of white gloves completed the look. The pinned-up hair exposed her pointed ears. She held a miniature clipboard and wore a bird-like metallic pin.

"So you're a stewardess now?" he grumbled.

She kicked him in the nose. It hurt, like a shock from a doorknob. "Excuse me, Mr. Troglodyte. I am a flight attendant."

She hopped down to his pillow as he sat up. He rubbed his nose, then his whole face, before inspecting her feet to see what pointy, plastic thing had poked—zapped?—him. She wiggled her bare toes.

"Doesn't that outfit come with shoes?" he asked.

She pursed her lips. "Have you ever seen Barbie shoes?"

"No, actually, I don't believe I have."

"Well, they're not designed for real feet."

He toyed with the idea of debating whether her feet counted as "real." As he looked more closely at her jacket, a bizarre nuance dawned on him. It so confused him he couldn't figure why he hadn't seen it yesterday, with the lab coat. "How do you..." He paused, pointing over his own shoulder with a thumb. "Uh, how do you get your wings...?"

After a few seconds, she replied, deadpan. "What wings?"

He waited a bit more than a couple seconds, long enough to evaluate pressing the point. "Never mind."

≡≡≡

That morning they hit the road. Harrison's provisions consisted of beef jerky and granola bars, along with four plastic bottles of water, which he would refill at streams or convenient spigots along the way. He had crammed two flashlights, two compasses, and many maps into an Adidas knapsack, along with a Walkman radio. Batteries, like water, would be available from numerous sources, or so he planned. These preparations, and a fair amount of luck, would see him through his thousand-mile hike.

The longest stretch of westbound road he had yet discovered consisted of a section of Route 2, which intersected I-91 in Greenfield, close to the Vermont border. The drive to Greenfield took the better part of an hour. The pixie rode along beside him.

Harrison tried the radio and for the second day in a row found nothing. He dismissed the idea Claudia's broadcast had been a dream, not yet ready to embrace a world where pixies turned up real and human voices on a radio were imaginary.

"Tell me a story," Glimmer held a dime in both hands, flipping it over and rotating it like a wheel.

He turned off the radio. "What kind of story?"

She shrugged. "Tell me a story that has you in it."

He thought for a moment, trying to remember any of his favorite anecdotes, but the only story in his head right then was one he had never told before.

"I was on my way to work. Sunday morning, no traffic. I was going to be early for once. I stopped at a traffic light, and that's when it hit." He paused, remembering the sensations. "At first, I felt like I was upside down. Then I saw all the cars waiting at the light in front of me, going up like smoke. Just dissolving into thin air. In a sort of wispy, swirly way. The ones further ahead went up first, and I had just enough time to realize I was next. Suddenly I was on the ground, no car. The cars behind me all disappeared, but none of the other drivers survived. The road was gone. The stoplights, the buildings, all gone. The ground was just bare dirt. Then the trees came up. I heard the roar before I saw them. They just tore straight up out of the ground in a huge wave.

33

The tree line came right up to me in seconds. I was sure it would kill me, but the trees went around me and kept going. Then it was over, and I was in a really, really big forest. I walked for a few hours until I found a Laundromat, standing out there, all by itself, in the middle of the woods. It was shelter, and it had a bunch of unlocked snack machines, so I lived there for a while."

Spoken out loud for the first time, the sound of the story gave it a power and a reality for which he was not prepared. He looked at Glimmer. She wore a curious expression. "What did you see that day?" he asked.

She shook her head in a rapid shiver. "Not a whole lot. Big flash. Everything changed. Did you steal this car?"

For the second or third time, he had asked her a reasonable question, only to have her deflect it. If she wanted him to trust her, she was off to a poor start. "I salvaged it."

"Hmm." She inspected the upholstery. "It's nice."

"I guess." He had owned several cars in his life and had driven them all to scrap. After only four weeks of his ownership, this current ride already showed signs of wear.

"Somebody just up and left the keys in it, did they?"

"Didn't need keys. It wasn't locked when I found it, and the ignition lock's busted." He held up his right hand to show her the absence of a key in the ignition, but when he looked down to gauge her response, she was playing with the ashtray. He scowled and changed the subject. "Why aren't you all high and squeaky?"

"I beg your pardon?"

"Your voice," he said. "I've been thinking about it. Your vocal cords have got to be microscopic, but you sound like a normal person."

"Oh, um…" She tapped the side of her head. "It's not really a 'voice.' It's kind of complicated. Here, watch." She pinched both of her lips between her thumbs and forefingers, then sang, "Twinkle, Twinkle, Little Star," without opening her mouth. He tried to watch her do this and keep an eye on the road. The complete absence of any other traffic facilitated this. She finished her song and released her mouth. "Get it?"

"Not even a little bit." He had finally stumbled on a question she would answer in detail, but he had no way to determine what made this question different, and its answer made no sense. "Ventriloquism?"

She shook her head. "I'm not really talking. I'm stimulating your inner ear directly, so you hear me, even though I'm not making any sounds. If we had a microphone, I could show you. I only do the moving-my-lips thing because otherwise it creeps people out."

"What? You're in my head? Like telepathy?"

She rolled her eyes. "No. Like magic."

"Oh. Right. Can you?" he asked.

"Can I what?"

"Can you talk?"

"Oh!" she said. "Uh, yes. Sort of."

He waited. She climbed up on the armrest of the passenger side door and stared out the window. After a moment, she hummed a little tune.

"I meant," he said, "can you talk right now?"

She stopped humming. "See, the thing is, I don't use my voice much. And I'm a little self-conscious about it."

"I promise I won't laugh."

The better part of a minute went by. Finally, she cleared her throat.

"To be, or not to be," she said, and this time she sounded precisely the way he expected her to sound: like a chipmunk. "That is the question. Whether 'tis nobler in the mind to suffer the slings and arrows of out—" She made a choking noise and coughed, then slumped down on the seat, and hid her face in her arms.

Harrison, dumbstruck, felt foolish and cruel. After too much time, he said, "I just wanted to hear what you really sound like."

"Well," she said without looking up, in the fuller, alto voice she had explained was not a true voice. "I guess you got what you wanted." She climbed down to the floor and crawled under the seat, where she spent the rest of the drive.

Harrison got off the interstate at Greenfield. The exit led to a traffic circle, which took him to Route 2 West. He drove it all the way to the end, a little less than ten miles, where the road led straight into a dense cluster of trees and became unnavigable.

He parked the car and took a moment to roll down all the windows. Glimmer might or might not have any intention of coming out from under the seat, but Harrison would not be responsible for cooking her to death in an unventilated car. He got out and looked westward. Like much of the rest of the world—or at least the rest of New England—forest lay before him. The ground appeared level. Hopefully it would stay that way for a while. He had not found anywhere to salvage a decent pair of hiking boots, and therefore wore the only pair of shoes he had: sneakers. As long as he didn't have to climb on rough stones or step in anything wet, they would hold out for at least a few weeks.

He pulled one of the dashboard compasses out of his backpack. It wobbled in indecision, then pointed back to his car, the closest sign of civilization. If his luck held, he could use the device to find buildings, roads, maybe even another car or a place to spend the night.

He looked back at the car. This would be a great moment to ask the pixie how she had found the K-Mart, if he could figure out how to talk to her without understanding less than when he started. It would be helpful for her to be his scout, but he had a feeling whatever she had to offer would be on her own whimsical terms, or not at all.

He put the compass back in the knapsack, pulled out a granola bar, unwrapped it, and put the empty wrapper back in the bag. Like many other behaviors, his aversion to littering gave him focus in an unfocused environment.

He ate with slow care, taking the time to taste the sweetness, savor the chewiness, and feel the crunchiness. His mouth rejoiced at the pleasure of a chocolate chip as it melted, dissolved on his tongue, smeared itself across his taste buds, and infused them with its unique bittersweet flavor. This moment might well be the last pure, sensual opportunity he would have until he made it to Chicago, and he refused to waste it. There would be more granola bars, but by the time he ate the next one, he would be tired and filthy, and it would not be the same.

He flicked the last bit of oat out from between his teeth with his tongue. It took several tries, and he relished the relief and the freedom of success. He called back to the car. "This is it! I'm going!" He waited. Nothing happened. "Right now!" Still nothing. He turned and walked, trying not to appear reluctant. When he reached the edge of the forest, a green, sparkly streak shot over his shoulder and out of sight into the trees. The streak hung in midair, faded to yellow, then rained out as sparks and vanished. He nodded. "All right, then. Here we go."

His walk began pleasantly enough with inviting, even terrain. It gave the impression of not being a real forest at all, but a set or a soundstage dressed up to look like nature without any of the pesky chaos. Upon the soft, dry ground, his sneakers, which he had assumed would become a liability, now felt like the wisest choice. The air was unusually dry for mid-August, and the forest canopy provided excellent shade. Wind swept the top of the trees with a comforting sound. What little breeze filtered through to him carried the improbable scent of fresh-mown grass, along with something floral. Every now and then, he caught sight of a pale glow in the distance ahead. Its color varied, but reassured him he still had company.

From time to time, he took out the compass to check it and see if it had anything new to tell him. So far, all it did was point behind him, presumably at the car. He took comfort in the optimistic fantasy he was already making good time. The world had rolled out a carpet for him, offering gracious bows as he passed. Or perhaps it simply lured him. Perhaps it had granted him absurd hope and an unwarranted presumption of security. The incredible events of the last couple days drove him to reexamine the new state of the Earth. It started to feel less like something that had happened and more like something that had been done. A seed germinated in the dark places of his mind, growing into a suspicion

At last, he came to the inevitable hill.

He felt a slight but noticeable incline initially, but soon understood the honeymoon had ended. The ground grew not only steeper, but more textured. He encountered more rocks, and it got harder to walk around them. Eventually, he needed to climb to keep moving. At the leading edge of fatigue, he stopped and sat on a rock. As he pondered whether to keep going or change course, he ate a piece of beef jerky and drank the entire contents of one bottle of water. From where he sat, he could not estimate the width of the hill, and whether it would make more sense to soldier on or try to walk around it.

Standing, he shouted, "Glimmer!"

No response.

"Nice work," he said in a soft voice. "First remotely viable companion you find, and how long did it take you?" He looked around again, this time with more care, squinting, looking for anything not forest colored. A flash of blue presented itself a short way farther up the hill. He climbed for it. A tiny blue jacket, pseudo-military style, hung from a twig. He plucked it off and inspected the back. No wing slits. "Damn, but that's weird."

Up he went. If she would speak to him, he would ask her to scout ahead, though it appeared she was already doing so. He took out the compass for a second opinion, and for the first time it encouraged him to go forward. "Really? There's something up there?" He climbed with new energy.

At the top of the hill, the world shifted again. The incline ended on a grassy plateau, maybe fifty feet wide, and on the other side, descended to a vast, sprawling plain. Like the crest where he stood, this plain lay covered with grass, suburban-lawn quality: lush, thick, deep green, with nary a clover or dandelion to be found. And vast, possibly hundreds of square miles. At the horizon, the plain terminated in brush and more forest. At the bottom of the hill, and a considerable distance off, lay a baseball diamond.

He took off his shoes.

Down the hill he went. Accepting the world's continuing invitation and hospitality, he made for the only observable contour in the land, the baseball field. As he approached it, he pulled out the compass and confirmed it counted as civilization. Details became clearer as he got closer. In addition to the fence behind home plate, the benches in place of dugouts, and the bases themselves, he discovered an artifact, something without question man-made: a drinking fountain. The pixie stood on it, trying to make it work. She had lost the little hat, the jacket, and the gloves, but still wore the blouse and skirt.

"Hey," he said.

"Hey. Give me a hand with this, would you? My hands are too small to work the button."

He stepped up and placed his thumb squarely on the smooth, round knob. A double column of water shot forth in an arching, textured stream.

Glimmer hovered above it, dipped her face into it several times, then sighed with satisfaction. "Ah! That hits the spot."

Harrison drank as well, and indeed it did hit the spot. The cold water had a mild, metallic aftertaste, the exact same flavor he had always complained about in high school. Drinking triggered a nostalgia to which he had thought himself immune. He gulped, relishing the bitter flavor of his childhood.

"So…" He filled his empty bottle. "Now where to?"

She pointed to a dirt path leading away from the ball field, too narrow for him to have recognized it from the hilltop. It led straight to the overgrowth on the horizon. "Somebody wants you to go that way."

"Yup," he said, "and that somebody is me."

───

The dirt trail eventually led into the brush, at which point it became a gravel path, and after that, a paved walkway. The walkway led to a driveway, which led to half a house.

They stood outside what once must have been a mansion. One side of it appeared to be sliced clean off, exposing half-rooms containing partial furniture.

Propriety drove Harrison to the front door. He rang the bell, out of more than habit. He didn't want to risk or presume anything. Nevertheless, when no one answered, he tried the front door. Unlocked, as expected. Nothing was locked anymore.

"Is this your house now?" Glimmer asked. "Salvage again?"

Harrison shook his head. "Homestead Act."

Nonperishable food items lined the shelves of a well-stocked pantry. The electric and water still worked. He made himself a spaghetti dinner and devoured it. They found a giant television and an admirable library of movies. The home entertainment center and the collection of DVDs established this house hailed from his own time, or close to it. He and Glimmer watched *The Shawshank Redemption*, and they talked about it until after midnight.

On his room-to-room quest for the most comfortable bed (before he settled on the gorgeous king-sized one in the master bedroom), he voiced a concern. "This should be harder."

Glimmer kissed him on the cheek with a tiny, electric shock. "It will be," she whispered. "Go to sleep."

8

PLANS

The ball made it almost three-quarters of the way down the alley before tipping over into the gutter. It drifted lazily past seven pins still standing, no threat to them whatsoever, and disappeared from view. The sweeper dropped down to clear the remaining pins, and seconds later, the pinsetter planted a fresh set of ten in formation.

A 3 appeared in John's fourth frame on the automatic scoreboard.

"Definitely rusty," he said, flopping down onto the bench.

"I'm sure it will come back to you," said Dorothy. This trip had been her idea. In the week since John arrived at her strip mall home, he had managed to jury rig a drainage pipe from the tub that dumped water onto a completely different part of the hardware store floor, and little else. As the days wore on, his mood—already dour enough the day she met him—declined considerably. She suggested exploring the bowling alley primarily as an excuse to give him a chance to succeed at something, but as with his plumbing skills, Dorothy had overestimated his sporting prowess.

She picked up a marbled purple ball and felt its twelve-pound heft with both hands. Her feet constrained in the unfamiliar rental shoes, she took her few steps forward, and when she released the ball, it hit with an unexpectedly loud *thump*. It meandered down the alley in a straight line, and collided with the pins dead center, toppling most of them. The pinsetter descended to grasp the two remaining pins and hold them steady while the others were swept away.

"Oh! Seven ten split! Good luck with that." He grinned at her with new enthusiasm, and a completely unwarranted arrogance.

Dorothy did not wait for her ball to return. She pulled the nearest one off the rack and made her best effort to send it to one of the pins. It dropped into the gutter less than halfway to its target.

"Ha! Tough break." He laughed, and stood, grabbing a ball.

"Maybe you could wait until you are ahead before you start gloating," said Dorothy.

John did not respond, and when she turned to look at him, he was not smiling, and would not make eye contact. Inwardly, Dorothy groaned. Her plan of making John feel competent had so far backfired spectacularly, and she was part of the problem. She returned to the bench and picked at the plate of French fries waiting there. They were still warm, but too soft. John had insisted on starting up the fryer in the snack bar and had succeeded in not injuring himself or burning the building down, which would have to be sufficient.

John's next ball scored a strike.

"Thank God," muttered Dorothy.

He returned to the bench, still scowling and not looking at her.

"Now you can gloat," she said.

His face relaxed a bit.

Dorothy ate another French fry. "We should talk about winter."

John frowned, finally looking at her. "It's August."

"It won't always be August. We need to make sure we have enough food."

"Wait, are you saying that store is going to run out of food before winter?"

"I don't think so," she said. "But we should move what's there before it snows. Take it all back to where we live."

He made a sour face. "That's going to be a lot of work."

"Do I need to tell you the story of the ant and the grasshopper?"

"The what?"

She shook her head. "Never mind."

They got an early start the next morning on the first of what she expected to be many food runs over the next few days.

"Should we bring a shopping cart?" John eyed the rack full of them outside the hardware store entrance.

"I tried that once," said Dorothy. "It's still out there somewhere, at the bottom of a hill. The packs are easier. Trust me."

Dorothy took the lead. She knew the trail from memory, but John still needed her guidance, or the ribbons. He followed in silence, and after five minutes or so had fallen considerably behind. Dorothy looked back occasionally to see if he was still there, but found no compelling reason to wait up for him.

Forty minutes into their hike, Dorothy came upon her favorite sitting rock and took a break. As she waited for John, she took a sip from her water bottle, and idly tossed a few small stones and twigs into a nearby brook.

Her lead on John had grown substantial by that point, and while still visible to her, it took him some time to catch up. From a distance, it looked like he was holding some object and inspecting it, but by the time he arrived at Dorothy's rock, his hands were empty.

"Are you having trouble keeping up?" she asked.

He shrugged. "You're moving pretty fast."

"But your legs are longer," she countered.

He looked behind himself, then glanced at the trail ahead of them. "Maybe I'm just trying to save my energy. We're going to do a lot of these, right?"

Dorothy couldn't argue with that. Besides, she wasn't particularly concerned with how closely John followed her. As long as he carried his fair share of the canned goods back to their home base, he could do it as slowly as he liked.

After a few minutes, she got up again and set off without comment. John followed.

Dorothy arrived at the store well ahead of John. She paused briefly to wait outside for him, but with the amount of work ahead of them, she could not afford to let him hold her back from it. Entering through the gaping hole in the wall, she found everything as she had left it. Fewer rats this time, doubtless as a result of her taking their only sources of accessible foods. They fled from her, into the shadows.

A quick survey of cans confirmed her rough estimate of one thousand. These would take priority over goods in glass jars or plastic bottles. The glass had been difficult for her to transport, given the added weight and the occasional breakage. Plastic bottles were easy to carry, but generally contained pop, juice, or salad dressing, all non-essential.

She knew from experience she could average between twenty and thirty cans in her knapsack. Even assuming John could carry more—and she was well past the point of assuming John had any capabilities whatsoever—they were still looking at about fifteen trips, possibly more. If they planned to do at least one run per day, they would be finished in close to two weeks. A plethora of utility shelves sat in the hardware store where they could set up a proper pantry, then inventory and ration everything.

In the interest of playing it safe, Dorothy decided to start with transporting foods she preferred. She was in the process of separating items into categories of delicious and disgusting when John finally found his way inside.

"Hey. Wow. This place is a wreck." He pulled a can of chocolate frosting off a shelf and turned it over to look at the back. "What's the plan?"

"Fill your backpack with as much as you can. Take it home. Repeat." Dorothy set aside several cans of peas for a later trip.

"Gotcha." John pulled off his knapsack, unzipped it, and dropped the can of frosting inside.

Dorothy winced and debated giving him more specific instructions. "I'm sorting right now. The first few trips I want to bring only essentials. That way if we can't make it back for some reason, we won't leave anything important here.

"Gotcha." He looked around. The frosting stayed in his pack. He wandered down the aisle, moving his finger along labels. Occasionally he picked up a can or jar and put it in the bag. Ravioli. Sardines. Fruit cocktail. Alfredo sauce. He selected these items one at a time.

Dorothy tried to find a way of describing the difference between grocery shopping and gathering provisions, but ultimately gave up. As long as his bag was full of calories when they set out for home, it would be good enough. Hopefully they would be able to come back for all of it, but if they couldn't, she resigned herself to do the thinking for both of them. She loaded her pack with cans of chicken for protein, and tomatoes to fight off scurvy. She had recently learned about scurvy at school, along with a list of foods that had vitamin C. The lesson was presented as a what-if scenario, placing her class on a pretend ship voyage several hundred years in the past. While most of her peers complacently listed lemons on their inventory sheet, she wanted more variety than that, even for an imaginary trip. She silently thanked Mr. Winter, her social studies teacher, for helping her learn tomatoes provide vitamin C. He could not have known how valuable the lesson proved to be, which made his teaching it all the more valuable to Dorothy.

"I'm full," said John.

Dorothy looked up from her nostalgic classroom musings. "That was fast. Let me see your pack."

He brought it over and placed it on the floor next to her. Inside she found a variety of snack foods, including a can of honey roasted peanuts, several jars of assorted jellies, and a six-pack of Miller Lite. She silently berated him for being impractical. On reflection, she conceded survival without joy was itself impractical. If he needed these comforts to get him through the next few months, then so be it. She would have to be sure he got enough real food to maintain some base level of health. And she wouldn't be shy about eating those peanuts.

"There's room in here for ten more cans," she said.

"Ten?" He stepped back, eyes wide.

"Yes, ten. And I don't mean ten more cans of sardines. I mean ten more cans this size." She held up a can of concentrated cream of mushroom soup for his inspection. "Anything smaller than this, and you'll need to put in two of each."

"That's going to be heavy."

"No heavier than mine, and I'm just a little girl."

He looked around the store, uncertain concern on his face.

"I'm working on dinners here," she said. "How about you find us some desserts. There's plenty of fruit left. I like pears."

"Gotcha. Pears." He picked up his pack with an obvious new sense of purpose.

Dorothy topped off her pack with one last can of chicken. She had to put almost her full weight on the bag to get the zipper to completely close. Once sealed, she picked it up and slipped it on her shoulders. The hiking knapsack included a belt, which she clicked into place and tightened. The full pack weighed enough to give her pause, and she bounced up and down on her knees gently to get a feel for the load. John's would be as heavy. He seemed about the age where some of her adult acquaintances had complained of back trouble, and she hoped that wasn't a standard part of the growing old experience.

"Okay, I got ten more," said John. He had also donned his pack.

Dorothy walked over to him and buckled and tightened his belt. "Let's go home then."

≡≡≡

On the way back, John straggled again. Unaccustomed to walking with her pack this full, Dorothy moved at a pace more sluggish than usual. And yet he still managed not to keep up with her.

She stopped at her favorite sitting rock again, much closer to the grocer than the Hallmark store. The fact she already felt the need to rest there did not bode well for the plan. If this weight exceeded her reasonable limits, they would have to make a lot more trips, which would be more exhausting and time-consuming. She tried to rationalize this as her job, and plenty of people worked longer hours than she would spend transporting goods. At least, they did when jobs still existed.

She had lost sight of John completely by that point, and so she waited at the rock for him to catch up. Within a few minutes, he came around a bend in the trail. This time the object in his hand was clearly visible, and glowing, and when he looked up and saw her, he quickly shut it off and stuck it back in his pocket.

"Hey," he said when he got close enough to communicate without shouting.

"Hi," said Dorothy. "What's that in your pocket?"

"Nothing."

Dorothy sighed. "If you don't want to tell me what's in your pocket, that's your business. But please don't treat me like I'm stupid."

He shrugged. "Maybe I'm just happy to see you."

Dorothy met this remark with a cold stare.

"It was a joke," he said.

"It was an unfunny joke."

His face turned an awkward shade of red, and he looked away. Reaching into his pocket, he produced a rectangular solid roughly the size of a chalkboard eraser and handed it to her.

It was polished black metal, with a glass screen on one face, and a smattering of unmarked buttons along one side. Dorothy turned it over in her hands, not quite sure what to make of it. "What is this?"

"It's a map thing," said John, still not looking at her. "Push one of the buttons."

"Which one?" she asked, trying to tell them apart.

"Any one."

She lightly pressed a random button and felt a tiny inaudible click. The glass screen came to life, showing a relief map of the great lakes region in shades of green. The image lacked marked boundaries, but she recognized the area corresponding to Wisconsin easily enough. A glowing blue marker hovered toward the lower right side of that area. The waypoint sat close enough to her former hometown, Sheboygan, that she assumed it indicated her current location. How far she'd moved from the lake in her travels surprised her. With a mixture of fascination and homesickness, she touched her finger to the screen on the location of her old house. As soon as she made contact, a red circle appeared there, ringing her fingertip. She lifted her finger off the screen and the map followed it. The flat map became a three-dimensional projection, whose height varied along the contours of the land it represented.

"Whoa!" said Dorothy. "Is it supposed to do that?"

"Yeah. Not really sure how it works though."

"This is amazing! I didn't think this technology existed. It looks... expensive."

"I didn't exactly buy it," said John.

She looked up at him. He still faced away from her. "Where did you find this? Was there anything else like it there?"

He shrugged again. "It was a ways off from here. Couldn't tell you exactly."

"Could this?" asked Dorothy, holding up the map projector.

John turned around. The red had faded from his face, which now looked deprived of blood. "I ain't going back there, okay?"

Dorothy lowered the map, as well as her voice. "Is that where your friend—"

"She ain't my friend! Just... forget it." He started walking again toward the strip mall, leaving Dorothy behind.

"Do you want this back?" she called after him.

"Keep it!" he shouted.

Whatever demons he battled there, she chose to let him walk them off, and made no move to catch up to him. If he had been using this device as a guide, he could get lost on the way back, but he had the ribbons to follow. Besides, he was an adult, and shouldn't need her to take care of him. As she thought this, she silently acknowledged how many times those words had run through her head of late.

She turned her attention back to the map and experimented with it. Certain hand gestures caused it to zoom in or out, rotate, expand and contract, but repeating these gestures did not have consistent results. It would be some time before she mastered the subtleties.

The side buttons brought menus up onto the screen. Unlike the map, they lay flat against it, even when touched. Most of the commands at her disposal read as gibberish, but the few she understood, she explored. One gave the option to update the map, and she chose that. Unfortunately, it returned the all too clear "Unable to connect to Network" message. An information option popped up inside this menu, and she selected this. Two more layers down, she found a command to show the most recent update. When she selected that, it gave her a date.

June 17, 2053.

She stopped there. Surely that was an error.

Back up two layers and over to software version. 10.3.1. Released September 2052.

She wiped the accumulated moisture from her forehead, vaguely aware on this milder than usual early August day, this was her first recollection of perspiring.

2053.

Forty-nine years from now.

This was new. The world as she knew it was nearly devoid of civilization. In its place lay vast, untamed forest, newly populated with odd creatures like multicolored rats and (evidently) at least one werewolf. As tricky as that had been to get accustomed to, she had to start over.

This device, or perhaps John, or perhaps she herself, had traveled through time.

[9]

ARTIFACTS AND GADGETS

I t did get harder. **The night after finding the half-house,** Harrison and Glimmer slept in a log cabin. The night after that, in a shanty made from welded, corrugated tin roofing. The night after that, they slept under the stars and took turns keeping watch.

Harrison watched Glimmer sleep, his high-tech sunglasses set for night vision. Glimmer slept curled on a tiny bed of leaves she had spread on the ground. Without the aid of the glasses, Harrison saw her for what she appeared to be. She radiated a glow too faint to be seen in broad daylight, but shone like a beacon at night. Her wings fluttered gracefully behind her each time she exhaled. She was unearthly and wondrous and impossible. The presence of pink satin pajamas with a stylized B embroidered on the jacket pocket only barely diluted the effect.

The glasses revealed a different Glimmer. Her glow, or aura, did not give off any heat rendering it, and her wings, invisible in infrared. These objective, clinical, machine eyes provided no clarity as to her true nature. A small, human-shaped object rested on the leaves, warmer than the ambient temperature. Beyond that, the glasses showed nothing spectacular. He cycled through settings and found she did show a heartbeat, but a random one, not the expected regular pulse.

Harrison turned from the glasses to his other source of information and hope—the Walkman radio. In his daily checks, nothing but static ever came out of it. He had no desire to call off his expedition, but its purpose grew more questionable with each day of radio silence.

He flipped the switch again. His headphones responded with a loud *Cha-ching*, introducing the Pink Floyd song, "Money."

Claudia was back on the air.

Every day greeted them with a variation of their first day. They walked through huge stretches of undisturbed wilderness interrupted by the occasional building or other structure, many intact, but some, like the house where they spent the first night, at least partly destroyed.

Every evening at sundown, Harrison turned on the radio and listened to Claudia's broadcasts. For whatever reason, the station came in only after dark.

The compass proved an invaluable tool for locating manmade objects and buildings, and Harrison usually pulled it out late in the afternoon to find a secure place to sleep that night. So far, every time they found a building designed to accommodate some level of technology, everything in it worked. He grew accustomed to this as a constant, although at any time the next house might be the one with no power or the next office building might have toilets that didn't flush.

They also found more portable things. A week in, they came across the remains of a shoe store. Harrison picked out a new pair of boots and left his sneakers tied together, hanging over a cable that led from the store to a telephone pole. Once, in the middle of an empty parking lot, he found a briefcase filled with cash. Although it had two locks on it, it opened on the first try. He took a band of twenties, leaving the rest behind uncounted.

After that, they found a sporting goods store. Looking for a better compass, he found one with a wrist strap so he wouldn't have to keep fumbling for it in his pocket. This compass had the same pointing preference as the ones he had been using.

He traded in his knapsack for a larger backpack with a metal frame and some interesting properties. The pack itself had mass, and therefore weight, but the material had an impenetrable gravity shield built into it. Anything placed inside the pack acquired zero weight, allowing him to fill it, but bear only the burden of the pack itself. He found no obvious sign of a power source for this feature, but a small circuit board concealed behind a Velcro flap indicated advanced technology.

Other artifacts, also perhaps manmade, perhaps not, but not made by or from any technology Harrison understood, presented themselves along the way.

Once, on a gravel path, he found a stone much larger and darker than its neighbors. He picked it up, planning to throw it, a simple act of ennui. Almost the size of his hand, but much lighter than it looked, it felt right somehow. Comfortable.

"Leave it," said Glimmer, who wore an uncharacteristically serious expression.

"This?" He held out the stone. "Why?"

"You won't need it."

He frowned. "It's a rock. Obviously I don't need it." He turned it over in his hand. Someone had etched several faint lines of text into it. Trying to clean it so he could read it, he rubbed some of the dust with his thumb and blew on it gently. A pronounced breeze tickled his nose and tossed his hair up. Glimmer flew around him.

"Leave it," she said again.

He stared at the rock, then blew on it again, with more force.

A gust hit him in the chest and he wobbled. Behind him, a visible wave of force rippled through the foliage away from him and down the path. He looked at the stone, and at the pixie, who admonished him with her silence. The stone went into his pack.

He found a copper ring, and when he put it on, the right side of his body became stronger, and the left weaker. Once he came across a pedestal with a small, wooden box on top of it. The box contained an ordinary deck of playing cards. Experimentation revealed sometimes they would all become the ace of spades, and without fail, if he drew a card at random and then reshuffled it into the deck, no matter how many times he shuffled, he would deal that card right off the top.

He kept these curiosities. After the stone, Glimmer did not bother to advise him.

Some days were better than others. They found a stretch of brick road heading mostly west and followed it for two days. They lost an entire day walking around a swampy lake. Harrison found a bicycle and rode it for a few miles over flat terrain before he ran over a piece of glass and punctured a tire.

The days wore on into weeks.

"So," Glimmer asked enthusiastically, "are we looking for anything specific?"

In the middle of another dense forest, they had come across another ruined and uninhabited building the size of a large house, and stopped to investigate. The walls on one whole side had been torn away, leaving ragged and crumbling edges. Objects of an unknown design and technology, evidently intact, were strewn about the floors of every room.

Harrison picked up a small, cubical object and scrutinized it. "I'm not sure."

"Then are we looking for anything vague?" she asked with equal eagerness. She wore gym shorts and a white T-shirt that said Jell-O in red letters across the front. Her elbows and knees had pads strapped to them, and on her head sat an ovoid helmet. She flitted around the room.

Harrison shrugged. "Anything useful." He dropped the cube and shuffled through the room, scooting things out of his way with his feet. "What do you think this place was?"

"Like I would know?" She zipped past his head and grabbed a cord that hung from some apparatus on the ceiling. She tugged straight down on it twice with great exertion, to no effect.

"I was just thinking out loud. I've almost gotten used to the experience of finding future stuff, but it still seems weird to see it just lying around like this. I feel like I'm looting the Batcave." He picked up a silvery blue gadget, U-shaped and palm-sized, with a large, inviting switch on one side. A symbol had been etched into its otherwise unmarked face, presumably a company logo: a simple vertical line segment that connected at the bottom to an elaborate curve. "Well, this has got to be something, right?"

Glimmer merely cocked an eyebrow in response.

He sighed and turned the object around in his hands three times. Holding it out at arms' length, he looked away from it, gritted his teeth, closed his eyes tightly, and thumbed the switch.

"Like I would know?" Glimmer said. He opened his eyes. The pixie hovered over the U-shaped thing, flickering. "Like I would know?"

"Hey! What's the big idea?" demanded another Glimmer from behind him.

"Hmm," said Harrison. "Looks like I found a camera."

"Turn it off!" the pixie ordered.

He complied, weighing the object in his hand for a moment. Heavy for its size, in his pack its weight would make no difference. He looked up.

She pouted. "Do I really look like that?"

"Uh, no," he said. "You're much prettier."

"Oh!" She beamed. "Good."

Harrison continued sifting through the ruins, sorting treasure from junk, an unsatisfying process. "That's it. We're done."

"Did you find what you needed?" asked Glimmer.

Harrison did not answer right away. He climbed down from the ruins and back into the forest, where he wandered for some time. "This is starting to bug me."

She looked puzzled. "I'm not sure I know what you mean."

He frowned. "I'm not sure I do, either. This just..." He stopped talking, and they traveled in silence for a while until frustration boiled over and he blurted, "Oh, hell! We've been on our way to Chicago for almost three weeks, and I have no clue where we are. And as if that's not bad enough, I feel like my whole plan has been, I don't know, co-opted, or something."

"Still not following you," she said from right behind him.

"The stuff! All these treasure troves we keep stumbling into. I feel like we started out looking for Chicago, and now we're on some damned scavenger hunt!" He stopped himself, then said in a quieter, more measured tone, "I can't shake the feeling that I'm a mouse. A mouse running around collecting cheese, and I'm not supposed to worry about why there's cheese everywhere, except one of these times the cheese will jump on me and snap my neck."

"Ew." Glimmer scratched her head. "Sounds like good ol' paranoia to me. Why would anyone set Harrison traps all over the countryside? Seems like a lot of trouble."

"No more trouble than setting the entire freaking world on shuffle play." After a minute, he asked, "Where were you three months ago?"

"I don't like your tone."

"Seriously, where were you when you first started following me?"

"Stalking you," she corrected.

"Stalking me."

She became quiet. Her habit of giving obfuscatory answers to simple questions had now crept over the edge that separated foible from liability. Before he could explain this to her she gave him an unexpectedly straight answer.

"I was right near that motel where you were staying."

"Really?"

She nodded. "Only there wasn't a motel there. It appeared for the first time when the world went haywire."

So much for the straight answer. "Then what was there before?"

"A tree," she said, "and about a thousand pixies. Not counting me, of course."

"I feel like someone would have noticed that. Are they still there?" he asked.

"Not anymore."

"Well, where did they go?"

She scowled. "Where did all the people go?"

"I have no idea. I thought we had been over—" He stood still, staring into space for a few seconds. "Oh, my God. They're all gone?"

She nodded.

"You're the last one?"

She nodded again.

"Wow," he said. "I'm sorry."

"Don't worry about it." Without looking at him, she flew on ahead.

It took Harrison a few minutes to catch up with her, followed by a stretch of silence. He finally broke it. "Hold up. That motel was there before everything changed. I remembered it when I found it. It's not that far from where I used to work."

She shook her head. "No, it wasn't. It turned up with all the other weird buildings, the same time you did."

"But I've always been here," he muttered. He checked the compass on his wrist. It pointed behind him, at the wrecked building they had plundered. The needle wavered and rotated almost half a turn, pointing in front of him and off to the left. "That was fast."

Fifteen minutes later, they broke through the brush and found a divided highway.

"Awesome," said Harrison.

"This is good?" Glimmer asked.

"If this is what I think it is, yeah, it's super good. This looks like an interstate, and if I'm right, it's Route 90. If it holds out, this will take us all the way to Chicago. If we're really lucky, we might even find a car. We should be well into New York by now, maybe even halfway across."

They had gone about a mile when the familiar red and blue shield of an interstate highway became visible, paired with another sign, a green sign, on the same post. As it came closer, and more into focus, Harrison recognized it as a picture of a pilgrim hat.

"Oh, crap," he whispered.

"What?" Glimmer asked.

"Oh. Crap!"

"What's wrong?" Glimmer looked back and forth from Harrison to the sign, confusion in her eyes. "This isn't Route 90?"

"Crap! Crap, crap, crap! Yeah, it's Route 90, but it's the Massachusetts Turnpike."

After a few moments of silence, she ventured, "So that's crap, then?"

"We haven't even left Massachusetts yet! We've been drifting south this whole time! We're about 200 miles short of where I thought we were! Damn it!" He stopped walking. "This is insane. If we turned around right now? Followed this road east? We'd be back at the motel in about three days."

"Is that what you want to do?" she asked, no criticism in her voice.

He paused, staring in the approximate direction of his most recent home. "I want to go where the people are. Let's keep moving."

[10]

DEBATE

John's pack sat on the walk in front of the Hallmark store door, its owner nowhere in sight. Dorothy set her pack down and unzipped his. Ten cans of pears sat right on top of the jumble of merchandise inside. She zipped it closed and left the two packs to go find John.

He turned out to be in the first place she looked, true to his pattern. Seated in a lawn chair, feet propped up on another, he snored quietly. Dorothy pulled another chair alongside him, scraping it as loudly across the floor as she could.

"John," she said. Then a little more assertively, "John!"

He snorted, not opening his eyes. "Hmm."

"Do you want to nap before we go back out, or do you want to eat?"

"Nap," he said.

She gave him a few seconds.

His eyes opened.

"Wait, what do you mean go back out? I thought we were done for the day."

"No," said Dorothy. "I said we were going to do two runs every day."

"Ugh." He closed his eyes again. "Maybe we can start that plan tomorrow."

Dorothy's sore legs suggested agreement with this idea. She had never before attempted two food runs in one day, and was only guessing she and John were up to the task. "What year were you born?"

"I'm forty-two, if that's what you're asking."

"It's not," she said.

It took John a few seconds to respond to that. When he did, he sat up. "1962. Why are you asking me that?"

Dorothy pulled the mapping device out of her pocket and handed it to him. "When was this made?"

He stared at it. "How should I know?"

She reached for it, and he surrendered it without any apparent interest. "You would know by bothering to check." She tapped through the same menus she had discovered earlier and handed it back to him, with the apropos screen showing.

He stared at it some more. "I don't get it. Why are you showing me this?"

The ache in her legs crept up her spine and into her neck. She ignored it. "John, this thing is from the future."

"Yeah, lots of stuff is." His eyebrows went up. "Wait a minute, is this the first future thing you seen?"

A chill went through her. "You knew?"

"Sure I knew! Not that it did me any good."

"Are you saying we've traveled through time? Is this the future? Is that why everything is gone or destroyed? Can we get back? Can we prevent all this?"

He waved his hands. "Slow down. No, this ain't the future. Whatever happened, this is still 2004. That stuff is just part of the change. Like your colorful rats."

She paused. "And your werewolf?"

"Yeah," he said quietly. "Look, that future stuff, it don't mean nothing. None of this means nothing. It's just stuff."

Dorothy looked down at the simple device, with so much information at her fingertips and no idea how to take advantage of it. "Where did you get this?"

"I told you, I ain't going back there."

"John," she said as calmly as she could, "if there's more of this technology there, we might be able to do something with it. Maybe even use it to find other people."

"Other people suck!" Getting no response to that, he added, "I mean, you're all right. But I'm two for three so far on meeting people I don't ever want to meet again. This is a nice place to crash, and I feel safe for the first time since the thing happened. I ain't eager to stir up any trouble at this point."

"And what about me? Maybe you've completely given up on the world, but I haven't. I want to find other survivors. Or find anything that will make a better life for me. Can't you help me do that?"

"What's the matter with the life you got right here? This place is great."

"Augh!" she shouted. "You are so useless!"

John said nothing.

Dorothy winced. "I'm sorry. That came out wrong."

"This ain't working out." John propped his feet back up and closed his eyes.

"John, don't say that."

"I said you weren't gonna want me here, and I was right. Thanks for the hospitality, but I should go. Gonna finish my nap, then I'm out."

Dorothy's throat constricted. "You're really just going to leave me here alone?"

"Sounds like I'm not doing you too much good anyway."

"I'm sorry, okay?" said Dorothy. "I just got frustrated. You're not useless. Please don't go."

"You just want me to haul more food for you. You think that's all I'm good for, and you're probably right."

"To be honest, it is nice to have someone helping with the food runs. But you know what's nicer?" Dorothy paused for a response and got none. "What's nicer is sharing the food."

John said nothing and did not move from his napping position in the chairs.

Dorothy stood to leave.

"Gimme the thing." His eyes remained shut.

Dorothy extended her hand, offering up the mapping device. She waited in vain for him to open his eyes. "Here."

He reached for it, and she placed it in his hand. He opened his eyes long enough to fiddle with it for a few seconds and hand it back to her. "Green dot."

Dorothy looked at the holographic projection sitting in the air above the little screen. It showed a red relief map, with a single green dot in the center, and sufficiently zoomed out for her to recognize her location relative to it.

"Will you come with me?" she asked.

"Maybe," he said. "Now leave me alone."

Dorothy walked back to the Hallmark store, map in hand, mentally calculating distance and making note of the terrain. John could sleep to his heart's content. She had an expedition to plan.

GRILLED CHICKEN SANDWICH

They made it to the New York border by nightfall, and slept in a tollbooth. The next day, Harrison awoke to find himself alone. A note had been stuck to the window, with no visible tape or any other adhesive. He peeled it off to read it.

Dear Harry,
I woke up early and saw something I wanted
to check out. Don't wait for me. I'll catch up.
Stay on the road!
Love,
Glimmer

He read the note twice, in its neat and curvy handwriting, in letters bigger than her hands, each *i* dotted with a little heart.

Trusting she would indeed catch up, he set out down the highway, keeping to the shoulder. According to his maps, Route 90 passed through Albany, jiggering through Route 87. If that junction were no longer intact, the Hudson River would be a problem. "I'll cross that bridge when I come to it." He laughed at his joke, grateful no one heard it.

He walked for three hours, stopping to rest only once. Twice he tried the radio, but both times got nothing. Periodically he scanned the sky looking for a spark trail, but did not alter his pace. He had seen how fast she could fly.

After some time, he found a rest stop.

Rather than an exit ramp, a small dirt road, perpendicular to the highway and lacking any sign or marker, led to the facility. It consisted of a small gas station and a McDonald's restaurant, all ordinary enough. The moat surrounding it, and drawbridge lowered across it, struck him as quaint. Harrison crossed this bridge, lured by the prospect of a video game, or perhaps a functioning freezer filled with ice cream bars.

Inside the door sat a huge, glass-enclosed gear box with a giant wheel on the outside. For two quarters, plus one penny, a tourist could create a token that said, I ♥ NY or the Lord's Prayer. Harrison opted for the former, a gift for his traveling companion. He had pilfered some change from the tollbooth, and used it to create the charm, enjoying the sensation of spinning the large wheel, especially the resistance at the moment the press bit into the penny. The finished product hit bottom with a little metallic *clink* and he fished it out. He held it up to admire it, and froze.

Silently, behind the counter, stood a man in a McDonald's uniform. He offered no indication of noticing Harrison, who approached with slow caution.

Harrison gulped. "Hello?"

The man did not respond.

Harrison moved closer and brought himself right up to the counter. He made eye contact. "Hello?"

The man appeared to be in his early twenties, tidy, but with a vacant look. "Can I help you?"

After over two months of wandering through the unexpected and the impossible, Harrison found himself embedded in the quintessential familiar American experience. This couldn't be right. And yet.

"How long have you...?" he began, then stopped himself.

The man behind the counter stared at him, but not in amazement, or in wonder at the discovery of another human being. He stared in boredom, the stare of a man taking no joy in his job. Somehow, that stare added to the familiar warmth of the environment.

Harrison's question died on his tongue as his attention shifted to the menu overhead.

"Can I help you?" the man repeated.

Harrison thought for a second. "Yes." Speaking the word sent a flood of comfort through him. This was McDonald's, the friendliest sanctuary in the world, a sanctuary Harrison desperately needed. His uneasiness faded to irrelevance. "Can I have a... a grilled chicken sandwich? And a vanilla shake?" He waited, breathless and eager.

"Would you like fries with that?"

Harrison squeezed his eyes tight, tears of joy leaking from them. "Yes," he whispered. "Yes, please."

"For here?"

He nodded. Given his total, he paid with a twenty and counted the change.

The man behind the counter laid a tray down in front of him and covered it with a paper placemat. He scooped some French fries into a paper box and set it down. Then he went into the back. After two frustratingly long minutes, he returned with a sandwich wrapped in paper, which he placed next to the fries. Finally, he filled a cup with a cold vanilla shake and snapped a lid on it.

"Thank you." He slid the completed meal toward Harrison.

Harrison hesitated, drawing out the moment. A question nagged at the edges of his awareness, but he couldn't articulate it. Hunger prevailed, and he took his meal to a table.

The sandwich tasted about how he remembered them, but not quite delicious, which took some of the magic out of the experience. The shake tasted peculiar as well, like artificial sweetener. It felt strange to make the food a priority over the person, and Harrison wrestled with this discomfort and fear, right to the end of the sandwich. He resolved to get up on his last bite, but the man had already come out to talk, saving him the trouble.

The server opened his mouth, perhaps about to say something, when a beam of orange light shot through his chest. He looked down at it, a curious expression of surprise on his face. The beam extended beyond the man's back, well into the restaurant. Then came the blood.

Harrison had never seen that much blood before, counting all the times he had ever seen blood combined. It sprayed out the server's back in a grotesquely huge fan and spattered every surface behind him. The tables, the floor, even the ceiling and the counter twenty feet away from him were slick with the dark, viscous fluid.

Harrison took in all of this in a minuscule fraction of a second, the lag time between when he first understood this sight and when his shock and horror responses kicked in. While he tried to remember how to scream, he looked at the only other person he had yet met in an abandoned world as that person collapsed and died in slow motion.

As the man fell, tar-colored blood poured out of the hole in his chest and ran down the length of his McDonald's uniform. Simultaneously, globules of orange light leaked out of the same hole, rose upward, and dispersed. The beam of light remained poised in air, with a person-sized gap in it.

The scream formed at last, and Harrison leapt out of his seat, knocking his tray to the floor. He fell over, a part of him awestruck by the horrible beauty of the light. As it hung there, the beam faded from orange to white and dissolved in a shower of sparks.

All at once, he understood. The raw, awful violence paled in the light of this recognition, and of the fear that chased it. There she hovered, her wings purple and sparkly and beautiful, fluttering lightly.

And the entire rest of her body covered in gore.

Not some harmless, magical companion after all, but an evil, murderous monster. Had she seen him as prey this whole time? He had been a fool. Now he would be a dead fool.

"Don't kill me. Don't kill me. Don't kill me." He repeated this mantra and wept.

She wiped blood away from her eyes and stared at him with unveiled rage and loathing. "Did you eat anything?"

He shook his head, sobbing. "Don't kill me."

She flew straight at his face, too fast for him to throw his arms up to guard himself. "Did you eat anything!" she screamed

"Yes. I ate a chicken sandwich."

She turned and flew in a huge arc around the inside of the restaurant, and although she moved swiftly, Harrison perceived her flight as a prolonged and sickening crawl. She picked up speed. The arc would end with him detonated against the front windows.

He remembered a dog from his childhood, the best game of miniature golf he ever played, his first kiss. He remembered telling his father to go to hell at six years old, and his regret over that incident at his father's funeral, eighteen years later.

Glimmer came around for the coup de grace, her arms outstretched, her palms spread, no doubt to inflict maximum damage on her way through.

He remembered his favorite book, a secret hiding place he hadn't thought of in years, and his most embarrassing fart.

She hit him, the tiniest punch in the gut.

He looked down, ready to see the hole, but instead saw her hands laid flat against his intact belly. She glowed white, and from where she touched him, a radiant stain spread to his whole torso. He felt warm and uncomfortable, but strangely not dead.

The nausea came. Glimmer flitted away and he pulled himself up to his knees, in time to throw up, painfully. He felt detached and dizzy, reminiscent of the regret that followed the one time he had gotten puking drunk. Between the illness and loss of control, that had been the most unpleasant experience in his life until now. He coughed, spat, and sat back down on the floor, scooting away from the vomit, as far as he could.

Bloody Glimmer returned, holding a child-sized cup in both hands. "Drink this."

"Oh, God," he moaned.

The rage came back. "Drink it!"

He drank it. It burned. Pure fear drove him to finish it. It scorched his throat, and right before he threw it up again, he identified it as warm cola. It splashed, foul and hot, on his pants.

"Oh, God." His throat felt like it had been scoured with a wire brush. He thought he could feel his teeth dissolving. "Oh, God," he rasped. "Oh, God."

"It will pass. We have to get you out of here." She pulled on his finger. "Harry? Come on, Harry, we're going." She flew into his face and snapped her fingers. "Seriously, cupcake, time to go. Can you walk?"

He nodded in dull, hopeless confusion. "What just happened?"

"Everything is fine, sweetheart, we just need to get you up and out."

He stood, his legs shaking.

"Attaboy. Come on." She flew as he walked, slowly, leading him to the door.

As they passed the second or third table, he paused and looked back.

"Don't stop! Harry! Eyes forward."

Blood coated everything. For a moment, it renewed his terror of the pixie, until he saw his own vomit. It steamed and bubbled. Boiled? Hard to tell. It crept toward him. More than creeping, it writhed and flopped.

"Okay," he croaked, "let's go."

As they reached the front door, she blocked him "We need the pack, honey, and I can't carry it."

He bent down to pick it up, briefly disoriented it weighed almost nothing. He was stable enough to get it on, but only just.

Outside, the drawbridge had been raised, held up by two ropes. Glimmer flew through them and snapped them both. The bridge crashed down, sending an explosion of dust outward. Harrison jumped at the loud *bang*, but the bridge did not break. She led him across, and as soon as they reached dry land, she ordered him to sit down. He did. She flew back to the drawbridge, and across it, back and forth, with more and more speed. Her trail of sparks covered the bridge in denser zigzags until the wood smoldered and burst into flames.

She landed on the grass next to him. "Are you feeling coherent?"

He thought about this, then nodded.

"Good," she said. "I need you to focus for a minute. I have to get this stuff off me. Right now. I want you to get a bottle of water out of your pack and pour it on me."

"Pour it on you," he repeated.

"That's right. I need a shower, and it has to be right away."

"Moat?"

She shook her head. "No. That water's no good."

"Shower. Got it." He opened the pack and rooted for a few seconds, before producing one of the plastic water bottles. He stared at the pop-up nozzle.

"Just unscrew the cap and dump," she said.

He did so. The water glugged out, and she extended her arms and turned under the flow. Instead of simply rinsing off, the blood reacted to the water by hissing and sizzling against her flesh. If it hurt, she gave no indication of it. The water had no visible effect on her wings. They did not bend under its weight, and stayed dry. After a few seconds, the hissing stopped. The blood had washed away. At that point, something impossible to see through the gore became clear: she was naked.

In spite of everything, he found himself staring. Somehow, he had always imagined fairies to be lithe and svelte creatures, and her Barbie wardrobe had cemented that impression. The doll clothes gone, he could see her curviness, and the softness of her build. That she did not conform to the American cultural standard of idealized perfection made her more believable, somehow. She was, as she had pointed out to him when they first met, quite lovely. After what he had endured, the vision of her provided a tonic to his eyes, calming and centering him.

It took his brain a couple seconds to catch up with the fact he had run out of water. Glimmer looked up at him. She grinned and curtsied. "Ta-dah!"

He covered his eyes. "Sorry." His ravaged throat choked on the word.

"Don't be. I enjoy the attention. Towel."

He uncovered his eyes. She held her hand out. He reached into the pack and produced a washcloth, and she wrapped it around her body. Her wings emerged through the fabric.

Harrison dropped down onto his back and lay still with his eyes closed for a full minute. When the adrenaline receded, he opened his eyes, and rocked his head back and forth, looking for the pixie. She stood a couple feet away from his head, still wearing the washcloth, her expression tender and concerned.

"Hi," she said. "How are you feeling?"

He coughed. "Not so good," he whispered. "What did you do?"

"You needed a purge."

"The food... Poisoned?" His head still fuzzy, he struggled to assemble the puzzle. "I thought you were going to kill me."

"Kill you? I like you!" she said, her eyes wide with shock.

"You killed that man."

"Yes, I did, and, no, you weren't poisoned. But you had a stomach full of demon larvae." She walked closer to him and sat. "That man wasn't a man, Harry. It was a monster, and it was feeding you its young. They would have eaten you alive. From the inside out."

Harrison closed his eyes. He didn't want there to be demons. It made sense, though. If pixies existed, so would demons. The good came with the bad. And the ugly. He struggled for something to say. "They tasted like chicken."

"I've heard that," she said.

"How did you know? He looked human to me. He acted human."

"It was a homunculus demon. They can make themselves look like humans, or trolls, or whatever they're trying to fool. They can't sustain it, but they usually don't have to for very long."

"How do you tell when you see one?" he asked.

"Their magic smells like skunk. I detected this one from over two miles away." She paused. "The way you can tell one is that you stick with me."

He nodded in obedience. "Why the Coke?"

"Caffeine is a magic detergent. It's not strong, but mixed with carbon dioxide, it helps flush evil toxins. That, and the sugar, which is a demonicide. I had to make sure the larvae were all out. Coke is a great magical emetic for certain ailments." She offered a sympathetic face. "Sorry it was warm. I got it from a bottle in your pack. The soda fountain probably wouldn't have had any sugar in it."

"The shake tasted funny. Like artificial sweetener."

"Sounds about right."

He nodded. "Thank you."

She smiled. "All in a day's work."

Harrison sat up. He pulled another bottle of water out of his pack and, after rinsing and spitting twice, gulped it down. The tepid, marvelous water soothed his scratchy throat, and his voice took its first step on the long road to recovery. "I'm sorry I doubted you in there." His voice remained hoarse, but had a little more volume.

"Oh," she said. "Don't. I understand."

He shook his head. "That was..." He paused, looking for the right word. "Alarming. You did that thing... that thing where you made yourself a bullet. I didn't know you could be so... aggressive. That first day or two after you found me, you seemed so fragile."

"What? Fragile? That's how you see me?" Her huge eyes welled with tears.

"No, no, no!" The words sent him into new coughs. "No, not fragile. Wrong word. Ah... Sensitive. That's all. Nice. Sweet. Not the sort of pixie who would use violence."

"Oh," she sniffed. "Well, I am. Mostly."

"Mostly," he repeated, incredulous.

"Listen," she said, "I want you to sit still for a minute. Then come with me. I have something to show you that might cheer you up."

"I think I could use some cheer right now." He got up and wobbled a bit.

She took him back to the highway and further west. Whatever she wanted to show him was not close, and Harrison had to stop several times for rest and water. Finally, she took him off the side of the road, where they walked up a small hill. It overlooked a meadow, and what he saw there nearly crushed Harrison's fragile psyche.

On the grass, its back to him, sprawled the body of a dinosaur, like the one he had seen the day he first heard Claudia, apart from the detail of it being about twice as big.

"Okay," he said. "I'm cheered up. Can we go now?"

"Shh. Keep watching."

He kept watching, insofar as he could watch a dinosaur corpse. It twitched.

"There!" said Glimmer. "See?"

He did. "It's moving. Please, let's go now."

"Not yet," she whispered.

The beast rustled again, but the movement came from behind it. A larger predator, perhaps, chewing its guts out. After one more lurch, a head emerged.

The reptilian animal differed visually from the dinosaur it ate. Its long and toothy snout more resembled an alligator than a lizard. It sparkled when it moved, flashing both red and green. White puffs of breath spouted from its nostrils, despite the warm weather.

It looked right at Harrison.

He froze. If what he had learned from watching *Jurassic Park* had any validity, they could avoid its gaze with immobility.

Glimmer foiled this plan by waving at it. More than that, she zipped up and down, back and forth, cycling through the color spectrum.

Harrison stared in stupefied disbelief. "What are you doing?" he whispered.

"Oh, don't be a big baby." She pointed to the beast. "Look!"

He looked. It waved back, its limb drawing a huge brown flap of skin back and forth. A wing.

"I thought I saw him fly by early this morning," said Glimmer. "Spent most of the day tracking him. His name's Gustav. I wanted you to meet him."

"Gustav," Harrison said slowly, "is a dragon?"

"Duh," said Glimmer. "Let's go down!"

"Wait. Can you... uh, can you tell him I've had a really bad day? That maybe we could take a rain check?"

Glimmer put her little tingly hands on his cheekbones and looked into his tired, frightened eyes. "Do you trust me?"

He touched her hands with his fingers. She did not move them. His throat still burned from the demon larvae and the warm Coke. From Glimmer saving his life.

"Yes."

"Then come and meet my friend."

[12]

EXPLORING

Dorothy reached up and tied a silver ribbon to a branch. The map projector had reliably reported her position so far, but she would never trust getting back home to faith in this technology. She scrutinized the readout. Her present location was a little more than four kilometers from the store. She had never wandered this far south before; all her supply routes ran west from her home base.

She continued on. John had declined her invitation to explore, choosing instead to watch TV in the video store. Probably for the best anyway. Without having to monitor him, Dorothy could test her new equipment in peace.

About fifty more yards down her new path, she stopped to tie another ribbon. A small, cooling breeze trickled past her. As she took the moment to enjoy it, the tinkle of wind chimes sounded downwind from her. She jerked the ribbon tight around a branch and took off after the sound.

Absent any further wind, she soon lost the music. She slowed her pace, taking extra time to scan her surroundings. Wind chimes might indicate a house, which would be a great step up from her current dwelling. Or they might indicate wind chimes, hanging alone in the middle of a forest with no further context. It wouldn't be the first time she had found such an object.

New wind tickled the back of her neck, and she froze, listening intently. The wind chimes sounded again, behind her and a bit off to the left. Slowly, she backtracked. If she had managed to walk right past them, that greatly reduced the probability they were attached to something, but she enjoyed the pretty music, and wind chimes would be a lovely addition to her home.

A gust of wind came through, and the chimes resounded boldly, colliding and plinking in beautiful, melancholy chords. At that volume, she must have been right on top of them, but still they were nowhere to be seen.

Another breeze, another cascade of harmony, but this time, a small flash of light from the ground accompanied them. Dorothy moved in.

Behind a thorn bush, a circle of packed dirt lay in a small clearing. A cluster of clear white crystals, irregularly shaped, had been jammed into the ground in no obvious pattern. She crouched down to inspect them more closely. Perhaps reacting to her proximity, or the motion, a small wave of multicolored light rippled over the crystals, and they sang softly to her.

She laughed. "You're not a house."

The crystals responded with a trickling vaguely like a giggle.

She sat on the ground next to the circle. Reaching across, she touched one of the crystals cautiously. It tingled a little. She pulled at it, trying to rock it or dislodge it, but it would not budge. She flicked it with her finger, and it made a satisfying *ping*.

Impatient for more wind, Dorothy experimented with blowing on the crystals. They rippled and tinkled away in their wind chime chorus. She cleared her throat. The crystals reacted to that, too, with little staccato bursts of pitch.

A chipmunk zipped out of the thorn bush behind her and skirted around the circle. She giggled at that, too. When the crystals reacted to her laughter this time, the chipmunk stopped abruptly and crept back toward them.

"Hello there," said Dorothy cheerily.

The chipmunk gave no indication it heard her, but the crystals did. As they lit up and sang, the little ground squirrel moved closer.

"It's pretty, isn't it?" said Dorothy.

The chipmunk sat. Dorothy could not recall ever seeing a chipmunk hold still, let alone sit. A rabbit joined them, also sitting still, also entranced. She could not recall whether the rabbit had always been there, or if it arrived after the chipmunk, but the two animals appeared quite content in each other's company, and in no way put off by the presence of a person sitting right there laughing with them.

On the other side of the circle, close to the rabbit, sat two brown lumps. Dorothy leaned over the circle to look at them more closely. A small but swift downdraft brought her face closer to the crystals. It also brought her closer to the lumps, clearly piles of fur. No, not quite fur. Pelts. Pelts of tiny animals. Pelts with skulls.

Dorothy gasped, and stood so rapidly she gave herself a momentary head rush. Shaking it off, she looked around the circle in sober awareness of the dozen or so such dead animals, some small as mice, at least one big enough to be an opossum.

The chipmunk and rabbit offered no reaction to her sudden movement.

"Get out of here!" she shouted. The rabbit looked up at her, ears at alert. "I mean it! Go!" At that command, the rabbit bolted. The chipmunk remained where it sat, staring at the crystals, its jaw trembling slightly. Dorothy got down on her knees and moved her face to within inches of it. "I said go!"

At last, the rodent snapped out of its trance, wobbled, and zipped off with less grace than it arrived.

Getting to her feet, Dorothy rubbed her face. "Ugh!" she shouted, and kicked the nearest crystal, her only reward for the gesture a sharp pain in her toe. "Ow!" A brief search for rocks to use as smashing tools came up empty, so she used both hands to scoop duff off the forest floor and shovel as much of it as she could into the circle to cover the crystals. With that task as complete as she could accomplish, she turned her attention back to the map projector.

Or would have, if she still had it.

Her panic was brief, but severe. The device turned up only ten yards or so away. She hadn't thrown it, so it made no sense how it had gotten away from her at all. She looked back to the circle of crystals under their dead leaf tomb. The thorn bush that had been right next to it had disappeared.

Dorothy activated the map device, which had somehow turned itself off. A quick check of her position put her eleven kilometers from the Hallmark store, nearly three times as far as when she sat down.

"What?" she cried, smacking the little box. She looked up. The sun, which had been almost directly overhead, now sat unnervingly low. "Oh, God!"

She ran.

Dorothy reached the parking lot as the last half-light of dusk faded to darkness. Her entire body ached, her mouth completely dry. She made straight for the bathroom in the back of the store, turned the faucet on, and scooped water into her mouth. The first two scoops she rinsed and spat out. The third, she gargled. Once her mouth and throat were suitably moist, she took a fourth handful and sipped it without gulping. After stabilizing herself, she went in search of John.

The TV in the video store played nothing but snow to an empty room. Dorothy turned it off before heading to the hardware store. John lounged in the area he had carved out to be his room, reading a magazine about paint.

"Did you even notice I was gone?" she asked.

He looked up from his magazine. "Yeah. I thought you were out learning how to use the thing. Jesus, you look terrible."

"Thank you so much. There are crystals out there." She pointed, in no particular direction. "They hypnotized me or something. I think they eat small animals. Oh my God, I think I just got caught in a horror story Venus flytrap."

"Where are they?" he asked.

"About eleven kilometers from here, according to the map, which, by the way, got me the whole way home, thank God."

"Oh. Well, let's not go there." He went back to his magazine.

"Can you please listen to me?" She grabbed the magazine and threw it on the floor. "I think something out there just tried to kill me! I think it was alive or something! There are living crystals out there, eating things!"

"Okay, okay." He held up his hands. "I'm sorry. You made it back all right, though. Just don't go back there."

"That's not the point! What were those things?"

"Don't know. Never seen anything like that. Seen other magic stuff, but not crystals that eat people."

Dorothy's jaw dropped. "I'm sorry, other what stuff?"

"Magic?" he said. "There's magic out there. Just like the future stuff. Freaked me out at first too, but you get used to it. How long have you been holed up in here? You gotta get out more."

"Magic? That's your explanation? Magic!"

"You said you had those rats," he said. "What do you think did that? You think rats just turn fancy colors for the hell of it? I'm telling you, that's magic."

"Magic isn't real."

"None of this ain't real! You think what happened to us was real? You

70

think future stuff is real? You think werewolves are real? What's magic on top of that? Nothing! Now do you get it? You still want to go on your little mission to find more technology?"

She picked his magazine up off the floor and dropped it in his lap. "More than ever." She stormed back to her room.

[PART 2]
INTERSTITIAL

GUSTAV

As Harrison approached the dragon, it put off a smell somewhere between the tangy sweetness of barbeque and the vile sweetness of rotten meat. While they were still at least a hundred yards away, a spray of light and smoke poured out of the back of the dead dinosaur, followed by a hissing, roaring sound.

The smell emanated not from the dragon, but from the dragon's lunch. Gustav roasted the carcass as he went along. A loud, wet snap resounded from behind the dinosaur. Gustav spat out a huge bone.

"Come on," Glimmer whispered.

Harrison more easily discerned the dragon's form from closer up. It resembled a large reptile, not quite a lizard, not quite an alligator. Something else. It rested on enormous, bulky hind legs and had slimmer forelegs the same length. These full-fledged arms ended in distinct hands complete with opposable thumbs. Severe claws tipped their fingers, which Gustav used to grasp and tear. His wings lay folded across his back, though they unfurled and collapsed as he ate in a manner that looked unconscious rather than deliberate. They must have spanned at least fifty feet. No earthly vertebrate compared to this. Birds, bats, even pterosaurs had wings homologous to front limbs, yet on Gustav, wings and arms were distinct. He had the best of both worlds.

A thick, snakelike tail, ornamented with a row of fins, flipped back and forth casually. His head, wide and long, from flared (and smoking) nostrils to the crest in the back, lifted a bit before ending in two short, curved horns. Bony, protective ridges sheltered colossal black eyes.

Rather than the pebbly, scaly skin of a snake or lizard, the dragon wore a coat of genuine scales, each one the size of a human hand. They scraped against each other as he moved. This formidable armor plating raised the daunting question of what natural enemy would require him to have such a defense. The scales showed as red when viewed in one direction and green in another. Iridescence, apparently, was the natural state of magical creatures.

Down to every detail, this dragon exactly matched Harrison's expectations. Before him stood the archetypical dragon, the quintessence of dragonness. He was Smaug, as Harrison had pictured him from *The Hobbit*. He was Draco from *Dragonheart*, but with some of the obvious (to Harrison) flaws corrected. He looked so much like what Harrison thought the perfect dragon should look like, it forced him to confront the horrible possibility Gustav was another shape-shifting demon, pulling the image of a dragon straight out of Harrison's mind. If Harrison were to imagine a dragon, after all, this would be it. Conversely, perhaps dragons simply looked like this. Perhaps on some deep, submerged level, the idea of dragons embedded in Harrison's cultural consciousness came from a true source. Somehow, people simply knew what dragons were.

"Hey!" Glimmer no longer whispered. "Come on!" She stared at him impatiently.

So did Gustav.

The dragon had stopped eating. He inspected Harrison, turning his head from one side to the other, focusing with one eye at a time. Harrison did not grasp what information one eye gave the other did not, but he refrained from asking. Gustav lowered his snout to the ground and looked at Harrison straight on.

"Hello," said Harrison.

"I thought you vould be taller," said the dragon in a voice loud and deep. Even from a distance, his breath put out a powerful odor. Gustav spoke in an Eastern European accent , not quite familiar. Several half-formed ideas vied for the role of Harrison's possible response to being called short. The most immediate and pragmatic question bubbled to the top.

"Do you eat people?" He stole a glance at Glimmer.

She clapped one had to her forehead.

"Ach!" Gustav reared up, clarifying his actual size, like a living skyscraper. "No." The dragon patted his stomach. "I'm stuffed."

Not quite the reassuring reply Harrison had hoped for. Gustav looked down at him again in silence, and Harrison calculated the dreary unlikelihood of outrunning those wings.

"Is joke," said the dragon.

Harrison took a few seconds to process that. "Ah. Right. That's... ah, that's good."

Gustav brought his head down and walked to Harrison on all four legs, moving like a cat. He came to within about ten feet and stopped. "Ja. I eat people."

"Oh, shit," Harrison whispered.

"I don't eat you, though. You been vouched for."

Harrison looked at Glimmer. She grinned.

As Gustav continued to study him, Harrison stood still and tried not to feel like food. If this was to be Harrison's defense against dragons, Glimmer would somehow have to find every existing dragon and vouch for him to all of them. An unlikely prospect.

"You're not from around here, are you?" He hoped, too late, this did not sound patronizing, but Gustav showed no sign he took offense. Instead, he looked up, and stared over Harrison's head at something behind him. Harrison held still.

"No. No, I am not." Gustav stared a bit longer. "I had a cave. Deep in the heart of Prussia. It vas perfect. Is gone now."

What Harrison had taken to be staring now clarified itself as pining. Behind Harrison, the land stretched eastward to the sea and beyond. This dragon had come a long way. More than that. The Kingdom of Prussia had not been a distinct political entity for almost a century, which meant Gustav hadn't merely come across the sea; he had come from another world. Like Glimmer. Like Harrison, in fact. He had lost his world, no doubt trying to find his place in the new world before him.

"You could come with us!" Glimmer bobbed up and down in excitement. "We're—"

"Glimmer!" Harrison stepped back a couple paces. "May I have a word, please?"

She stopped bobbing and flew closer to his face. "What's the matter?" she whispered.

"Are you willing to vouch for Claudia?" he whispered back.

"Sure." She gave him a cheery grin.

"What about anyone else we might meet along the way? What about everyone in—" He caught himself. "Where we're going?"

"Oh," said the pixie, grim realization in her eyes. "I didn't think of that."

"If it's all right with you, I'd rather not have anyone I meet get eaten. Don't get me wrong. I'm sure Gustav is a wonderful—"

"I can't," said Gustav.

77

The sound of his voice, sudden and loud, startled Harrison, who forgot what he had been about to say to the pixie. He turned back to the dragon. "You can't?"

Gustav looked away and gave an enormous shrug. "Vell, I don't vant to, really. I came here looking for other dragons. Instead, I found zese." He indicated the dinosaur corpse. "Dey taste good. I'm happy here. And I'm tired. I don't vant to start over again."

Harrison nodded. "That's all right. We understand."

Gustav looked at them with sad eyes. "Ja. Me, too."

[14]

MISSION

Dorothy's eyes snapped open at the sound of her alarm clock. It took less than a second for her to shake off whatever dream had been interrupted. She made her way to the front of the store through the pre-dawn darkness and found the light switch.

She cracked open a can of cold corned beef hash for breakfast before changing out of her pajamas into hiking gear. Two knapsacks, each loaded the previous evening with a day's worth of food and water and a roll of toilet paper, waited patiently by the front door. One pack also included a bag of dark purple ribbon cut into eight-inch strips. After brushing and flossing her teeth, Dorothy took a flashlight and ventured next door.

The hardware store, cavernous even in full daylight, lay dauntingly dark. She tried the door and found it locked. After a minute or so of knocking, she banged on the glass with the butt end of her flashlight. The window proved sturdy enough to withstand her initial tentative taps, so she got progressively more assertive.

In the sudden illumination of the store lights, John appeared at the door in his underwear. Despite this being her goal, Dorothy jumped, and let out a little scream. The deadbolt clacked open, and the automatic door slid aside. John poked his head out.

"What's the matter? Are you okay?" he asked, his face a curious mixture of half-awake and deeply concerned.

"It's time to get up," she said. "Can I make you something for breakfast?"

John met this input with a blank stare. "What? What time is it?"

"A little after five. The sun should be up in the next half hour or so."

John yawned. He dragged both hands down the length of his face, and rubbed his eyes. "Jesus. I thought you were in trouble. What are you doing up this early?"

"I want to get moving as soon as it's light," she said. "Can I get you something to eat?"

"What? Yeah, I guess so. Lemme get dressed."

John had a can of hash for breakfast as well, though Dorothy took the time to heat his up on a stove in the hardware store. The aroma of fried beef and potatoes drifting off the skillet made her regret eating hers cold, but the Hallmark store had no kitchen appliances, and she stood by her decision to let John sleep a little longer.

She sat with him while he ate. He was about as talkative as usual, with an additional lethargy from the early wake-up call.

"Didn't think we were gonna get up this early," he said after a bout of silence.

"I want to be sure we can get the whole way there and back again in one day," said Dorothy. "We talked about this."

"Yeah, I remember. Just didn't think you meant this early."

"When did you go to sleep last night?" she asked.

"No idea," he said. "Midnightish, maybe. Maybe later."

Wonderful. A lengthy hike with a sleep-deprived partner. Dorothy had been to bed by eight o'clock the night before, though she silently conceded she had calmed down enough to fall asleep around ten. "Are you okay to do this today?"

"If I say no, are you gonna do it anyway without me?"

"Probably."

"Then I guess I'm okay," he said.

Dorothy suppressed a smile. The first hint of sunrise crept in through the storefront. She chose to attribute the warmth she felt to the daylight.

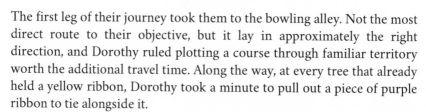

The first leg of their journey took them to the bowling alley. Not the most direct route to their objective, but it lay in approximately the right direction, and Dorothy ruled plotting a course through familiar territory worth the additional travel time. Along the way, at every tree that already held a yellow ribbon, Dorothy took a minute to pull out a piece of purple ribbon to tie alongside it.

They arrived at the bowling alley after two hours. Considering his apparent fatigue, John kept up with her, and they made decent time. They went inside to take a break on the benches in the air conditioning.

"Wanna bowl a frame while we're here?" he asked.

Dorothy had expected the question, and prepared a response. "I'd like that, but we should probably save our energy. How about we play a game on the way home?"

John nodded. "Yeah, that sounds good."

Dorothy smiled, anticipating the end of their day. By the time they made it back here, they would be in no shape to bowl. She looked around at the relatively comfortable environment. "Maybe we could even spend the night here if it gets late."

"We probably should have spent last night here," said John. "Would've cut four hours off our day if we used this place as a base."

Dorothy's heart sank. "Oh, no. You're right. Why didn't you say that before? We could have planned that."

"Hey, this was your plan, kid. I'm just along for the ride."

Dorothy nearly let loose a rant about which one of them was supposed to be the adult, but in the wake of her comment about him being useless, bit her tongue. "Stupid, stupid, stupid! I can't believe I didn't think of this."

"Yeah," said John. "We could've slept a little longer, too."

She whirled on him. "Don't!"

He held his hands up. "Whoa. Settle down. It's fine. Maybe we should just stay here for the day and start again tomorrow."

"I only brought food for one day!"

"There's food here."

"No!" she shouted. "We do this today!"

"Why does it matter?"

"Augh!" Dorothy stormed away. She charged into the bowling alley office and slammed the door behind her. A large black leather desk chair sat behind a pile of papers. Dorothy flopped herself into it, swept the papers onto the floor, and put her head down on the desk, arms folded beneath it. Torn between hoping John would stay away and hoping he would come in so she should scream at him, she sat there without moving for five minutes.

When she finally got tired of being angry, she made her way out to the alley. John was nowhere to be seen, but the unmistakable smell of French fries permeated the air. Behind the snack bar, she found him standing over a basket in the deep fryer. A droplet spattered onto his arm, and he jumped back, brushing at it.

"Don't stand so close," said Dorothy.

"No shit."

"You should leave those in a little longer than you did last time. I like them crunchier."

"Anything else you want to tell me how to do it?"

She frowned. "What's that supposed to mean?"

"Come on," said John. "You and me both know who's in charge here. Let's just agree to it and be done with it."

"I don't want to be in charge," said Dorothy. "I want us to work together."

"Well, that ain't working out so great. Probably easier to just let you be the boss."

She thought about this for a moment. "That's hard for you to admit."

"I'm forty-two," he said. "Supposed to be a grown-up by now."

"You're not very good at it," she said plainly.

"No, I ain't." He picked up the basket with care, and shook it gently to look at the fries. "Done?"

She watched them jiggle as he agitated them. "Little longer."

He lowered the basket. "See? That's easier than arguing. You gotta make the calls, kid. I do my best, but my best ain't any good. And you're like the brainiest kid I ever met. Anybody ever tell you that?"

"It has come up," she said.

"Well, you are. So let's quit with all this back and forth. Truth is, I'm a lot better off with you than I was before that."

"I'm better off too."

He shrugged. "If you say so. I'm just saying thanks for taking me in. And I don't want you to regret it, which I'm pretty sure you do half the time."

"Not quite half," she said.

"Right. So, why don't we just say you're the mom, and I'll try to do better not to piss you off. Deal?"

She hesitated. "I don't know how to be a mom, but I'm an awesome big sister. Is that acceptable?"

He smiled. "Sure. Never had one of those. Sounds like a sweet deal."

They stood there for a moment, both unsure what to say next.

"I... um," said Dorothy. "Do you want a hug?"

"Never was much of a hugger."

"Me either."

John offered his hand. She took it. They shook once, firmly, and released.

"Done deal," he said. "So, do we stay here, or head back out? Your call."

She nodded to the fryer. "Your fries are probably ready. Let's talk about it over some food."

===

The journey from the bowling alley began late morning. Every hundred yards or so, Dorothy would stop and tie a purple ribbon to a tree. This added time to their trip out, but would greatly speed along their trip back. When John pointed out the mapping device made the ribbons unnecessary, Dorothy pointed out it was her decision, and the conversation ended. This new arrangement was proving quite satisfactory.

Sometime around mid-afternoon, John stopped and looked around. "This looks familiar."

"The map says we're still five kilometers out," said Dorothy.

"Yeah, but I definitely been here before."

"Well, that's good, right?"

He hesitated. "Yeah. Just... Let's make this quick, okay?"

"It will probably be at least another hour before we're there."

John said nothing, and started walking again.

"What does it look like?" asked Dorothy. "A building? Like the mall?"

"It's more of a door," said John.

Dorothy frowned. "Just a door?"

"A door in a wall. You'll understand when we get there."

"How long were you there?"

"Not long," said John. "Me and Linda found it. We were trying to get the door open when she... I don't know, wolfed out? What do you call that?"

"I wouldn't know." John's sudden willingness to talk about his werewolf friend took her by surprise, and she ran with it. "What happened?"

He shrugged. "Not much to tell. One minute she was talking to me, the next she was screaming. I don't think she knew it was gonna happen."

"What did you do?"

He looked away. "I don't really remember. I wanted to help her, but when she started to change... I panicked. It happened so fast. She was screaming, then she was howling. So I ran."

"That was probably the smartest thing you could have done."

"Yeah," he said. "Maybe. How fast you think a wolf can run?"

"I've never seen a wolf," said Dorothy.

"No, but you seen a dog, right? How fast can a big dog run? You think you could outrun one?"

"Probably not."

"Me neither," said John. "So how come she didn't catch me? How come I'm not dead?"

"I don't know. You said she was screaming. Maybe she was in pain? Maybe she couldn't run?"

"Maybe." He paused. "Maybe. I kinda think she didn't want to chase me though. I kinda think she still knew who I was. I feel like I probably shoulda stuck around."

"You can't know that," said Dorothy. "You can't beat yourself up about this. Anyone would have run."

"Maybe. But maybe it's just all part of me not being very good at anything. What if she needed me? What if I let her down? What if she's pissed now?"

He left unspoken the question: what if she's dead. Dorothy did not supply it for him. "I thought you said she wasn't your friend."

"Yeah, well." He paused. "Sometimes I say stuff."

▰▰▰▰▰▰▰▰▰

John's description of a door in a wall proved accurate. The wall in question composed part of a small, trapezoidal structure, about the size of a small shed. Its surface of smooth, unpainted, white metal held no windows or any other features apart from the door, itself similarly featureless, of the same material, and sunken about four inches into the surface of a sloped face.

"What is this?" asked Dorothy.

"No clue. I kinda figured it was storage or something."

"And you found this here?" She held up the mapping device.

"Over there." He pointed to spot behind the structure. "It was just lying on the ground."

"Was there anything else?"

"I told you, I wasn't here very long. I found that, Linda found some other thing, then we tried to open the door, then I ran away. Whole story."

Dorothy walked around the structure, running her finger along it. The metal had been baking in the August sun all day, but remained cool to the touch. She looked up to gauge if the tree cover was sufficient to shade it for most of the day, and in that moment something snapped under her shoe. "Oh, no." She scooped up an object about the size of her thumb, mostly glass and shattered beyond identification. "John, keep your eyes on the ground. I just stepped on exactly what we came here to find."

It took them half an hour to comb the grounds around the structure, extending about twenty yards in every direction. At the end of that time, they had a pile of seven objects, all clearly manmade, and of uncertain purpose.

"This is good," said Dorothy, after lining their finds up in a neat row, sorted by approximate shape and size.

"Are we done?" asked John. His demeanor had gone from edgy to partially relaxed, the longer they lingered here with no sign of an angry (or scorned) wolf.

"We should still try to open that." Dorothy pointed to the door. "What did you try?"

"We got as far as pushing on it. Like I said—"

"You weren't here long. Got it." She approached the door, looking for anything resembling a latch, or a button, but found nothing. The longer she looked at it, the more she wondered if it even was a door, and not simply a recessed section of wall. "Open Sesame?"

Unsurprisingly, this had no effect.

"Maybe one of these things opens it," said John, looking at their small array of booty.

Dorothy looked over her shoulder.

John stood, apparently waiting for direction.

"Try fiddling with them," she said. "See if anything happens."

John picked up a small blue rod, tapped it, and swished it back and forth.

Dorothy turned her attention back to the door. In an attempt to determine whether the structure was hollow or solid, she pounded on it three times with her fist.

The door swung inward.

Dorothy gazed into the opening, at a stairway leading down into darkness.

John walked up behind her and looked over her shoulder. "I guess we should have knocked."

15

QUESTIONS

Harrison and Glimmer rode westward in a station wagon they found at a rest stop. If the road held out, they would be in Buffalo well before sundown. After that point, even if the road gave out, it would be a simple, if time-consuming, task to follow the lakes. As long as they kept a huge body of water to their right at all times, they would walk straight to Chicago. Eventually.

"So," Glimmer asked, "who made all the decisions?"

Harrison shrugged. "It was a democracy. The people made the decisions."

Glimmer eyed him with suspicion. "Oh, come on." She wore a blue denim jacket with the stylized B on the pocket over a pink shirt and bell-bottom blue jeans with the cuffs rolled up. No shoes.

"Well, okay," he admitted. "It was a representative government, not a true democracy. Still, the president, the senate, the house of reps, the governors, the state legislatures, they were all elected, which meant we could choose leaders who would make the decisions we would have made. So the people had a hand in the decisions, if not really a voice."

"That's stupid," she said. "Wouldn't people just lie to get elected? Then do whatever they wanted once they were in power?"

Harrison sighed. "I know it sounds dumb, but even though most of the politicians were liars, the system worked, mostly."

"Mm-hmm. Who did you vote for?"

"The loser, usually."

"Okay," said the pixie. "That's good enough. Your turn."

"All right, I'll follow a political question with another political question."

"Fire away."

"You had a king," he said.

"Oberon."

"Right. Oberon. And he ruled over all the pixies and fairies and... gnomes?"

She shook her head. "Gnomes are anarchists."

"Oh. Uh." He frowned in thought. "Um, oh! Brownies!"

She nodded, smiling. "And...?"

"Wait. Um..."

"And elves and sprites," she finished.

"Elves," he said with a knowing nod, "and sprites."

"Mm-hmm?"

"So. Oberon makes all the rules. Let's say a sprite goes rogue—"

"Never happen."

Harrison pursed his lips and tried to be patient about Glimmer completely missing the point. "Okay, let's say it's a brownie."

"Ooooh!" Her eyes went wide, and she covered her mouth with her hand, scandalized. "A rogue brownie! Yeah?"

"Well, what would happen? What kind of law enforcement did you have? Were there police? Little prisons?"

She deflated a bit. "Oh. Um. Well... he would... if we ever broke a rule..." As she struggled to finish the sentence, Harrison again felt the frustration of his inability to find her boundaries. "He would play tricks on us."

Harrison waited for more. "Tricks?" He tried to hold back the smile, and failed.

"Don't laugh!" she cried. "It was humiliating!"

He struggled to straighten his face.

She pouted. "I hear."

"Your turn," he said.

"Oh!" she said, brightening at once. "I've got one! Bicycles!"

"Bicycles?"

"When you ride a bicycle, why don't you fall over all the time?"

"Oh. Ah, that's actually a physics question. I used to know this." He paused, composing his answer. "Crap. It's either something to do with the wheels generating force vectors perpendicular to gravity or where you place the steering axis relative to the front wheel. I swear I used to know this. I learned it in college. I almost minored in physics, you know, until I had a run-in with the department head."

Glimmer's blank stare did not reveal how far back he lost her. "We'll just file that under 'something to do with physics,' and move on. Your turn again."

"How does magic work?"

"Wow." Glimmer frowned, as though considering the question for the first time. "Um, gee. Well, um, it just does. You may as well ask how a light bulb works."

"Take a tungsten filament and run electricity through it. It converts most of the energy to heat, but it also generates light. Enclose it in a vacuum so it doesn't catch on fire, and voilà! Light bulb."

"Oh," she said in a quiet voice. "Um, I mean… it would be like asking someone who didn't know."

"Yes, well… it's my turn again, and you still owe me the answer about magic."

"Foul!" she cried. "I didn't ask about the light bulb! Besides, your bicycle answer hardly counted."

"You said you would count it."

"I take it back."

Harrison scowled.

She held her hands out in surrender. "Okay, you can take another turn, but I can't owe you the answer about magic because I really don't understand a lot about it. Magic is all intuition. And the stuff I do understand…" She paused. "Well, no offense, but you don't have the vocabulary to understand it."

"All right," he said. "Then I'm going to try this one again. How do you get your clothes on over your wings?"

"They're intersubstantial," she said.

Harrison stared. He hadn't expected a straight answer and was still unsure if she had given him one.

"You know," she added, "like an angel's halo."

Harrison let that settle. "Pretend for a moment I have no idea what that means."

"Which part?"

"Interwhatever. And the thing about the angel."

"Um, okay. Intersubstantial means between states of being. Somewhere between real and imaginary. It also means stuff can't touch it. The angel part means you can't touch his halo. He can put on a hat, or whatever, and the halo doesn't move. I thought people knew stuff about angels." She frowned, surprised at this hole in his education.

He shook his head. "I always thought the halo thing was, I don't know, a metaphor or something." In truth, he had always thought angels themselves were metaphors.

Glimmer shook her head. "No, they're made out of pure Divine Glory. Intersubstantial, but literal."

"Okay," he said, "so what are your wings made of?"

"Mischief, mostly." She gave him one of her wide, toothy grins. "And glee."

"Wait, if they're intangible, how do they beat against the air?"

Her eyes went wide and indignant. "Against the air? What, like a *bird*? Do you have any idea how much *drag* that would create?"

"Wait, what? So how do they work?"

"They beat against the ether, of course!" She harrumphed, then added at a barely audible volume, "Thought I was a *bird*."

"I'm sorry. I'm still running on a physical world paradigm over here." He frowned. "Speaking of which, how is it you understand aerodynamics, but you don't know how a bicycle stays up?"

She gave him a baffled look. "They really don't have anything to do with each other." She tapped her chin. "Now, counting, 'how do they work,' you just got two turns. So there."

Harrison grinned. "Fine. Your turn."

"Fine," she echoed. Then she shifted to a far more serious tone. "Tell me about Claudia."

"Foul!" For the first time since the game began, he found himself uncomfortable. "The questions were supposed to be about what it was like before."

"Unless you can prove she wasn't here before, she's fair game." She folded her hands under her chin and glared at him, her lips curved into a wicked smile.

Harrison squirmed in his seat, silent for a long while. "I don't know anything about her. I heard her voice for the first time the day before I met you. Everything I know about her, I get from her broadcasts, and she doesn't share much." He thought on that. "About herself, that is." He left unspoken the fact she hadn't shared much about anything else, either. She announced her location, but left out what it would mean to find her.

"All right," the pixie continued, her smile growing wickeder. "What do you think she's like?"

Harrison smiled. "I think she's the most beautiful woman I'll ever meet. Mid-twenties. Tall, leggy, wavy blonde hair all the way down to her butt. I think she's a Harvard graduate, with a degree in, oh, philosophy or something." He paused to craft and refine this idealized Claudia. "She has a dog, extremely well behaved, show quality. Something expensive... I don't know breeds. On weekends, she paints, mostly landscapes, but also portraits of her friends. She plays the violin like a virtuoso, but gave it up to follow her heart and be the guitarist in a rock band. And there is nothing, but nothing sexier than her up on stage with that guitar."

Glimmer said nothing, perhaps waiting for more, perhaps having heard enough.

Harrison sighed. "Or she's a housewife. Lonely, sad." He let that image roll around, too. "Misses her kids."

Glimmer blinked as Harrison lurched from adolescent fantasy to melancholy without any transition. In that moment, she broke the silence with a tender question, her smile gone. "What do you hope she's like?"

Her probe took him somewhere he wasn't ready to go. The tone of the game had spun away from their intent, and he tried to find a way to nudge it back, without success. The silence grew. Glimmer respected it. Well after the point when he could give an answer without it being awkward, he added one word. "Human."

And having come up for that gasp of air, the conversation went under for the last time. Harrison did not offer his next question. Glimmer did not prompt him to do so. She turned her back to him. He watched her wings open and close, slowly, several times, before returning his attention to the road.

———

They made camp on the grassy median. He planned to drive as long as possible and sleep in the back of the car, but late in the afternoon, they discovered a wide chasm in the highway, at least two hundred feet across and a hundred feet deep. The crack went well beyond the road itself on both sides, like a miniature canyon. Its rocky walls provided plenty of footholds, so Harrison could climb it with ease. The car lacked that skill, however, so they abandoned it.

They walked on, hoping to find any building to spend the night in, but when the sun set before that happened, they quit walking. They had not spent the night out in the open in more than a week, but they had accumulated enough supplies to render the prospect only a mild inconvenience. Harrison had collected a lamp, bright enough to illuminate their entire campsite but frosted so one could look straight at it and not be uncomfortable, and a heater, which would come in handy since the first cold snap of the season had arrived. Although Glimmer preferred to sleep in the grass, Harrison did not. Thankfully, his supplies also included a cot that could collapse down to the size of his hand.

As he set about unfolding it and setting it up, he listened to the Walkman. Glimmer watched him as he sang along to a Who song. He did his best Pete Townshend air guitar lick, then let himself be Keith Moon for a few bars. He turned, and seeing Glimmer watching him, lost the moment.

She motioned for him to take the headphones off. He lifted one pad off his ear. "Whatcha listening to?"

He grinned to make a show of not being embarrassed. "It's a song by The Who. 'Bargain.'" He pulled off the phones and hung them around his neck.

A puzzled look came over her face. "Are you still humming?"

"No, humming sounds like this." He hummed the song he had been singing.

"Shhh!" Because of the way she made him hear her, the hush came through loud and clear. She frowned, tilted her head, and pulled her hair back from her pointy ears. "Do you hear that?" For the first time since he had met her, she said it without moving her lips. As she predicted, it did creep him out.

"What?"

"Humming," she said, still not moving her lips. "Inane, pointless humming."

"No," he whispered, exaggerating his own lip movements, offering a hint she did not take.

"Don't look at me," she said.

"What?" he asked, staring at her.

"Shh! Do not look at me." She faded. After a few seconds, he could almost see right through her. He could make out her outline and wings as a cloudy silhouette, but nothing more. Despite her orders to the contrary, he kept staring straight at her. The sight of this pixie becoming translucent transfixed him. She darted away.

The urge to track her with his eyes compelled him, but he did what she insisted by focusing straight ahead. Surely, she had an excellent reason for him to be silent and not draw attention to her.

He made a dutiful show of going about his business for the benefit of whoever (whatever?) found them so interesting. Nothing to see here, he mimed for all the world to see. Nothing. Nada. Sweat poured down his forehead, threatening to shatter the illusion.

A pair of hands clapped behind his head. The sound might as well have been a cannon firing.

"Ghaaah!" He turned, throwing his hands over his face. When he lowered them, Glimmer hovered in front of him, looking at her hands.

From her expression, they likely contained something akin to a handkerchief filled with snot. Or a dead animal.

"Fuck. Have you ever seen one of these?" She thrust her palms out to him, glowing brightly, and covered in luminescent goo, like what one might expect to find inside a Halloween glow stick.

"One of what?" he asked.

She sighed impatiently and pushed her palms closer to his face.

Upon closer inspection, he confirmed his original analysis, that she held glowing slime, although he now upgraded that to glowing pus. "Oh. No. No, I've never seen that before." Mixed in with the goo were a pair of crushed insect wings, and it came together she had a squished firefly. This insect posed no threat, but it must have been too mundane for Glimmer to identify it as harmless.

"Fuck." She wiped her hands on her pants, now strikingly cute with phosphorescent streaks on them. "Fuck, fuck, fuck." She looked up. "Get your pack."

His heart flushed, and his relief swirled down and out. Not a firefly. Something horrible. In seconds, he had scooped up his pack and donned it, ready to light out in an instant.

"Put that down!" she said. "We need what's in it."

He pulled it off and dumped the contents onto the grass. She swooped down, grabbed a random device, carried it about ten feet from the standing lamp, and dropped it on the ground. She flew back, grabbed something else, and dropped it a few feet away from the first.

"Make a circle," she instructed as she came back for a third thing.

"What's happening?"

"Circle first," she said. "Questions later."

They had enough items in the pack to make most of a circle wide enough to contain them, though leaving a gap on one side.

"What about the pack itself?" he asked.

"Let me see it." She touched down next to it. "Yes. Yes, this is technology, not just a bag, right? This will do fine." After using it to plug the hole, she went to his Walkman, also part of the circle, and pulled out the headphones. She yanked the wires out of the ear pads, then peeled them apart, all the way to the jack.

"Hey!" shouted Harrison, as she destroyed his only link to their actual goal.

"We need a binder," she said. "Do you have any more wire?"

He stared at his ruined headphones. No more Claudia. Just like that.

Glimmer snapped her fingers in his face. "Wire? More?" Her urgency transitioned into an uncharacteristic fear, and it sobered him.

He made a frantic search for wire, then grabbed a rock and smashed a device whose purpose he had not yet determined. Whatever it did apparently did not require internal wiring. He smashed another, no luck. The third one had a core wrapped with a long filament. Once he unwound it, they had more than enough to go around the whole circle. He picked up the remains of his headphones, their death now rendered meaningless.

Glimmer tied off the filament, then dropped down to the ground to catch her breath.

"What just happened?" he asked.

"Voyeur."

"I'm sorry, come again?"

"Somebody's avatar. A fucking voyeur," she said, shaking.

"That thing you wiped on your pants?"

"That thing I wiped on my pants was a spy. It was spying on you. It has likely been spying on you for a very long time, and come tomorrow, it will likely be replaced."

"A spy? Who would spy on me? What's worth spying on about me?"

Still shivering, she said quietly, "I wish I knew."

16

CRITTERS

The flashlight beam splashed across another door, thankfully at the bottom of only one flight of stairs. Shining it upward revealed a row of light fixtures on the ceiling, with no obvious switch to activate them. The cool air in the stairwell smelled musty.

"Should we go down there?" asked John.

"I have no idea," said Dorothy. "Maybe. It is why we came here, right?"

"I thought we came here for the stuff." John pointed to their small cache of new equipment to emphasize his point.

Dorothy gave him her best annoyed look.

"Okay, right, sorry. Your call, boss."

"We did come here for the stuff. Don't you think there's likely to be even more stuff down there than what we found lying around on the ground?"

"So, we go?"

Dorothy shined the light on the downstairs door, as featureless as the one they had already opened. "If that one opens when we pound on it, this will be the easiest break-in in history."

It turned out to be even easier than that. As soon as Dorothy reached the bottom step, she tripped some invisible sensor. The door slid open of its own accord. On the other side, they found themselves in a broad, mostly empty room.

"Let's find a light switch," she whispered.

"What?" said John.

Dorothy flinched. "Find a light switch," she said in a normal volume. "Sorry, I forgot we weren't actually sneaking."

About a minute into their quest for light, a bank of fluorescents on the ceiling came to life. John had found a panel of controls on the wall, which he toggled experimentally.

"Thank you," said Dorothy.

"No problem."

Apart from one desk, the room was devoid of furniture. Stacks of unopened cartons sat against the far wall. Two doors hung open on that wall, and to their left, a hallway extended further into the complex. John walked over to one of the stacks of boxes, pulled a knife from his pocket and cut the top one open.

"What's in there?" asked Dorothy.

John pulled handfuls of packing peanuts out and tossed them to the floor before reaching in and extracting a length of rubber tubing, sealed in a plastic bag. "Sciencey stuff."

Dorothy walked to another stack to read the labels, all marked with codes she had no way of interpreting. John worked his way down to the next box in his stack. "This one has test tubes in it."

"Leave that stuff," said Dorothy. "Let's see what's in the rooms."

Consistent with the supplies, the rooms proved to be laboratories. The first had nothing in it but barren tables and more cartons of supplies. The second held considerably more than that.

One entire wall consisted entirely of cages, vaguely reminiscent of a pet store, assuming the store only dealt in dead pets. Each cage contained the mummified remains of anywhere from one to a dozen animals, some common rodents, others less identifiable, none of them larger than a large rat.

"Oh, God. This is awful. These poor babies." She rested her hand against the bars of a cage containing six expired mice. "What happened here?" she asked their corpses.

"Looks like somebody left them here to die," said John bluntly.

"I bet their people all disappeared when the world changed," said Dorothy. "One day the food just stopped coming and they all starved to death."

"Yeah, well, you don't know what they were doing to these things. Maybe they were better off dead."

"Maybe. It's still sad."

"How much longer are we gonna stay here?" asked John. "We're not finding any more cool stuff."

Dorothy sighed. "I don't know. You're probably right. Let's just poke our heads in the last few rooms and then head home."

The next lab contained more cages, only some occupied, and many empty ones hanging open. The few animals housed there were also dead, but considerably larger than mice. Dorothy found a cage with two cats in it and one that held a small primate.

"Holy shit," said John. "Look at this one."

Dorothy joined him and found herself staring into a cage containing a medium-sized dog-like animal. From a head and body approximately German Shepherd-shaped extended tiny hind legs, and forelegs long, spindly, and covered in broad sheets of skin.

"What the hell is this?" said John.

"Those are bat wings," said Dorothy, struggling to maintain an even voice.

"Damn," said John. "That's messed up, right there. See? Better off dead, right?"

"I don't want to talk about it," said Dorothy quietly. "I think we should go now."

"Yeah, yeah," said John, with a strange new enthusiasm. "Let's just check out one more room and then head out, right?"

"No," said Dorothy. "We are finished here. I don't want to waste any more daylight."

"Right," said John. "I'll catch right up. I just wanna see what else is down here, okay?"

"If you feel the need to find more monsters, go right ahead," said Dorothy. "I want nothing else to do with this. Just make it quick."

John grinned. "Got it!" He left her alone with the bat-dog and its deceased ilk.

Dorothy found a chair and sat in it, looking at the floor instead of the cages. "I'm so sorry. They shouldn't have done this to you. I hope you all died in peace."

"Jesus!" shouted John so loudly she could hear him clear as a bell from two rooms away. Dorothy hoped in vain he would not share the particulars of his discovery. "Dorothy! You gotta come see this!"

She did not respond to this directive. John came back.

"There's a huge cage in there with an eight-legged horse in it! For real!"

"That's great," said Dorothy. "We can go now, right?"

"There's like two more labs," said John. "Do I have time to at least take a look?"

As Dorothy grappled with how best to tell him no, something moved

96

behind him. With his body in the way, she could not tell how big a something, or what kind of something. They had left both doors open on their way in, so anything could have followed them down here. Probably a raccoon or a groundhog. Probably not a monster.

"John," she said as calmly as she could, "please come in here."

"What? Why?" he said. "Am I in trouble?"

"I hope not." She looked around the room for a weapon. Something shifted in the hall. At least two (probable) raccoons/groundhogs shuffled around back there. On the floor near the cages lay several lengths of copper pipe. It would take her at least two seconds to make it over there and grab one of them. "Just come in, please, slowly."

The probably-actually-not-raccoons-or-groundhogs hissed.

John turned around. "Oh, shit!"

At that point, Dorothy had an excellent view of the animals because John bolted straight for the exit. One of the creatures charged after him. Four others entered the lab.

Dorothy's jaw dropped. "John?"

No response.

Before her, into the room, their eyes locked on her, crept four modified cats. Their heads accounted for about a third of their total body volume. These absurdly inflated crania displayed shark-like mouths, excessively wide, lips pulled back, and filled with hundreds of pointed teeth. Each animal was oversized and obese, easily forty pounds. Despite their hefty builds, they expertly slinked toward her with focus and grace, and did so on six legs.

John had fled, abandoning her to face these beasts on her own.

17

WORM

Harrison spent most of the night interrogating Glimmer and found every scrap of information he could glean from her to be less reassuring than the last. She explained the glowing snot on her pants to be the remains of a magical creature, not entirely unlike a pixie (much more like a faerie, she insisted). Sentient, after a fashion, but not autonomous. These creatures were linked directly to the beings that created them, transmitting all the sensory information they experienced.

The circle had been to shield them from any further intrusion, but it would buy them only a few hours. Technology was alien to the world Glimmer had come from and appeared to be incompatible with magic. Another avatar would not be able to see into the circle of tech they had created. With luck, it would look for them there, not find them, and move on, perhaps giving them enough time to change course and avoid detection altogether.

In addition to their small size, these creatures could become invisible and inaudible at will, making them excellent spies. Because of this, their masters referred to them as keyholes, spyglasses, and other labels of that nature. Often they were simply called bugs, in two senses of the word.

"Why did you call that one a voyeur?" Harrison asked at one point.

"The spying they do?" replied Glimmer. "Lurking? Watching? They get off on it."

After that, he stopped asking questions for a while.

Fortunately for Harrison, faeries and pixies were closely related, in a magical sense, to the little spies. As a result, Glimmer had the rare ability not only to detect them but also to render herself invisible to them.

The other, far more crucial information he obtained concerned the reason faeries and related beings had this unique connection to the avatars. Avatars were never created by noble creatures, or for noble causes, for a simple cost-benefit reason. The magic used to create one required the sacrifice of a living faerie.

Someone wanted to watch Harrison badly enough to murder for it.

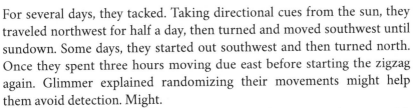

For several days, they tacked. Taking directional cues from the sun, they traveled northwest for half a day, then turned and moved southwest until sundown. Some days, they started out southwest and then turned north. Once they spent three hours moving due east before starting the zigzag again. Glimmer explained randomizing their movements might help them avoid detection. Might.

They came upon a small structure in a hilly forest, a single room with one glass door and no windows. It looked new, with a bright white exterior and a large, stylized logo sign fixed above the door. It read, in garish blue letters, GLTW, punctuated with a small icon in the form of a curvy squiggle connected to a short vertical line. The glass door revealed the entrance to a functioning escalator, going down.

"Well," said Harrison. "My, my, my. Isn't that inviting."

"What's a gltw?" the pixie asked. She wore tights, purple at the waist and sheer black all the way down from there, and a multicolored jacket with sheer black sleeves. Around her neck, on a red, white and blue ribbon, hung a tiny plastic Olympic gold medal, with a white sticker on one side indicating she had won it at the 2002 Winter Games, for the US team. Conspicuous by their absence from her naked feet were small plastic figure skates.

"It's probably not a word," he said, patiently. "It's got to be an abbreviation for something."

"Oh," she said, sounding disappointed. "An abbreviation for what?"

Harrison shrugged. "My first guess would be Obvious Trap of Certain Doom, but that doesn't have all the right letters. How about Gratuitous Lure to Torture and Woe?"

Glimmer studied his face. "You don't trust this thing. What are you afraid of?"

"What's not to be afraid of? This is a door to some underground, I don't know, something. That can't be good. We're basically on the lam now, right? Do we really want to stroll into some bunker, possibly with only one entrance or exit, without knowing what's down there? Doesn't this just shout trap to you?"

"Actually, I was just thinking the exact opposite."

"What? You think this is a lucky-break sanctuary? Ride the escalator into the bowels of the Earth, and all will be well? Why are we not already walking away from here?"

"It's not magic," she said.

"What's not?"

"The door. The room. The escalator. It's a real escalator."

"So what?"

She heaved a frustrated sigh. "Let's get on the same page here, Harry. So far, the only thing we know about whoever was watching you is he's using magical tools. If you recall, technology blinds the spies he uses. This is technology. They're not going to be down there. They're also not going to come down after us. The escalator alone will be enough to throw them off our scent, and there's no telling what might be down there we can use. It's worth checking out, and it's probably the safest place we could even be right now."

Harrison scrutinized the entrance again. It still looked like bait. "You can't possibly think this is a good idea."

"There's no one down there to fear," she said, "and we'll be invisible." They stared at each other for several long seconds. "I think..."

More staring happened.

As the door sensed his proximity and opened itself to invite him in, Harrison hesitated, then stepped through. "I really hope this isn't my first opportunity to say I told you so."

"It won't be," she said cheerfully. "I'm pretty sure."

The escalator went down the equivalent of two floors and ended at a short, narrow corridor, which led to another escalator. That one took Harrison down about two more floors. This time, the escalator opened out onto a much wider passageway, which, in turn, led to a cavernous enclosure.

It looked like a small, abandoned city.

They entered a well-lit, but strangely colorless chamber. Visible from the bottom of the escalator were maybe fifty small buildings laid out in rows. Wide walkways ran between them, a bit too narrow to be proper roads. On the ceiling several stories above hung a large, roughly trapezoidal solid, suspended over the center of the little faux town square, dark and smooth, its purpose not obvious. Everything looked remarkably clean, as though the entire place had been painstakingly constructed but never occupied. Lustrous tiles of ceramic and black glass covered the main walls, with no apparent graffiti. The letters GLTW ran across the top of one massive wall, in the same style and color as on the door topside.

"Welcome to Glitwuh," said Harrison under his breath. He frowned at his awkward pronunciation, envying Glimmer's ingenuous ability to read it naturally.

Most of the structures appeared to be storefronts. They found a newsstand (without a single periodical on display), a drug store (where Harrison traded in his depleted first aid kit for a fully stocked one), a bookstore, and more shops of that nature.

Some of the stores had alleys running between them, and a few of these had signs pointing down toward smaller tunnels that led out of the main chamber. The signs all proclaimed, in the same stylized blue letters, one word: WORM.

"Well. I know what a worm is." Glimmer smiled, quite pleased with herself.

"You don't really think these tunnels all lead to clearly labeled worms, do you? It has to be another abbreviation." Harrison looked back at all the shops. "Maybe it stands for Wonderful Offerings of Rich Merchandise."

"Oh! I like this game! Um, wait… let me think." Glimmer frowned and tapped her forehead. Her eyes popped wide. "Wrongful Ogres and Revolting Monsters!"

Harrison turned pale and moved on.

"What?" said the pixie. "What did I say?"

Harrison found a music store, and went in to look for replacement headphones for his Walkman. He found something much better. In a display marked simply "Media Players," he picked out an object about the size of a credit card, and nearly as thin. The display included a kiosk with instructions for how to preload music, and a cord that connected to a port on the player. It took him less than an hour to upload every album he remembered ever having owned, or heard of (including the one by the Treadles). A small display on the screen of the player indicated he had consumed zero-point-four percent of its storage capacity.

"Unreal," he whispered.

"Hey, Harry!" Glimmer had found another four-letter sign, in the same lettering, fixed above the entrance to a corridor. "What do you think this one means? I know it must have something to do with xylophones, but I can't think of a good one."

Harrison stared at the sign. "I think it says exit."

Glimmer squinted at the sign again. "Oh. I figured all the signs were initials. I didn't even read it." She smacked her forehead and giggled. "Duh. So, this one's just a word?"

"Maybe they're all words." He looked up at the enormous GLTW on the wall, back at the smaller WORM signs posted at various locations, then back at the clear and obvious EXIT sign in front of him. "Let's try to figure out where the hell we are before we touch anything else." He looked around. "Let's find an office, or an information booth. Something other than a store. We're so used to scavenging that's all we look for anymore, but this place can't be just for shopping." He waved his arms and spun in a circle. "No one would excavate a cavern to fill it with shops. It's got to be here for some other reason."

"But why would the shops be here, too?" she asked.

"I don't know." He looked around some more.

"What do they sell? Could that be important?"

Harrison pointed to his most recent stop. "Music." He pointed to the next one. "Pizza." Another. "Books and magazines." And another. "Toiletries. Stationery. Snacks. Toys. Magazines again." He looked back at her. "None of this stuff matters."

She nodded. "So now what?"

"We've only been down this one alley, right?" She nodded again. "Let's walk the whole square. Take every path, don't stop anywhere, just look around. If we see anything that looks administrative, we'll stop."

She saluted. "Aye, aye, Cap'n!"

After walking down one row of buildings and halfway up the next, they found a sizeable gap opening out onto the center of the square. In that center stood a single building, fenced in by a counter. Signs above the counter, in the familiar style, displayed the letters G, L, T, and W, but unlike every earlier sign, here followed each letter with the rest of a word, though in smaller type. "Great Lakes Transit Worm." He stopped, turned in a circle again to take in his surroundings, and slapped his forehead. "Oh, duh!"

"Duh?"

"This is a subway! This whole setup is a glorified subway station!" He looked at Glimmer. "A subway is a train that runs underground."

"I know what a subway is."

"Oh." He frowned. "Did you... were there subways where you came from?"

She rolled her eyes. "Of course not."

"Oh. Well. Um... Anyway, I think that's what this is. 'Transit' is a dead giveaway." He looked back up at the huge logos on the main walls and scanned further for more signs that read WORM. "The word 'worm' is a metaphor, I guess." He looked to Glimmer, who had no expression on her face at all. "You know, like an earthworm? Moves by burrowing underground? Like it's in a tunnel? Like a subway?" Her expression did not change. "That's why I didn't get it at first."

"So," she asked, "this subway is basically a big worm?"

The odious image of commuters riding a giant earthworm on an elongated, multi-seat saddle sprang uninvited to Harrison's mind. Revolted, he set it aside and shook his head. "No, no. It's called a Worm, but it's not really a worm. I think. I hope."

Further inspection of the counter area confirmed Harrison's assessment, more or less. The words "Great Lakes Transit Worm" appeared numerous times, printed on a variety of paperwork, tools, fixtures and furniture. Alternating small plastic tiles and large glass ones covered its surface. The counter area enclosed a square building set about fifteen feet behind it, and Harrison ventured in. The interior consisted of small offices, a break room, a time clock, and other banal trappings of a utilitarian industry.

"This doesn't sit right," he said after exploring several offices and having found nothing useful or especially informative. He looked back into the hall for Glimmer. She had pulled paper cups out of the dispenser on a water cooler, using them to build a castle on the carpeted hallway floor.

"What doesn't sit right?" she asked, putting the finishing touches on a turret.

"This just seems like a stupid way to design a train station," he said.

"What would a not-stupid train station look like?" She strolled through the opening in the front of her castle, lowering a paper portcullis behind her. She flew up and over the wall to get back out, and sat on the floor, giving Harrison her undivided attention.

"There should be maps," he said. "Maps of the train route and maps of the station itself."

"Maybe there are maps out there and you missed them," she said.

He frowned. "I don't see how. How would I miss one if I saw it?" She shrugged unhelpfully, and he sighed. "Let's poke around some more. If we don't find anything else useful in here, I think we should call it quits and go back topside." He looked up and down the hall. "I'm starting to get claustrophobic in here."

The next office they explored had the promising distinction of a sign on the door: Administrator. In addition to the same types of office paraphernalia they had found everywhere else, it included an extra piece of furniture, approximately a desk, but overrun and consumed by a computer terminal and many panels of readouts and controls. Harrison sat down at the station and tried to make sense of the screen. Overlaid on top of a complicated program sat a box with a question in it. It looked like a warning in any Windows program.

It read, "Idle time exceeds standard maximum. System switching to Standby Mode. Override?" On the screen, beneath the question, were the images of two buttons, officiously labeled YES and NO.

"It can't possibly be this easy." He reached out and touched the screen.

And the little city came alive.

Multicolored lights trickled into the office where he sat, and the unnatural silence that had pervaded the entire chamber gave way to quiet but invasive background noise. Harrison and Glimmer emerged from the office into a sea of activity. Displays lit up on every wall and surface, many showing data, many more showing movies. The lack of informative displays of which Harrison had complained now made sense. Information flowed freely from the glass tiles in the walls.

The little screens saturated the environment with instructions, entertainment, and advertisements galore. The trapezoidal structure on the ceiling comprised IMAX-sized screens on which ads for the various shops alternated with schedule information. As he watched, they cycled through to show the one thing he wanted to see most badly: the train.

Beautiful, sleek, and without doubt, a vehicle. Not an animal.

The silver Worm had windows and doors, constructed not by magic, not by God, but by human endeavor. It was a train. An actual, ridable train. The next steps would be to find out where it went, where it was, and how to get the hell on it. As Harrison pored over the deluge of new input, he heard a new sound and stopped. The sound hadn't come from a speaker, nor did it feel like the memorized sensation of having his eardrums magically stimulated.

"Cool!" said the sound.

Said the voice.

Said the boy.

On the other side of the counter and quite a way beyond, gazing, nearly hypnotized, at the oversized, overhead screen, stood a boy. This boy did not appear to have taken note of Harrison or Glimmer, at least not yet. Filthy, clothes worn through in several places, he showed no sign of self-consciousness over his appearance. Like the pixie, but, for presumably different reasons, he wore no shoes. His long, black hair hung halfway to his shoulders, clumpy with grease. His bangs had been cut off, unprofessionally.

Harrison asked Glimmer quietly, "Does he smell like skunk?"

"No," she said, her eyes also locked on the child. "Oh, good question."

"Hide," he said calmly.

It took Glimmer a full five seconds to pick up he was talking about her. "Why?"

"Just hide!" he whispered through his teeth.

She glared, venomously, then saluted. "Aye, aye, Cap'n." She zipped away.

Harrison cleared his throat. "Excuse me?"

The boy did not react.

Harrison would have a rough go competing against the gargantuan TV. He tried again, louder. "Excuse me?"

This time the boy looked right at him. "Hey! Did you do that?" He pointed up at the screen.

"Yeah," said Harrison. Ice broken. Now what? "My name's Harrison!" He waited.

The boy took the cue and walked to the counter. He stayed on the other side of it, and as he came closer, his extreme youth became more apparent. "I'm Mitchell."

"Hi, Mitchell," said Harrison.

Mitchell went back to looking up at the screen. "How did you do that?"

"I touched the screen in the administrator's office."

"How'd you get in? All the doors are locked."

Harrison shook his head. "Not the one I found. Have you been down here long?"

Mitchell nodded. "A while."

Great. "Do you know how long?"

Mitchell shook his head.

"A few days?" He deliberately aimed low.

"Longer, I think."

"Weeks?"

The boy thought before responding. "Maybe."

Time to risk the big question. "Is there anyone else here?"

The boy simply shook his head. "Not now. At least, I don't think so. Not counting you."

"Have you seen anybody else since you've been here?"

Mitchell shrugged and looked down.

"Mitchell?" said Harrison softly. "It's okay. You don't have to be scared. I just want—"

"There was a lady."

Harrison waited for more, got nothing. A lady. Human survivor

105

number four. In five minutes, his census of the planet had doubled. "Did she leave?" He didn't dare ask his real question, did she die?

Mitchell nodded. "She was nice. She came in a while back. She was pretty cool. Didn't want to stay, though."

Hearing that shocked Harrison. He had already adopted Mitchell, whether the boy knew it or not. The idea an adult would come down here, find him, and walk away was appalling. Inhuman. "Did she ask you to go with her?"

Mitchell nodded again.

So, she didn't just walk away. She tried to take him, but somehow took no for an answer. "And what did you do?"

"I hid."

"Why?"

Mitchell hesitated. "I dunno."

Harrison blinked at that. Some undisclosed anxiety had kept this kid trapped, on his own, in a dungeon, no doubt living on Cheetos. "What did she do when you hid?"

He shrugged again. "She looked for me, I guess. She shouted a lot." He looked away, and rocked his head to one side. "I think she was maybe crying a little bit, too."

"How old are you?"

"Is it August yet?" the boy asked.

It was late September. "Yes," said Harrison in an even voice.

"Then I'm nine."

Nine. Alone, and nine years old.

"Mitchell," said Harrison, "I want you to trust me. Can you do that?"

Mitchell shrank back a bit. "Are you going to try to get me to go with you, too?"

"Yes." Harrison braced himself for Mitchell to run. He didn't.

"She was nice," the boy said. "The lady who was here for a while. She took care of me. I really liked her." His voice shook. "She was all right, wasn't she?"

Harrison said, "I don't know her, but if you thought she was all right, she was probably all right."

Mitchell said nothing. It looked entirely possible he would cry, obviously struggling with whatever had kept him here the last time someone had tried to rescue him. Harrison may well have just given this boy his first real lesson in regret.

"Hey," he said, urgently hoping to break the mood. "I want you to meet someone."

Mitchell looked up, a bit brighter. "There's someone else here?"

Harrison nodded. "Her name's Glimmer. She's... well, she's going to be a little bit different than anybody else you've ever met." He thought for a moment, and for the sake of accuracy, added, "Probably."

"Where is she?"

"She's hiding," Harrison said loudly. "Glimmer? There's someone out here who wants to meet you. Can you come out?"

Without warning, the pixie appeared right in front of his face. "Right here, boss," she said without moving her lips, and no doubt not including Mitchell in on the sound of her voice.

"Whoa!" Mitchell wore an expression of unbridled wonder. "Is she real?"

Harrison smiled. "She sure is."

Mitchell stared, wide-eyed. "Can I touch her?"

Glimmer responded, "Why don't you ask her?"

"Can he touch you?" Harrison asked her softly.

"Yes." She looked straight at Mitchell. Her face softened. This moment surely mattered as much to her as it did to Harrison, and so far, he had shut her out of it. She differed from him in so many ways she made it easy to forget the one thing they had in common: loneliness.

Mitchell reached out.

"Wait!" cried Harrison, surprising both boy and pixie.

"What?" they both asked.

He directed his comments to Mitchell. "You know what it feels like when you rub your sneakers on the carpet and then touch a doorknob?"

The boy nodded.

"That's what it feels like to touch a pixie. I just didn't want you to be surprised."

"Does it hurt?"

"Yes. A little. But in an okay kind of way." Harrison looked at Glimmer, who smiled softly at this admission.

Mitchell touched her cheek, creating a tiny, visible spark.

18

SPEAKING

As the cat-things advanced, Dorothy stole a glance at the pipes with which she hoped to beat them to death. One of the creatures turned his gaze in that direction as well and moved toward them, cutting her off.

They showed no sign of haste. Gradually, they took up positions around her in a roughly semicircular form of about a ten-foot radius. Once in formation, two of them sat on their haunches. The other two paced back and forth in front of her. At least one of them growled.

Dorothy rose from her seat calculating a route to the door least likely to end in disaster. As she did so, the two sitting beasts stood as well. Experimentally, she sat back down. One of those two sat again. The other paced. Not a net improvement.

The only object left in the room still within Dorothy's reach rested beneath her, a small, rolling desk chair. Without taking her eyes off the cats, she ran her fingers along the edges of the seat beneath her, to get a sense of their thickness, and by extension, the weight of the chair. Options included holding the chair as a shield in front of her, wielding it as a bludgeoning weapon, or hurling it as a missile. For any of those scenarios, the wheels would surely throw off the balance, rendering it clumsy. She attempted to calculate which one of those uses would be least awkward, and minimize danger or maximize cat damage. The missile would take out at most one cat, but the right cat could open a passage to the door. The shield would only protect her in one direction; if they outflanked her, she would be defenseless. Swinging it to hit them would be exceptionally difficult, and if she lost control of it for even an instant, she would be done for.

One resource. Three perfectly terrible choices for how to employ it.

She braced herself, preparing for her one shot at freedom and life. As she cautiously shifted her orientation to best launch the chair at the cat nearest the door, she offered a quiet and futile plea.

"Please don't kill me."

One of the cats responded, "Please don't kill me."

Dorothy froze. The creature had repeated her words back to her in a wispy, scratchy voice, but with identical cadence and inflection to her own.

"Please don't kill me," said another cat.

"Please don't kill me," said a third.

They all started to talk over each other. "Please don't kill me. Please don't kill me. Please don't kill. Don't kill me. Please don't. Don't kill. Please me. Don't me."

"Please kill me," said the cat nearest the pipes.

The other three turned to face him, and loudly in unison, said, "Please *don't* kill me."

They all went silent, staring at each other.

"Please don't kill me," said the one by the pipes.

"Please don't kill me," the other three chanted one more time. Then all four went silent again and turned their gazes to Dorothy. The ones that had been pacing all sat down.

Dorothy weighed her escape plan against her astonishment. "What just happened?" She asked, uncertain if she addressed the cats or the universe.

They fell to babbling again. "What just happened? What just happened? What happened? What just? Just happened? Just what? What just? What happened? Just what? What? What? What? What? What?"

They stopped. The cat closest to the door, the one Dorothy had been hoping to take out of commission on her way to safety, looked her in the eye and said, "What?"

Dorothy took a deep breath and let it out. She maintained her grip on the chair, poised to strike. "Are you just repeating my words, or are you actually speaking?"

As expected, they followed the prompt. "Are you just repeating my words, or are you actually speaking? Are you just repeating my words, or are you actually speaking?" Their behavior became more complex as they mimicked her, rocking back and forth, standing and sitting, and generally interacting with each other as they ignored her. "Are you just repeating my words? Just repeating? Repeating? Repeating? Are you just repeating my words, or are you actually speaking? Are you actually speaking? Actually speaking? Actually speaking. Speaking. Speaking. Speaking."

They went silent again. The cat by the door, identifying himself as the leader, said directly to Dorothy, "Are actually speaking."

Grasping this small purchase of communication, she asked, "Are you going to kill me?"

This triggered a dramatic flurry of activity, and a cacophony of raised voices. "Are you going to kill me? Are you going to kill me? Are going to kill. Going to kill. Are don't going to kill. Don't kill. Are speaking. Actually speaking. Please don't kill. Just don't. What? Are going to kill. What? What just happened? Are speaking. Please don't kill."

With all of them talking over each other, Dorothy had difficulty assigning specific words to specific cats. But she did recognize an argument, and a heated one at that. As it rose in volume and aggression, two of the cats dropped out. The cat by the pipes and the cat by the door faced off as the other two slinked back.

"Are going to kill," said pipes cat.

"Are don't going to kill," said door cat.

"What? What just happened?" said Pipes.

"Are don't kill," said Door. "Are speaking."

"Don't speaking," said Pipes. "Are going to kill me." As the cat said these words, he looked directly at Dorothy, then at the pipes on the floor, then back to Dorothy.

She released her grip on the chair, relaxing her body into the least aggressive pose she could imagine.

"I am not going to kill you," she said to Pipes. "Please don't kill me."

The cat stared at her, exposing all its teeth and narrowing its eyes.

"Are don't going to kill," said Door.

"Are don't kill," said Pipes quietly before flopping down on the floor and facing away from Dorothy.

"Are not going to kill you," said Door to Dorothy.

"Thank you," said Dorothy.

Three of the four cats, in chorus, said, "Thank you. Thank you. Thank you. Thank thank thank thank."

This elicited a nervous giggle from Dorothy. The tension, if not exactly broken, had shifted.

"Thank you," said Pipes, still facing away from her.

"Thank you," she said to Pipes, who turned and hissed at her in reply.

"You understand me," she said to Door. "You are learning my language, just from hearing the words. Is that right?"

All the cats but Pipes muttered variations of that statement and question, incorporating words from earlier in the conversation.

After some time, Door said, "Is that right. Are understand you."

"Do you need context to learn the words, or just vocabulary?"

The cats conferred again. "Do you need context to learn the words, or just vocabulary? Do you need context to learn the words, or just vocabulary? Need context to learn? Need context? Need context or vocabulary? Or just vocabulary?"

From across the room, Pipes said, "Need to learn?" They all struggled with syntax, but at least one had already mastered sarcasm.

"Need to learn!" said Door pointedly to Pipes. Then, to Dorothy, it said, "Just vocabulary."

Dorothy took a moment to collect herself, then took a deep breath. "I, you, we, he, she, it, they. Me, him, her, them. My, mine, your, yours, his, hers, its, their, theirs."

The cats went to work assimilating these pronouns. After some collective muttering, they paused, and Door said, "Thank you. Words?"

She took this as a request for more. "And, but, or, if, so, as, to, for, from, by, in, into, onto, unto." She paused there, scanning her inventory of conjunctions and prepositions. "Um..."

"Um," said Door.

"Um," the others repeated. "Um. Um. Um. Um. Um. Um. Um."

"Oh." Dorothy hung her head. "Great."

"Great, great, great, great, great."

―――――――

Dorothy's conversation with the cats lasted about an hour. During that time, they picked up hundreds of new English vocabulary words, though by the time she left, they still couldn't put together a proper sentence.

She also learned a great deal about them. It turned out their original plan was in fact to eat her. She took that as an opportunity to teach them the word "forgive." While their English vocabulary was limited to whatever she had provided (and, she learned, John's contribution of "shit"), they communicated extensively with each other in Russian. They did not provide much information about their origins, or their lives before that day, as they clearly did not want to relive any of that.

In addition to their language skills, the cats were also highly intelligent. The outside door opened when Dorothy knocked on it because they had rigged it to do so. This made it easier for them to come and go as they pleased. Dorothy asked them why they would want to continue living in the lab complex if they hated it so much, and they said something about watching over their fallen comrades. She did not fully understand, but she did not press.

When she did finally make her goodbyes and return to the surface, both knapsacks and the pile of tech devices they had found were gone.

[19]

RIDE

Harrison spent the next several hours absorbing as much information as he could about the Great Lakes Transit Worm. The GLTW had been part of a much larger network, with junctions connecting it to an Atlantic Seaboard Transit Worm and a Mississippi Basin Transit Worm, both of which connected to other Worms down their own lines. That network was not, at the moment, whole. The system featured real-time monitoring of every station in the network, with most of those monitors currently blank or snowy. A station in Baton Rouge still fed a real-time image of its empty self from several perspectives that rotated through in a set pattern, but no other station on the Mississippi line reported in.

Glimmer and Mitchell emerged from the office building a few minutes later, the boy substantially cleaner. A locker room in the building included working showers, and Glimmer had insisted the boy avail himself of one. He wore a pair of pajamas with the GLTW logo emblazoned across the top and down both legs. While Harrison focused on exploring the train system, Glimmer had slipped easily, if not quite expectedly, into the role of babysitter. Mitchell hadn't had any trouble accepting the reality of her at all. He apparently perceived her as an adult.

"What's up?" she asked.

"I think I can make this thing work," said Harrison.

"The train?" asked Mitchell. "How? Do you know how to get to it?"

"There's one parked right downstairs, which is pretty fortunate, actually, because I can only find four trains total on the whole line, and one of them happens to be here." He motioned to them. "Come here. I want to show you both a few things."

Glimmer lighted on the counter, and Mitchell hoisted himself up into one of the tall chairs.

"Okay, first off, take a look at these." Harrison pointed to a bank of small screens built into the counter. Each screen showed an empty Worm station, and displayed a label, in small unobtrusive type, across the bottom. The first screen in the upper left corner of the bank, the only one that showed activity in the station, read *Buffalo*. He pointed to it. "This is us." As he said that, the image helpfully shifted to a different perspective, which happened to include, tiny and in the distance, the three of them sitting at the counter.

"Buffalo?" Glimmer asked. "Isn't that where we were trying to get in the car?"

"You had a car? I thought all the cars were gone. I thought all the roads were gone."

Harrison held up his hand. "They're not," he said to Mitchell, "and yes," he said to Glimmer. "Turns out we made it." He pointed to the next screen. "This one is Erie, Pennsylvania. It's still there, and so is the one in Cleveland, and the one in Toledo. There were also stations in Fort Wayne and South Bend, but I'm not getting anything from them, so we have to assume they're gone." He brought up a map of the entire Great Lakes Transit Worm line. "In fact, something like half the stations on the line are down. Without Fort Wayne, we can't ride this thing any farther west than Toledo, but look here." He traced a route with his finger. "There's a tunnel that cuts from Toledo to Detroit. Detroit connects to Owen Sound, farther north. From there, it's another hop north to Sault Ste. Marie, down the Michigan Upper Peninsula to Green Bay, and then to Milwaukee, all of which are intact." He tapped each monitor in that order, letting his finger rest nonchalantly on the one that said Milwaukee. He tapped it several times.

"I can read, Harry," said Glimmer. "The next one says Chicago. I get it."

Harrison, with flourish, lifted his finger from the Milwaukee monitor and placed it on the Chicago monitor. "And the next one says Chicago. Right here." He tapped it again. "See?"

"How far away is that?" Mitchell asked.

"Going that route, about a thousand miles."

"A thousand miles! That's like the other side of the world! That's gonna take years to get there."

"No," said Harrison, "it's like the other side of the lake, and in this baby, we'll be there in under two hours."

"Harry," said Glimmer, "not to burst your bubble or anything, but what makes you think the tunnels are intact? I mean, couldn't the stations be just sitting there, like, totally unconnected?"

He shook his head. "Take a look at this." He touched a spot on the main screen, and the image changed to a diagram of the train itself, sitting in a cutaway view of the tunnel. It was smooth, tapering at both ends. About twenty cars were visible, with no external connections between them. Instead, the train showed a contiguous surface, with flexible joints between cars giving it its segmented look. It had no wheels, nor did it make contact with the tunnel walls at any point.

"The train is a Maglev. It rides suspended on a magnetic cushion, repelled off the bottom three-quarters of the tube. The tube is a permanent magnet, so even in a total power failure, the train goes right on hovering. There's a whole thing they do with gyroscopes and ballast that keeps the Worm from rolling in the tube. Here along the top of the tunnels is the actual propulsion, what they call the 'rail.' It's another series of magnets, designed to attract the front of the train. The magnetic field is always one step ahead of the train, like a hare on a dog track. Once it gets up to speed, the train coasts almost the entire way. They use the rail mostly to pull it around turns or up inclines. It's energy efficient, it's comfy, and it's super-fast."

"And so this all makes you sure the tunnels are intact because?" asked Glimmer.

He held one hand up while tapping the screen with the other. "I'm getting to that. The tunnels themselves aren't just tunnels. They're vacuums. The trains are zipping through a frictionless environment, which is one of the reasons they move so fast. Do you see these stats?" He pointed to the monitors.

Mitchell nodded.

Glimmer rolled her hands in an impatient gesture.

"Every station is connected to the tunnels through a series of airlocks. The locks are all equipped with pressure gauges on both sides." He swept his arm proudly across his tidy collection of displays. "I ran a diagnostic on every gauge on every airlock on every one of these stations. They all report they are functioning normally, and they all report zero air pressure in the tunnels I mapped out. If there were breaches anywhere on the line, the tubes would be flooded with air."

"What if there's an obstruction in the tube?" she asked. "What if something, I don't know, materialized in there? Or what if the tube was cut off by a huge wall of rock? Isn't it possible the tunnels are still impassable?"

"Yes, it is. Which is why all Worms are equipped with obstacle detectors, which operate at a range of over 200 miles. If they spot anything in the tunnels, they automatically return the train to the last station and divert it to a different route. I'm telling you, Glimmer, this thing is foolproof and chimp simple! I thought you would be thrilled about this. Is there a problem?"

"What would you say," she asked, "if I told you I had found a lovely pumpkin and eight mice, and it would be child's play to turn them into a carriage that would hustle us all to Chicago in no time at all?"

He thought about that for a moment. "I guess I'd say I'd rather walk."

"That's right. I'd rather walk than ride your Worm."

"What? Why?"

"Because it's tech, Harry! I don't understand any of what you just said! What the hell is a magnetic field? What do you mean by air pressure? How am I supposed to trust this thing if it doesn't make any sense to me?"

"I know what a magnet is," said Mitchell to Glimmer. "They stick to metal. They stick to refrigerators, too. Which is weird, because refrigerators aren't really metal, but magnets work on them anyway. So, they stick to metal and refrigerators. Oh! And chalkboards."

"Refrigerators are made out of metal," Harrison said.

"They are?"

Harrison nodded. "And so is the train," he continued, still talking to Mitchell, but drawing Glimmer in, too. "That's how the magnets in the ceiling make the train move. The magnets in the train are trying to stick to them, so it moves toward them."

"Hey, don't compasses use magnets, too?" the boy asked.

Glimmer seized the opening. "Oh, sweet! Why don't we all just get our compasses out, and then..." She paused, feigning alarm. "Oh, my! I just remembered! Those don't work right anymore, do they?"

"Okay," Harrison whispered to Mitchell, "now you're not helping."

"Sorry."

"So now what?" asked Glimmer. "What makes you think this will work?"

"Come." He got up and marched into the building. They followed him into a room with several long tables and a wall of snack machines and drink dispensers. A sink, a counter, a microwave oven, and a refrigerator occupied one corner of the room. Affixed to the refrigerator were several small labels, one bearing the GLTW logo, others advertising shops outside. He peeled one label off and handed it to Mitchell, peeled another off and handed it to Glimmer. "Magnets. They work just fine. The problem with the compasses isn't magnetism. It's magic."

116

Glimmer said nothing.

Harrison pulled up a chair and flopped into it. "Okay... I get this thing makes you uncomfortable. I guess I'd feel the same way, like you said about the pumpkin. But the thing is, I'm ready to be done walking. We're in Buffalo, New York, right now, which means we've come halfway, and we've been on the move for over two months. That stinks. If this thing works, we'll be there today. Not two months from now, not next week, today." He paused, glancing at the child. "Also, if we're looking for a way to travel surreptitiously, we'd have a hard time finding a better method."

"I already thought of that," she said.

"And you'd still rather take your chances up on the surface?"

She looked down. "No, not really." She looked up again. "This better not be my chance to say I told you so."

<hr>

Harrison programmed the entire route into the train from the station. He also cleared the tubes remotely by depressurizing and opening an airlock in every station along the way. Every time he cleared a path, a light on the monitor for that station changed from red to green. The entire process took about twenty minutes.

Mitchell explained, several times, he had been down the tunnels marked WORM, and every single one ended with a gate he could not open. Harrison forged fare cards for himself and Mitchell with more than enough credit on them to cover the trip they had planned. When they got to the gates, Harrison insisted on going first. He approached the gate, and rested his fingers on it, almost absent-mindedly. Before he could swipe his card, it buzzed lightly and opened for him.

Mitchell and Glimmer hung back until Harrison passed through, then Mitchell moved forward, Glimmer on his shoulder. The boy imitated Harrison and waited for the gate to open. It did not.

"Try swiping the card through the slot on the wall," Harrison called back through the gates. When Mitchell did this, it worked, and he walked through with the pixie in tow. From there, they proceeded down another escalator, which took them to the platform.

Smooth chrome covered the train, dotted with a series of tear-shaped windows that ran its whole length. All of this design served style more than function, however. Traveling through a vacuum made aerodynamics irrelevant, and there would not be much to see out a window moving over 600 miles per hour through a sealed tunnel. Apart from the brilliant metallic shine, the blue GLTW logo provided the only color, worked tastefully into a racing stripe applied under the row of windows. The train hovered behind an enormous curved wall made of glass with huge metal ribs, presumably part of the network of magnets, there to keep the train from repelling off the far wall and crashing through the glass. Small openings sat at several points in the wall, with boarding ramps leading to doors in segments of the train, all open.

They boarded, Harrison giddy, Glimmer reserved, Mitchell somewhere in between. They made their way to the front of the train. The last passenger car they passed through on their way to the bullet-shaped lead car included a lounge, presumably the Transit Worm's equivalent of first class. Mitchell picked a voluminous couch and stretched out on it.

"I need to do some stuff up front," Harrison said. "Are you okay here?"

Mitchell nodded, having already found the controls to the TV screen. He scrolled through prerecorded programs, most of them ads, information about the train, or news programs. Harrison's gaze lingered for a moment on a story about a war somewhere in Europe, events that had not yet happened and likely never would. When Mitchell changed the channel, the story vanished.

"Stay with him for a minute, would you?" he asked Glimmer. "Try to see he finds something, I don't know, wholesome to watch."

"Sure." She sat on the couch next to him and started asking questions about the remote control. Harrison passed through the doorway into the cockpit.

The sparse car held a number of seats, two of which faced front, situated behind a small panel of controls. Some of the seats faced tables that folded out from the walls. The control panel was several orders of magnitude less complex than he expected. Some gauges indicated speed, location, air pressure, and the like, and as in the station office, he found a touch screen and a bank of smaller monitors. Nothing else. What should have looked like the cockpit of a jumbo jet, or maybe some futuristic spaceship, instead looked like a room that had nothing whatsoever to do with the operation of the train. The touch screen clearly and helpfully read, "Course Downloaded. Proceed?" The same two YES/NO buttons he had seen when he had restarted the system back in the station awaited his command.

"Chimp simple." He reached forward and held his finger poised over the YES option, and hesitated. "This should be a bigger moment."

Glimmer appeared behind him. "Do it before I change my mind."

He did.

The message on the screen changed to "Course Accepted," and showed a graphic of the doors retracting and sealing and the boarding ramps folding back into the tunnel wall, which also sealed. "Station Lock Depressurizing," the screen read. It had begun. In less than two hours they would reach the end of their journey.

"Did you find Mitchell a good cartoon?" Harrison asked.

"I guess it was good," she answered. "It put him to sleep."

"Wow. That was fast."

She shrugged. "He had a big day. Besides, it's almost midnight."

"Man, I had a big day, too." He rubbed his eyes. "If I'd slowed down long enough to think about it, I probably would've said we should get a fresh start in the morning. It's going to be stupid late by the time we get there."

"Yeah, well, *carpe noctem*," said the pixie.

"Hmm. I wonder if I can score some coffee on this boat."

As he said this, the screen changed again, showing the message, "Lock Depressurized. Hatch Opening." No dramatic rumbling or clanking sound marked the grand event of the tunnel door opening, as the hard vacuum between the door and the hovering train would not convey any such noise. The sudden acceleration pulled Harrison's seat back from him, and the station receded from the window in front of him.

"Whoa," he said. "We're in the caboose!" The light of the station faded to a speck, then vanished. In addition to being soundless, the train cruised so smoothly as to render motion undetectable apart from the occasional light pull to one side or another as they rounded curves. "Well, this is it. I can't believe we're almost there."

"Given any thought as to what we should do when we get there?" Glimmer asked.

"No clue. The station there isn't running yet. I guess we could go out and explore the city in the middle of the night. Probably better to just get some sleep and head up in the morning."

"Aren't you eager to meet your Claudia?"

"She's not mine, and yes, I am. But I don't think I'm going to win any friends trying to track her down at two in the morning."

"Ah, yes." Glimmer smiled. "The moment must be perfect in every detail, right?" As Harrison rolled his eyes at her, she giggled. Then she pointed to the bank of monitors behind him. "One of your lights just went red."

"What? Where?" Harrison turned around and scanned the panel. "That's weird. Milwaukee Station is showing a closed airlock. I had them all open. Did you actually see the light turn red?"

"Yep," she said. "It was green. Now it's red."

"Shit." He tapped the main screen for a status report on that station. "Says the station's on lock-down. That doesn't make sense. I just opened it when we were upstairs. Why would it seal itself?" He double-checked the other stations on his route and found them all exactly as he left them. "This is screwed up. I can't get the lock back open."

"Is that one we can go around?"

"No. In fact, it's about the only station we can't get around somehow. It's also the only station that connects to Chicago, so if we want to take the Worm the whole way, we need to take it through Milwaukee." He tried to reopen the lock the same way he had opened it the first time. "It's not responding. I wonder if it's just gone idle. This would be the worst time for it to do that. Damn, this sucks."

"Now what?"

"Now we stop the train. If we can't ride this thing to Chicago, it's not worth taking it up and around the lakes." He looked at his map. "We'll stop in Toledo. That's going to mean going on foot again, but I don't see an alternative. Because of the route I marked out, that's where we turn around and start going way out of our way." He slapped the Milwaukee monitor with his palm. "Dammit! This sucks!"

"Well at least we'll get as far as Toledo, right?" said Glimmer.

"Yeah," he said quietly. "Yeah, and that alone will take weeks off the trip. I guess I should be thankful I got anywhere in this thing at all."

"That's the spirit. How soon until we get off?"

"You could sound a little more disappointed, you know."

"Yes."

He brought up the main menu on the screen and found an option for course revision. Canceling every part of the route after Toledo, he ordered the locks at that station to seal and pressurize once they were there. He submitted the final revisions and tapped a button that said, "Confirm Changes."

The system responded, "Unable To Proceed. Course Revision Not Accepted."

Harrison felt his stomach drop down to the track. "Oh... That's not what I want."

He tried again, giving the same commands as the first time, and got the same result. Then he tried to program the train to stop in Erie. Again, the system would not comply. He tried to program the train to stop in Detroit. This also didn't work.

"What's happening?" asked Glimmer.

"It's not letting me stop the train. It still wants to take us to Chicago." Harrison thought in silence for a few moments as he examined their situation. "As near as I can tell, the system is acknowledging the Milwaukee locks are closed. It still intends to send us through that station without flinching."

"What does that mean?"

"It means… I think, we are going to crash. In about…" He looked at a monitor that displayed a map of the route with a lighted indicator showing their location. "Ninety minutes or so."

Neither of them spoke for a few seconds.

Harrison broke the silence. "Is this where you say I told you so?"

Glimmer scowled. "I should think I deserve a bit more credit than that."

"Right. Sorry."

"Can't we just turn the train off?" she asked.

"You mean shut down the power? I don't know. I can try. The problem, though, is even if I can, we're in a frictionless environment. If I cut the power right now, I'm not sure how far we would coast. Maybe the whole way to Milwaukee." He thought for a minute. "What we really need is a way to stop the train at one of the stations as we pass through it." He looked around the sparsely equipped room. "I'll bet there's an emergency brake we can pull. There's got to be some way to stop the train manually."

Minutes later, he found a pull handle near the doorway, labeled discreetly, but with clear purpose. He went back to the monitors to check their position. They were already closing in on the Erie Station. He brought up a display that gave a running estimate of their arrival time. They would be there in under five minutes. "Damn. This thing is fast."

"What if we stop the train," Glimmer asked, "but we can't get the tunnel doors to close? You guys need air, don't you?"

"There's got to be a way to get out. Maybe there's an escape pod, or spacesuits, or something. We'll have plenty of time to sort that out." He got up, went to the handle, and rested his hand on it. "Tell me when we get within thirty seconds of Erie."

Glimmer stood on the control panel, watching the screen. "Soon. Very soon. Very, very soon. Very—now!"

Harrison squeezed the handle, hard. For a moment, he froze. The moment passed. Nothing happened.

"Harry? What's going on?"

"Nothing."

"Yes, dear," she said. "I can see that. I mean, why is nothing going on?"

"Not here," he said. "We'll do it at Toledo Station."

Glimmer scowled. "This is not a game you want to play right now, Harrison."

"It's not a game," he said without apology. "Look, if this works, then we're way better off doing it that much closer to where we're actually going, and if it doesn't work, it won't make a difference. It was the right call."

"And what is your backup plan if it doesn't work? I sure hope you don't need those extra few minutes to think of one."

"Relax, will you? We're going to be all right."

"Oh, really?" she asked. "That's very comforting. While you're basking in that certainty, I'll let you roll this bit of information around. If we hit that sealed door, at..." She checked a figure on the monitor. "305 meters per second? If this thing splits open, or crumples up like a wad of paper? Do you know what will happen to me?"

"No," he said simply, hoping she might not tell him.

She flew to his face, hovered right in front of his nose, and whispered, "Nothing at all. Not a scratch. So don't tell me to relax."

They rode in silence to Toledo. As they passed through Cleveland Station, intermittent light from the platform flashed into the train, a sharp reminder of their speed. As they approached their goal, Glimmer again gave Harrison a countdown, of sorts. "Wait for it. Almost. Almost. Wait for it. Aaaaaand—Now!"

This time Harrison pulled, throwing his whole body weight into it. The handle came straight down and some internal mechanism engaged with a hefty metallic *click*.

And again, although it took them both some time to fully understand it, nothing happened.

"Oh, fuck," said Harrison.

"Watch the boy," said Glimmer. She shot out of the caboose toward the front of the train, leaving her signature sparkling trail, purple this time.

Mitchell slept on, curled up on the couch with a blanket draped over him. While he waited for her to do whatever she needed to do, Harrison paced and tried to reorganize his thoughts. In a little over an hour, he and Mitchell would be raspberry jam, and Glimmer would be inconsolably pissed.

Five minutes later, she came flitting back into the car. "Well, I was wrong about one thing. If we hit that door, I'm dead as a dishrag."

"Where were you?" he asked.

"Milwaukee," she said. "We have a problem."

"What? How fast can you fly?"

"Pretty fast. Listen, if we can't get this worm thingy stopped, we are seriously screwed."

Harrison raised his hands slightly to balance himself. "Wait, are you telling me you could have flown to Chicago any time—"

She snapped her fingers in his face. It sounded like a rifle shot. "Focus! The tunnel is magicked up! This is a major problem!"

Sweat beaded on his forehead. "Magicked up? What the hell does that mean?"

"I mean there's a spell in the tunnel, right in front of the door. You can see it shimmering. I'm pretty sure it's some variation on a shield curse, which means if we make contact with it, we're toast. We won't even have to hit it all that hard." She spoke quickly, though with relative calm. "The bottom line is we either need to find a way off this thing or find a way to stop it."

Harrison took a deep breath, willing the blood back into his brain. "Please tell me this is the sort of thing that happens to tunnels all the time, by accident."

She shook her head.

"Are we at 'I told you so' yet?" he asked.

"Is that really where you want to be?" she replied acidly. "Snap out of it, Harry! We've got a big problem to solve, and about an hour to solve it. If you want, I'll rake you over the coals about this relentlessly all the way to Chicago. But not now."

"Right." He pushed through the dizziness, and wiped the sweat off his face. "Whether we get off or stop, we have to do it near a station. Mitchell and I won't be able to walk hundreds of miles through the tunnel."

"Yeah, I thought of that, too," she said. "Would you rather abandon ship or try to stop it?"

Harrison mulled those two options. "I don't remember seeing any provisions for escape in the information I looked at. I'm sure there are some, but I'm not sure I'd find them in time. You could cover more ground alone, so you should check out our escape options while I try to slow us down. I have a couple of ideas I want to try. Do you know what you're looking for?"

She nodded. "Lifeboats."

"Yeah. I'm going to get to work."

20

HIKE

"P lease come in here, John," said Dorothy. Ahead of her, up a short, rocky incline, a purple ribbon dangled from a tree branch.

She lowered her voice. "Sure thing, Boss. Whatever you say." She took several, zigzagging steps to maintain her balance, then stopped at the tree to rest. Scanning beyond it, she spotted another strip of purple and made for it.

"Oh, look," she said in her normal voice. "Monster-cats."

"Golly, Boss!" she said in the lower voice, now drawn out and cartoonish. "We should run away!" She hiked to the next ribbon over even terrain, slightly downhill. Her sore legs relished the relative break.

"Hang on, John," she said in her best attempt at a tone both nurturing and commanding. "Maybe we can talk our way out of this." Sunlight cut through the trees at a low enough angle to get in her eyes as she walked, but still beat down on her enough to make every step a burden. Near the next ribbon, an outcropping of rock presented itself as a suitable bench. She lowered herself onto it gently and took a few deep breaths.

"Gee, Boss," she said in the lower voice, "I guess you're right, as usual."

"As always," she said bitterly and shook her head. "No, I take that back. I was wrong to think this trip was a good idea. I was wrong to think we could make it in one day." She paused. "I was wrong to trust you."

Looking up and around, it took her more than a minute to find the next purple ribbon. As she stood, the flashlight in her front pocket bit into her leg, the one piece of equipment she managed to salvage from this expedition, having had it with her when the cats cornered her. She pulled it out and switched it on. The beam shone bright and sustained, as it had been the last four times she checked. Given the sun's position in the sky, this was the only scrap of good news she had at that point. Without the mapping device, she had no way to gauge how far she still had to go before reaching the bowling alley.

"Next time we do this, let's count ribbons." She said this in her normal voice, and not to her pretend version of John. Even as an imaginary target for venting, John still provided worse company than solitude. It was impossible for her to know what had become of him, with no sign of him outside the lab complex, nor of the fifth cat that had pursued him out of it. Perhaps he fled into the woods and got lost. Perhaps the animal took him down somewhere too far for Dorothy to find him in her quick search.

Perhaps. But the missing packs told the story of a different possibility.

If John had left her for dead and taken all their supplies, would he have gone home? And if she found him when she finally made it back there, what explanation would she accept for his abandonment? What excuse could he offer that would be anything other than abominable? As angry as she felt entitled to be, one inescapable fact confronted her: he had warned her of his own worthlessness.

In the wake of her new understanding of the extent of that worthlessness, things would be different from here out.

As she set out for the next ribbon, a refreshing breeze trickled past her sweat-covered neck, convecting away a little bit of her accumulated body heat. She sighed happily, until another, slightly stronger gust got her attention. Overhead, the sky darkened from more than the setting sun.

Dorothy staggered into the main entrance of the bowling alley well after dark. She shivered as the air conditioning enveloped her rain-soaked body. Her glasses fogged over, and wiping them on her damp shirttail only served to make them streaky. Most of the lights were off, rendering her eyesight moot anyway. Her sneakers squished beneath her as she advanced through the darkness. She felt her way to the switch for the lights over the front desk, and turned them on.

"John?" she called. No answer.

She returned to the front door and latched the deadbolt, as a flash of lightning illuminated the forest beyond. The thunder came quite a bit after, a low rumble in the distance. She made her way down to a bench, where she pulled off her shoes and peeled off her socks, leaving the latter draped over the ball return to dry. The cold hardwood floor pressed against her aching, saturated, bare feet. She made her way back to shoe rental across the scratchy carpet and picked out a pair of red and white shoes. She pulled them on without socks, in the hope they would protect her feet from the cold, but they proved to be the same temperature as the rest of the air-conditioned building. Off they went, and back on the shelf.

Feeling exposed in front of the glass doors, she ducked into the manager's office, away from any prying eyes, to remove her shirt. She wrung it out directly onto the floor, where it left a sizable puddle, her plan to put the shirt back on now ill-advised in the face of how much moisture it retained. She laid it over a chair to drip before hunting for some alternative. The office closet housed a musty smelling Green Bay Packers jacket, which she pulled on. Before leaving the office, she pushed the wall thermostat control the whole way up to ninety degrees. An audible *thump* followed by a new and deeper silence indicated the air conditioning had turned off.

Emerging from the office, she called again. "John? Are you in here?" As expected, the question went unanswered. Her stomach growled. "I guess I'm making my own French fries, then."

Behind the snack bar, Dorothy looked over the deep fryer for the controls to turn the vat of stale oil into a vat of dangerously hot stale oil, before losing her courage. The freezer held a few hamburger patties covered in the snow of their own dehydration. Frying up one of those on the grill turned out to be simple, particularly given she had no intent to clean up afterward. She let it cool on a paper plate, and devoured it without utensils, along with a bottle of Sprite and a bag of potato chips, easily the most satisfying meal of her life.

Taking two more bags of chips with her into the manager's office, she paused near the front door, looking at the lock. If John were still out there, and still headed home, he would be locked out to spend the night in the rain.

"Well," she said to the version of him in her head, "isn't that just too bad." She retired to the office, closed the door, and curled up in the leather desk chair. Sleep took her in minutes.

The morning air was hot and sticky, saturated with evaporation from the previous night's rainfall. Dorothy trod on in her mostly dry clothing. Bowling shoes, in no way intended for hiking, bit into her heels through damp socks. Her sneakers, still too wet to use, but not damaged enough to discard, hung limply from her left arm in a plastic bag.

The two-hour hike from the bowling alley to the Hallmark store took nearly three hours. By the time she arrived, the sun stood overhead, beating her without mercy. Unlike the purple ribbons, the yellow felt familiar and welcoming as they merged with the other colors, and Dorothy counted them down to her destination. When she got down to ten, her pace picked up. Her right heel stabbed her with pain from the stiff shoes, which she ignored.

Finally, she broke from the brush to the empty parking lot and staggered through the door of her home, dropping her sneakers on the front walk on her way in. She made a beeline for a chair in the manager's office, where she delicately untied her shoes and pulled them off with care. Both feet had sizeable blisters on their arches and heels. The one on her right heel had burst and was extremely tender.

She walked on tiptoe back to her bedroom area, stripped off all her clothes and left them in a heap on the floor. With a clean towel, she gently patted and wiped down her entire body to pull off the layer of accumulated perspiration and rainwater, then dropped that on the heap as well. From her storage tubs, she pulled a clean set of underwear and clothing, and a pair of fluffy bunny slippers, and donned them all. Then she scooped up all her dirty clothing and dropped it in the laundry hamper. Selecting another complete, clean outfit and two towels, she piled them in a neat stack and carried them out the front door.

The hardware store door was unlocked, and the lights off. Turning them on, she shouted, "John!" By that point, the call was a formality.

She piled her clean clothes and towels on a small table next to the tub, then walked back to the spigot to get the water going. While the tub filled, she made a quick visit to the area John had staked out as his personal space, bringing two black trash bags with her. Like him, the area was a mess. Anything not obviously valuable went into one trash bag. Loose clothing went into the other. She reorganized the jumbled furniture, picked up throw pillows from the floor, and tidied the shelves.

Dorothy made two more trips before heading back to the tub: One to the dumpster, and one to the laundry area with the bag of clothing. After setting down the bag next to the washing machine, she removed all of her clothing and stuffed it inside. Normally reserved, her solitude and anger emboldened her, and she strode the length of the hardware store to the tub completely naked, apart from the bunny slippers. It was nearly full. She walked back to the sink, head held high, silently daring John to return unexpectedly so she could scream at him for violating her privacy. He did not accommodate.

When she finally shucked the slippers and climbed into the tub, the comforting blanket of the bathwater enveloped her. For that moment, all was right in the world.

21

BOOM

Over the next half hour, **Harrison made some progress** by cutting the power. He couldn't shut it down completely, but he persuaded the system the magnetic rail needed to be deactivated for maintenance. Without the constant pull, every corner bled a tiny bit of momentum from the Worm, and the speed gauge descended from 305 down to 299 meters per second.

Glimmer, meanwhile, had returned with bad news. The train did indeed have bays to hold several small escape vehicles, all of them, unfortunately, empty.

By this time, they had passed well into Canada. With the rail already deactivated and no means of escape, he turned to the only other thing he could influence, the air pressure in the tube.

"I think I've got it," he said after a few minutes of digging through menus.

"Tell me."

"It's here in the maintenance options. Every section of tunnel is peppered with hundreds of hatches to snorkel tubes leading to the surface. They're for emergencies or repair problems or any reason you might want to flood the tunnel with air. I've already got the system alerted to a maintenance problem, so it should be possible to pop all the hatches between Milwaukee and Green Bay."

"Are you doing that so you can breathe when you get out?" she asked.

"Partly that," he said. "But more to the point, if I'm right, having air in the tube will slow us down more, and if I vent the tunnel only ahead of us, it should send a pressure wave down the tube. Basically, a big wall of air which will swat the train. Maybe stop it."

"Swat it how hard?"

"Pretty hard. It's going to be coming at us at the speed of sound."

"Sound has a speed?" She started to look lost.

"Yes, it does," he said patiently. "It moves a little bit faster than we're going right now. If the pressure wave hits us that fast, we'll feel it, and it probably won't be fun."

"Do it. We're almost out of time."

He did. There would still be some lag time between opening the hatches and feeling the difference. "You should wake Mitchell up. It's about to get shaky in here."

A couple minutes later, Glimmer returned with the boy, bleary eyed, and still in his pajamas.

"What's going on?" He yawned. "Are we there yet?"

"Not yet," said Harrison. "But almost. We're about to hit a bump, and I wanted to be sure you were ready for it." Harrison escorted him back to the lounge and found a secure, well-cushioned seat facing the rear of the Worm. He planted Mitchell in it and then covered his lap with throw pillows. The boy started to nod off again.

"Hey, sport," said Harrison, "I need you to stay awake for a few minutes. Once we get over this bump, you can go back to sleep, okay?"

Mitchell nodded, eyes half open. That would have to do.

They sat and waited. "What happens now?" Glimmer asked.

"If I timed it right, we should run into some serious drag right about halfway between Sault Ste. Marie and Green Bay. Hopefully, that will bring us to a stop within walking distance of the station." He sat up sharply. "Oh my God. I just thought of something. That trick you do with eardrums, can you do it in reverse?"

"What do you mean?"

"I mean, can you block sound instead of creating it?"

She considered for a second. "Yeah, I guess I can do that, but it's not exactly the same trick. I can put up a barrier in your ears so your eardrums don't respond to anything."

"I need you to do that to me and Mitchell. When that wall of air hits, there's going to be a boom."

"Okay. You want me to do that now?"

"Please." His ears went blank. There had been subtle background noise before, now gone. He couldn't even hear the ocean-like sound of his own biology. He looked in on Mitchell, who had taken advantage of the silence by falling asleep again.

Harrison made it to his seat seconds before the sudden deceleration slammed him into its back and held him there. Though the sonic boom evaded his eardrums, it hit the rest of his body hard enough for him to black out. He came to as the Worm hit the side of the tunnel and scraped along it for several seconds, the combined forces of the wall of air and whatever turns they passed through briefly overtaking the magnets. The train righted itself, and Harrison strained to turn his head in Mitchell's direction. The boy, now wide awake, sat similarly pressed into his seat, eyes bugged, jaw wide open, surely screaming.

Several of the windows cracked, but none had shattered, testimony to their solid design. The train vibrated fiercely. Glimmer's eyes bugged out and she had her hands over her ears. He waved to get her attention, then pointed at Mitchell. She came to and gave him a thumbs-up, then lighted on Mitchell's lap, where she did something sparkly. Harrison pulled himself out of his seat and crawled into the caboose.

He managed to make it to the seat at the control panel. The speed gauge had dropped dramatically and continued to do so. So far, they had slowed to 220 meters per second. He checked their deceleration against his watch: 216, 212, 208. They were losing about four meters per second, squared. Almost half a gee. It felt awful, and he could only imagine what it felt like to the kid. The time between four-meter increments grew longer. After a full minute, the train slowed to 120 meters per second and leveled off. The sleek design, which he had thought for show, served a purpose after all. It worked against them. With the train no longer slowing, the gee forces abated. He got up with ease and walked back to the lounge.

Mitchell slept again. Glimmer had, presumably, given him a magical sedative. She chattered animatedly to Harrison. He pointed to his ear, and she slapped her forehead and waved her hands. As his hearing returned, the low rumble of the train speeding through air became audible.

Over that sound, Glimmer shouted, "Holy shit! That was loud!"

He nodded. "I didn't hear it, but that was a sonic boom. We just hit a wall of air with a combined velocity of almost Mach two. Are you all right?"

"I'm fine," she said. "I love surprises."

"It slowed us down," he said, "but nowhere near enough, and we've passed the point where our drag can overcome our momentum. We're not going to be able to stop at Green Bay, which means we need a plan for how to get into Milwaukee Station without hitting that damned barricade." As Mitchell fitfully slept away the crisis, Harrison's fear transformed into rage. Someone was trying to kill him. He could accept that, somehow. But that someone would sacrifice this little kid to do it was beyond horrific. "What happens when an object hits a shield curse?"

"Could be lots of things," said Glimmer. "Hard to say with something this big. The most likely is it would disintegrate." She gave it more thought. "Or maybe just shred. I've seen that. Sometimes they compress; that's a sight, let me tell you."

Harrison fought his nausea. "What happens to the shield?"

"Oh. It disappears. Pretty much always, if you hit it hard enough. They don't last long anyway, but as soon as they take one good smack, that's it."

"That's good."

"How is that good if we disappear, too?" she asked.

"It's good if we're not the object that hits the shield, that's how. If we can knock out the curse, I might be able to get the door open." He marched into the caboose. "I need to find something I can throw at it. A maintenance drone. A missile. Something."

A cursory examination of the specs for the Worm and the tunnel revealed no convenient robots for suicide runs, and the train completely unarmed.

"Wait a minute. This train is segmented. It looks contiguous from outside, but the cars are clearly separate." He brought up control menus, looking for anything that qualified as an emergency procedure. After a few minutes, he found what he sought.

"This is it," he said calmly. "We're going to cut the train in half."

At that moment, the train slipped into Green Bay Station. No longer their goal, Harrison had stopped thinking about it, but seeing it glide by sobered him. They traveled slowly enough to make out some details.

"Slowing down has bought us a little bit of time," he said, "but not much. Here's what we're going to do. I'm going to sever the connection between two cars in the middle of the train. We'll seal off the lounge car, but I'll leave the other hatches open. Try to increase drag on the back half of the train as much as possible. With luck, the front end will pull away from us, hit the barricade, and take it out. Then..." He paused and sighed. "Well, then we crash. But at least we crash into the station, and not some big magic bug lamp."

"That's a plan," she said.

Harrison followed the procedure for detaching cars, still marveling at the simplicity of operating the train. He would normally have thought one needed schooling to pilot a futuristic, underground, magnetic bullet. The bulkhead to the lounge shut with a pronounced *clank*, followed by a distant squealing.

"It's away," said Harrison, trying to sound triumphant. He checked their speed. Down to 112 meters per second. He brought up a diagnostic cutaway of the train to get a sense of whether the plan was working.

It wasn't.

The front half of the train had indeed severed from the back half, but it was still in contact. Harrison searched the system to determine why, but couldn't tell. The cars read as detached but touching.

"We need to push it off," he said. His fragile calm finally stretching.

"How?" the pixie asked. Harrison looked to her hopefully. "Hey, I can't even carry your pack."

He slammed the counter. "Dammit! We're so close to solving this I can feel it!" He grabbed bunches of hair with both hands. "Think! Think! God, what I wouldn't give for a box of dynamite right now!"

"What's a box of dynamite?"

He looked up, still surprised by her ingenuousness. "You blow stuff up with it. If I had enough, I could set it off in the joint, and it would push the front end of the train away from us. It might even slow us down some, like a rocket firing in reverse." He paused there. "My God, that would work! We have to find something on this train we can explode." He looked at the map, and the speed gauge, and his face sank. "In twenty minutes."

A horrible silence fell over them. It was highly unlikely the train carried explosives, and even if it did hold materials from which to fashion a bomb, neither he nor the pixie had the expertise to do so. He looked into her wide eyes. "Glimmer... You should go. Save yourself."

"I know a trick," she said.

Exhausted, defeated, and imagining Glimmer hoped to cheer him up, he decided to let her. "What kind of trick?"

"A pixie kind of trick." Her face went blank. "I can blow stuff up."

"What? How? No. Never mind. Can you make a big enough explosion to do what I'm talking about?"

"I think so," she said in a faint voice.

"Do it," he said. "What have we got to lose?"

Her tiny eyes lingered on his. She flew to his face, kissed his nose, and dropped something in his shirt pocket. Then she zipped away, leaving behind her little trail of sparks.

Harrison went back to the lounge and curled up next to Mitchell, who stirred in his sleep. In a few minutes, they would know. He wouldn't wake the boy until he was sure of their safety. Better that way. As he leaned into the seat, a small object scraped against his chest, and he absently reached into his breast pocket. He pulled out a tiny plastic replica of an Olympic gold medal on a ribbon.

"Oh, fuck!"

He jumped up as the middle of the train detonated. The force of the explosion threw him to the floor. Flaming wreckage streaked past the lounge windows. The rear of the train decelerated again, and the front had, no doubt, jumped ahead of them into certain oblivion.

A few minutes later, another explosion shook the train. It sounded like a hundred grand pianos being dropped onto a tower of glass. Light of every conceivable color streaked past the windows, and the air in the sealed compartment smelled of burning leaves. Mitchell was awake now. The first explosion had frightened him. This one had him captivated.

Shortly thereafter, they collided with the remains of the other half of the train and the door. By then, they cruised at a pokey 23 meters per second, well protected by the hastily erected mountain of cushions they had piled against the wall. It took them two hours to get into the station through a service hatchway in the tunnel. Neither of them sustained any injuries beyond the capacity of the first aid kit.

Four days later, they gave up looking for Glimmer and headed south.

[22]

RESOLVE

Dorothy woke after dawn, and before the alarm she had set. She changed from her pajamas into clothes and applied new Band-Aids to the blisters on her feet. The burst one on her heel had already begun to callous over. She took a moment to admire it, and vowed to follow its example. The other three blisters were soft and tender; the pressure had gone down overnight. Either they too would rupture today, or they would shrink to nothing soon enough. There would be no extended hikes before that, in either case. She glared at the bowling shoes nearby and silently cursed them before slipping into her fuzzy bunnies and launching into her to-do list.

First up: laundry. She sorted through the bag of John's clothing. Any garment with even the slightest sign of wear—ratty edges, missing buttons, or holes—went straight into the trash. The rest went into the washing machine. It made one large load, which she ran on warm without separating colors.

While the laundry cycled, she took the bag of John's retired clothing to the dumpster. The lid still up, it held no small volume of rain from two days earlier, and smelled inescapably horrid. Her original plan to keep it as dry as possible had conclusively failed, and she needed a plan B. Perhaps the trash within had sufficiently composted by now, and she could use it to grow something. Maybe if she simply sprinkled weed seeds into it, they would take over, consuming the nutrients and killing the stink. She found it difficult to imagine any way that could make it worse, but Dorothy's life had become a never-ending journey of discovery, so she would simply have to experiment and see what data would result.

Armored in large rubber gloves, she entered the hardware store men's bathroom, cleaner than her worst prediction, but still well in need of a polish. She took Lysol to every porcelain surface, glass cleaner to the mirrors, and a mop to the floor. She also refilled the soap dispensers, left fresh rolls of toilet paper in the stall, and sanitized the door handle. This all took about thirty minutes, after which she did the same to the women's room.

John's laundry had finished by then. She moved it to the dryer and put on a load of her own whites. Before leaving the hardware store, she took one last pass through John's area, to tidy up and sweep the floor.

The Hallmark store bathroom was already nearly spotless, but she took a few minutes to clean that as well. Two other stores in the strip mall stood intact, and she ventured into them to inspect and clean their bathrooms as well. The one in the video store required minimal attention, but the one in the UPS store was atrocious. By the time she finished with them, they both sparkled.

Around midmorning, she returned to the video store. A dozen times or so she had been here to watch a movie, but the experience of sitting by herself in a folding chair, looking up at a TV mounted near the ceiling, felt awkward. On this visit, she climbed onto the counter to inspect the mounting. The TV rested on a metal platform, and after disconnecting the cable, she lifted it down to the counter. Transporting it back to the Hallmark store proved simple enough once she found a suitable cart. She set it up in her bedroom area, complete with a DVD player, both still on the cart in the event she needed to relocate them at some point in the future.

She returned to the hardware store to move along her laundry. John's clothes had dried by then, and she folded them neatly into piles. The piles went into a plastic storage tub, which she left on the floor in his area, pushed off to the side.

After that, she returned to the video store, where she spent more than an hour browsing, and selecting a library of films to keep in her room. This brought her to about lunchtime, and she took a break to eat a can of tuna while watching the first half hour of *Harry Potter and the Chamber of Secrets*.

After lunch, she pulled up a stool at the front counter, and with a set of colored pencils, sketched a map of the network of ribbons she had laid out to mark paths to her various resources. Directions were approximate, the length of each colored branch proportional to the amount of time each walk took, at a scale of six inches to each hour. With this laid out, she connected each node on the map to all the others with a brown pencil, then measured the lines to approximate the walking time between them. In most cases, the direct routes were less than twenty minutes shorter than taking the ribbon routes; however, the distance between the clothing store and the pharmacy was almost an hour shorter. She went over this line boldly in black. Once her blisters healed, mapping this trail would be her next project.

She spent the next hour inventorying food to plan meals. After that, she rearranged the merchandise in the Hallmark store, clearing displays and shifting fixtures to partition out room areas. She furnished these areas with some of the more portable items from the hardware store. Every hour or so, she would check on her laundry, until eventually she had cleaned and neatly stored it all away.

By the time she quit for the day, the store had taken on a homier structure, though clearly still a work in progress. For dinner she had Kraft macaroni and cheese, minus the traditional milk and butter, which she served herself on a folding utility table in her makeshift dining room. She took a bath before retiring. From the comfort of her improvised bed, she watched the rest of the Harry Potter movie, or at least as much as she could before she fell asleep.

Starting from the pharmacy, and headed in the probable direction of the clothing store, it took Dorothy less than an hour to find it. Her estimated path intersected with the blue ribbon trail relatively close to her destination. She marked this shortcut with strips of black ribbon.

Once there, she prioritized replacing her lost backpack. She still planned to conduct daily food runs until she had moved all the cans to the Hallmark store. It would take her considerably more time to do that by herself than it would have with John, making it even more urgent for her to stick it out.

Though the late summer weather still supplied an uncomfortable amount of heat, autumn would arrive soon enough. Dorothy filled the backpack with sweaters, long underwear, and flannel pajamas. The selection of winter coats was sparse, given the stock reflecting the store's final day of operation in late May. She did find one coat that fit her well enough, but it wouldn't fit in the pack with her other clothing. She set it on the counter. There would eventually be a cold enough day she could wear the coat home.

The next day she set out for the grocery store with her new backpack. She moved from memory, barely aware of the ribbons as she passed them, and made better time than usual, with less fatigue. The rainbow rats greeted her by skittering away. A thorough inspection of the store showed no signs of rat damage to any of the canned goods, but plenty of evidence of rat occupation. Having exhausted the readily available food, they apparently used the store for shelter only.

"Hey, you," said Dorothy to a peach-colored rat looking down on her from a high shelf. "Do you want to come back with me? I could use some company. If you promise you don't have any diseases, I can set you up with a pretty good living space and some tasty meals."

The rat continued to stare, intermittently twitching its nose and flicking its tail.

"Well, at least think about it. You don't have to answer right away."

She stocked her bag with cans of vegetables and fish, being sure to include one can of cherry pie filling as her reward for being such a good sport about the work. The zipper barely closed over all the supplies; larger loads would mean fewer trips. The pack was heavier than any she had carried so far, but felt manageable once she had it on.

For the next three weeks, she made daily supply runs, most of them for food, some of them for medicine in anticipation of cold season, and some of them for additions to her sizable and growing wardrobe. And once a week, she sought entertainment. By her third trip, she bowled 120 or better consistently.

While her morning routine consisted of hikes, she devoted her afternoons to the ongoing project of home improvement. Using whatever materials she could find in the hardware store, she taught herself to build simple, improvised furniture. She moved the TV cart into the living room, once she had properly created one. After several days of attempts and several different strategies, she finally rigged a pipe from the tub that ran out the back door into a storm drain, including cutting a hole in the bottom of the door that would still allow it to open, close, and lock, with minimal loss of heat. She erected a set of blinds around the tub, providing her with a sense of privacy she knew to be an illusion, but still found comforting.

Once her pantry was sufficiently full, she worked ribbon replacement into her supply runs. In addition to tying fresh strips onto each tree (after snipping off the faded ones), she brought a small can of paint with her on each run and marked each trunk with a swipe of the appropriate color. After ruining an entire outfit on the blue run, she stocked up on XXL T-shirts to use as smocks. She did not refresh the purple trail. The ribbons on the silver trail, which led to nothing but an empty spot previously occupied by carnivorous crystals, she removed completely.

About a month after the only other person she had found in this depopulated world had abandoned her and left her for dead, Dorothy had established a home so well-equipped and comfortable, she came to peace with the idea she might not meet another person for a long time, if ever.

Naturally, someone chose that time to pound on the back door.

[PART 3]
INTERSECTIONAL

BOOT

While Mitchell slept, Harrison listened to the radio on his new media player, an excellent replacement for the discarded Walkman, with crisper sound. Claudia's broadcasts still only came in after dark, but lately she had been working the night shift, putting her on air for longer stretches of time. A song ended.

"That was 'Just What I Needed,' by the Cars," she said over his headphones. "For those of you just tuning in, this is Claudia, coming to you from Chicago with an open invitation to anyone who can hear it. Tell your friends. Come to Chicago. I'll be here." The opening chords to a song Harrison did not recognize followed.

Harrison yawned. After putting away the radio, he took a small flashlight from his pocket and used it to check on Mitchell before going to sleep. The boy slept soundly, with a peaceful look on his face. Harrison smiled. Mitchell's days had been anything but peaceful. He had walked a great distance, and it wore him out. They both had their fair share of scratches and insect bites, but Mitchell's inventory of those exceeded Harrison's considerably.

He rubbed the plastic medal resting on his chest. Fearing he might lose it, he had put it on a chain. He checked once more to be sure Mitchell slept soundly, then quietly pulled a small device from his pack and touched a button on it.

"Like I would know?" Glimmer asked. He offered her image a melancholy smile and reached out, almost touching it. "Like I would know?" she asked again. He switched the recorder off and gently replaced it in his pack.

———

"Let me see your arm."

Mitchell held his left arm out obediently, looking in the other direction.

Holding it gently, Harrison examined the strip of white cloth taped around Mitchell's forearm and frowned at the orange stain on it. "We should change this again."

Mitchell whimpered, but did not object. Harrison pulled another strip of cloth from his backpack. Their first aid kit had been sufficient until Mitchell fell and gashed his arm on a tree root. Though not deep, the wound was long, and while Harrison got the bleeding to stop fairly quickly, none of the small bandages at his disposal covered it. Ultimately, he had to improvise by tearing a white T-shirt into strips and attaching them with adhesive tape.

Harrison peeled back the dressing to expose the raised cut, covered in an angry yellow scab with reddened edges. He winced. The wound had not yet progressed to red streaks, but still presented trouble. It would have to be opened and drained. Performing that procedure on a child, in the woods, would not be pleasant. He had anti-bacterial ointment in his kit, but he needed a proper sink, soap, and a large sterile bandage.

He removed the cloth and dabbed at the wound with a clean corner, roughly, to get some of the pus out without making too big a deal out of it.

"Ow!" Mitchell cried, jerking his arm away.

Cleaning it would definitely be a challenge, but if Mitchell struggled and got dirt in it, it would get worse. Harrison sighed and dropped the soiled strip of cloth on the ground. "Hold it up," he said gently. "I won't touch it."

As Mitchell looked at him with suspicion, Harrison produced a bottle of water from his pack, opened it, and held it out to him. Mitchell held his arm up. Harrison poured some water over the wound. Water would do little good through that scab, but it soothed Mitchell, and that would be enough for the moment. He handed the boy a paper towel, which he used to dab his arm dry. Harrison smeared some of the ointment on the new bandage, wrapped the arm, and taped it securely.

"What's that?" asked Mitchell, pointing behind Harrison. A hiking boot lay on the ground, partially obscured by weeds.

"It's a shoe," said Harrison. A little further up a gap in the weeds revealed the edge of a pants leg. "Stay here."

Mitchell said nothing.

Brush concealed most of the body. If they hadn't stopped to redress Mitchell's arm, they would have walked right past it without seeing it. Harrison pushed aside some of the overgrowth to have a better look. It was the body of a man, probably a little bit smaller than Harrison, but he could not say with any certainty because it had been stripped of much of its flesh.

About a dozen creatures resembling large insects crawled over it. Vaguely scorpion-like, each one about the size of Mitchell's hand, they had far too many legs for insects or arachnids. Indigo spots and lines decorated their black carapaces. Fan-shaped tails reminiscent of lobsters covered secondary, longer tails with knobbed ends, twitching back and forth as they moved. Their forelimbs consisted of at least four visible pincers, their shape again more reminiscent of a crustacean. The bugs did not bite the flesh from the corpse; they pulled it loose with those claws and stuffed it into their mouths.

"Arthropods from hell," he whispered. He backed into Mitchell and gasped all over again. "I thought I told you to stay put!"

Mitchell gawked at the dead man and the scavengers, the first human they had found since leaving the Worm station. Harrison wanted to tell Mitchell something reassuring, that not everyone they found would be dead and scavenged. He couldn't find the words.

"Come on." He escorted Mitchell back into the woods.

———

Late afternoon they finally came across a building. They had been following Harrison's compass for almost two days. The first sign of civilization as they emerged from the forest was a vast windowless wall and a row of widely spaced dumpsters.

"Strip mall," Harrison said. He glanced at Mitchell's arm wound. Somewhere in this structure he would find a bathroom, and possibly the supplies he needed, too. A mall would surely have a drug store or a grocery store. Some of the shops here had signs, even though this was clearly the rear of the mall. The sign closest to them read Hallmark. Harrison ruled it out as a source of bandages.

As they came closer, the air soured, permeated with a familiar stench akin to the smell of kitchen garbage, but stronger. Harrison scanned up and down the mall, looking for the source of the odor, finding it in the nearest dumpster, the one belonging to the Hallmark store. Full, it gave off the same smell as the dumpster at the motel he had called home so long ago.

"I think someone lives here," he said to Mitchell.

"What should we do?" Mitchell asked.

"Generally," said Harrison, "the polite thing to do is knock."

Harrison and Mitchell walked to the door and knocked.

After almost a minute, a woman asked, "Who is it?"

"What the hell kind of a question is that?" whispered Harrison.

Mitchell giggled.

"My name is Harrison," he called through the door. "I have a friend here with me named Mitchell."

"Hello," Mitchell said loudly, and with enthusiasm.

After a short pause, the voice asked, "What do you want?"

"Can I borrow a cup of sugar?" muttered Harrison. Mitchell laughed, and Harrison gently put his hand up for silence. "You're the first person we've found in a very long time. We just wanted to say hello."

The door opened, revealing a girl in her early teens, her blonde hair pulled back in a ponytail and large glasses slightly magnifying her eyes. She wore a pink sweatshirt and blue jeans, and multicolored toe socks on her feet.

"Is Harrison your first name or your last name?" she asked.

Harrison laughed. "My first name."

She held out her hand. "I'm pleased to meet you, Harrison. My name is Dorothy O'Neill. Is that a Barbie medal around your neck?"

[24]

COMPANY

The two newcomers stood in the back doorway, amusingly twinned in blue jeans, T-shirts, plaid shirts tied around their waists, knapsacks, and boots, all covered in travel dirt, the colors of their shirts the only badge of originality they wore. Apart from that, they looked nothing like each other. The adult, Harrison, stood easily six feet tall, and noticeably younger and fitter than the last visitor to Dorothy's home. The boy, Mitchell, appeared older than Dorothy's youngest sister, but younger than her middle sister, which would put him about eight or nine. He had a strip of dirty white cloth wrapped around one arm, presumably a makeshift bandage. Both travelers had shaggy, tousled hair—Harrison's light brown, Mitchell's nearly black—well in need of a trim. Harrison's short beard, little more than rough stubble, implied a relatively recent shave.

And, again unlike her last visitor, they greeted her with warm, attentive smiles.

"Come in, please." Dorothy stepped aside. "Bathroom to the left, if you need it. Can I get you anything to eat or drink?"

"Sure!" said Mitchell, brightening one notch.

"Bathroom first, sport," said Harrison. "We need to get that arm cleaned up." He asked Dorothy quietly, "Do you have any first aid stuff?"

"Can I take a look?" she asked Mitchell, holding out her hand.

He hesitantly lifted his bandaged arm.

She took it by the wrist, and gently unwound the cloth. Underneath lay a long, narrow scab, surrounded by a halo of red, inflamed skin. "Oh!" She looked at Harrison with as even a face as she could manage. "Huh."

Harrison gave a slight grimace. "Yeah."

"Mitchell," said Dorothy, "we're going to get a warm compress on this, okay? It will help draw out some of the... dirt."

"What's a compress?" he asked.

She dropped the bandage into a lined trash can. "It's just a washcloth. I'm going to heat it up with some water, and I want you to hold it on your arm as long as you can. Think you can do that?"

"Is it gonna hurt?" he asked.

"Hmm." She tipped her head and looked at the wound again. "More than a bee sting, less than a broken nose. Does that sound like something you can handle?"

"I guess." His face, already pale, went one step further in that direction.

"Do you like movies?" she asked. "I have a TV in the other room and bunch of DVDs. Why don't you go pick something out? I'll be there in a minute."

"Okay." He perked up a bit. He took off his knapsack and left it on the floor near the back door, then went into the store.

Dorothy whispered, "Come here." She led Harrison into the bathroom, where she turned the tap on the sink to hot, and pulled a white washcloth off a stack of them, neatly arranged on an end table she had brought in to hold supplies. "How long ago did he do that?"

"Two days ago," said Harrison. "It's pretty badly infected."

"I can see that." The water in the sink put out a cloud of steam, and she dropped the cloth into it. "We need to soak that scab off and clean out the wound. It will probably take more than an hour using the compresses. We might be able to do it faster if he's willing to sit in a tub as long as it takes."

Harrison's eyebrows went up. "You have a bathtub?"

"Yes, I do. It's in the next shop over. Very little privacy, and no TV. You obviously know him better than I do. Will he sit still for that?"

"Probably not."

Dorothy lifted the washcloth by the corner and let some of the water drain out before wringing it. The scalding water bit into her fingers. She ignored it and folded the cloth into a smaller rectangle. She switched the water over to cold, let it run for a few seconds, then filled a small cup and shut it off. "There's Advil on that table." She nodded in the direction of the supplies. "Can you grab that, please?"

"Sure." Harrison inspected a couple bottles of medicine before picking up the correct one.

"Come on," she said.

Harrison followed her into the store, and into the living room she had partitioned off. Dorothy took a moment to watch the look on his face as he took in all the work she had done to make this store a home. She found his expression satisfactorily impressed and moved on.

"Did you find anything?" she asked the boy.

"Can I watch *Aladdin*?" He held out the disc.

"I love that one!" said Dorothy. After setting the cup of water on the coffee table, she took the disc and passed it to Harrison. He set up the player while she got to business. "Okay, Mitchell, look at me." She held up the cloth. "This is very hot. It's going to sting, but look, I'm holding it, so I know exactly how hot it is, and I know you can take it. Do you trust me?"

He nodded.

"Ready to be brave?" she asked with a conspiratorial smile.

He sat up, and nodded again, holding out his arm.

She slapped the cloth onto his wound and held it tightly down with both hands.

"Ow!" he shouted, trying unsuccessfully to pull his arm away from her. He was stronger than she expected, but still outmatched.

"I know," she said. "I've got you."

"Ow, ow, ow," he whimpered. Tears formed in his eyes, and one rolled down his face. He squinted and sniffed.

"You are doing so great!" she said.

He stopped pulling and wiped his eyes with his other hand.

"Are you okay?" she asked.

He nodded weakly.

"Okay, I'm going to let go on the count of three, but I want you to promise me you won't pull it off. I need you to hold it down with your hand, and I need you to keep it on there for a long time. Do you promise?"

Mitchell closed his eyes and screwed up his face. "Yes," he said through gritted teeth.

"Okay, here we go. One... Two... Three." She relaxed her grip without letting go. When he didn't jerk away, she slowly removed her hands from his arm.

He brought his free hand to the cloth and clamped it down.

"Oh, you are doing fantastic," said Dorothy.

"Can I have a sticker?" he asked.

She laughed. "Absolutely! Now, I want to give you something to make this hurt less. Do you know how to swallow a pill?"

He winced. "Do I have to?"

She shook her head. "You don't have to do anything you don't want to do, but I promise it will help."

Dorothy took the bottle of Advil from Harrison, opened it, and shook out one beige tablet. "These are sugar-coated. You'll probably taste it, but don't bite it. The sugar is just there to make it slippery. All you have to do is put it on your tongue, then drink this whole glass of water. The trick is to think about the water, not the pill. If you can drink all the water, the pill will go down on its own."

"I've swallowed pills before," he said.

"Then this should be easy." She held out the pill and waited.

Hesitantly, he took his arm off the compress, took the pill from her, looked at it closely, and put it in his mouth. He held his hand out again, and she put the cup in it. Wincing, he put the cup to his lips, then gulped down the contents. He handed back the cup, letting his breath out in a huge sigh. His extended tongue had no pill on it, and he offered no follow-up coughing noises.

By this time, Harrison had skipped past the previews and started the movie. "You're doing great, pal!"

Mitchell sat back in his chair, clamped his hand back on the compress and put his feet on the coffee table.

"Can I get you a pop?" asked Dorothy.

"Do you have root beer?" asked Mitchell.

"I think so. Harrison, can you come help me find Mitchell a root beer?"

"You okay here?" asked Harrison.

Mitchell nodded, already lost in the opening song of the cartoon.

Dorothy and Harrison returned to the back room, where she had set up a kitchenette area. "Pop's in the fridge." She pointed to a minibar. While Harrison fetched a can of A&W, Dorothy popped into the bathroom, where she found a mass market paperback with the letters PDR boldly centered on the cover.

"Do you have Bactine or peroxide or something for when the scab comes off?" Harrison asked when she returned to him.

"There's antibiotic ointment in the first aid kit," she said. "But it's not going to help much. That infection is under the skin, not on top of it. He's going to need something better."

"This isn't your first rodeo, is it?" asked Harrison.

"I have two little sisters and my mom's a nurse," she said. "There have been lots of rodeos."

"Any this bad?" he asked.

She shrugged, and held up the book. "There's a pharmacy about an hour and half hike from here. I gave him the Advil to make sure he could swallow a pill. You stay here and watch the movie with him. Make sure you change the compresses when they get cold. I'll get you a bucket from next door to put the dirty ones in."

"Whoa," said Harrison. "You're going out there alone to get antibiotics?"

Dorothy nodded. "I should be back in three hours. Less if I run part of it."

"No, no." He put his hands up. "You stay here. I'll go. Where is it?"

"It's okay," said Dorothy. "I don't mind. Go ahead and get comfortable. I can take care of this."

"Thank you for offering," said Harrison. "Really. You're wonderful. But I've got this. How old are you?"

"Fourteen."

"Damn. You are an amazing kid, Dorothy. But I can't just walk in here and lean on a kid. You're great with the fine details, so please keep doing that while I handle the heavy lifting. Where's the pharmacy?"

Dorothy hesitated. "You're sure?"

"Completely sure." He pointed back to the store. "That little boy is my responsibility. This is what I do."

For a moment, neither of them spoke. Then Dorothy threw her arms around him and held him tightly. He responded with a few pats on her back that felt awkward and confused.

"What was that for?" he asked as she pulled away.

"For being a grown-up." She opened the book and scanned the index before the tears making suggestions behind her eyes could make any headway. "You're looking for amoxicillin or erythromycin. I'm dog-earing the pages that have pictures of them." She handed him the book, and he passed her the can of root beer. "You want to go out the front door, and look for a tree at the edge of the parking lot with five colored ribbons on it, and four spots of paint. Each color leads to different place. Follow the green ones."

"Got it. Keep him happy. I'll be right back."

Her first and only tear finally broke through. She smiled at him. "I know you will."

BUG

With about fifteen minutes to assess Dorothy's character, Harrison ruled her trustworthy enough to leave alone with Mitchell for several hours. He found the ribbons she described easily enough, and he followed them at a brisker than usual pace. Periodically, he checked the compass. When it stopped pointing behind him and started pointing in front of him, he carved a quick H into the bark of the nearest green-ribboned tree to indicate the halfway point.

To his relief, he found the drug store, a small business, not a familiar chain, completely intact. Inside, he made for the pharmacy. It took about ten minutes for him to find the two drugs Dorothy prescribed for Mitchell. With a mostly empty backpack, he took a few more minutes to collect some other first aid supplies. Dorothy mentioned she already had a kit, but better to be over-prepared than unpleasantly surprised.

He found his supplies in short order. A box of sterile gauze pads. A new roll of adhesive tape. Surgical scissors. Alcohol to sterilize any other instruments they needed to use. Antibiotic ointment to treat Mitchell's wound. Candy to reward him for being a good patient.

Time check. So far, including gathering supplies, this trip was not quite ninety minutes old, putting him well ahead of Dorothy's predicted schedule. She had based her ninety-minute estimate to walk to the store on shorter legs, after all.

Slight familiarity made the return hike feel shorter. He greeted his halfway mark with renewed vigor as he made his way down the last stretch. Finally, shy of two and a half hours round trip, he emerged from forest to the strip mall parking lot.

As he stepped onto pavement, a loud *crack* came from the glass storefront. It startled him. He froze.

One of the four-clawed bug things that had been skeletonizing the body in the woods skittered to and fro on the walk in front of the strip mall, though considerably larger than the ones he had seen before. This one stood as tall and broad as a medium-sized dog, with a pattern of indigo spots and lines much more complex than on the smaller specimens, including decorative swirls. It lifted its tail up and swung it like a club against the window with an awful sound, though the glass held.

Its window of interest belonged to the Hallmark store. From this distance, he couldn't see the kids, but if they had any sense—and Dorothy certainly did—they would have retreated to the back room at the first sign of trouble.

With the creature's attention drawn to the window it battered, Harrison took a deep breath and sprinted for the small hardware store next door. When he got within a dozen yards or so, the creature turned in his direction. He pushed himself the rest of the distance and threw himself inside the hardware store door. It wouldn't lock, but with luck the bug would be too short and too stupid to trip the door sensor.

He had not gone in there for safety. Trying to breathe properly, he scanned his options. Tools as weapons. Most of the tools here were small enough they would require close proximity to the predator-scavenger. Not ideal. He picked up an axe, but it proved too awkward to wield. After experimenting with a few other choices, he settled on a garden rake, long enough he could strike from a relative distance, light enough to swing well, and as a bonus, capped with a row of deadly iron teeth. He swished it back and forth a few times to feel its heft and prepare himself for what he would have to do with it, then went back to the door.

The creature had gone back to whacking the windowpane, where it had left a visible crack. Harrison took a deep breath and braced himself. He planned to take advantage of some basic physics. Nature never produced bugs of this size. By the square-cube law, as size increases, the ratio of volume to surface area increases as well. Above a certain size, any organism supported entirely by its surface (such as the exoskeleton of a lobster or scorpion) would collapse under its own weight. Tarantulas, for example, could not survive falls, even short ones, because they already had so much stress on their frames they would split open. This nightmare outsized any tarantula. If he shoved it hard enough, it should hit the ground and splatter apart.

However, by the same principle, an arthropod of this magnitude could not exist. With luck, whatever horrible magic had spawned it had not given it properties that would negate Harrison's plan.

He reached into his pocket and pulled out the wind-stone Glimmer had (months ago) told him not to keep. Turning it over in his hand, he looked at the writing on it he could not read. He took a deep breath, looked directly at the monster, held the stone to his mouth, and blew. A potent gust of wind lifted the creature off the ground and flung it through the air at a fantastic speed.

Directly toward Harrison.

The same gust of wind knocked him to the pavement, and the creature slammed into him. Regrettably, it did not split open on impact, but pinned Harrison underneath it. It lay on its back, thrashing around. Its hard body dug into his skin through his clothes. A smell came off it, sickeningly reminiscent of seafood. The disgusting odor helped Harrison focus on his original impression that these animals resembled lobsters. In an act of desperation, he gambled the thing might be enough like a lobster for him to treat it like one.

He grabbed one of the creature's pincers with both hands and twisted with all the strength he could command. It popped out. He tossed it aside. He successfully repeated this procedure on six more of its limbs before it finally managed to club him in the head with its tail.

He blacked out.

When he came around, the creature was chewing on his neck. Screaming, he heaved the thing off and scurried backward, panic giving him speed. It crawled toward him, but the lost limbs gave it trouble.

Harrison felt his neck. No blood. These things fed by pulling flesh with their claws. Their mouthparts apparently didn't include anything that could tear skin. He accounted for all four of its pincers, several feet away. It continued to stagger toward him. He stood, brushed himself off, and picked up the rake. In that moment, its resemblance to an oversized potato masher inspired him.

He brought it down on the creature's head. Again. And again.

He left it there, a mass of crushed tissue, picked up his backpack of medicine and first aid supplies, and limped back to the Hallmark store. On the way, he passed his bruised reflection in a window, and the shocked faces of the two children behind it.

[26]

DECISIONS

Dorothy clutched her mug of chamomile tea with both hands, willing them to stop shaking. Harrison and Mitchell sat across from her at the dining room table she had constructed from boards and cinder blocks. The boy was on his second can of root beer. His arm bore a fresh patch of gauze bordered by white adhesive tape, conspicuously cleaner than the rest of his body. Harrison sipped from a warm can of Miller Lite, one of the few remaining artifacts of John's tenure.

"I've never seen one of those before," said Dorothy. It had been nearly half an hour since the monster bug attack, and what little conversation they shared in that time had not included any mention of it. As Dorothy finally broached the topic, Harrison and Mitchell silently glanced at each other. "You have."

"Yeah," said Harrison. "Nothing that big though. We saw a dozen or so this morning. They were about the size of mice."

"I've been here since May," said Dorothy. "Why would they suddenly show up today?"

Harrison shrugged. "I'm not exactly an expert on this stuff. The good news is they're easy to kill."

"That... didn't look easy."

"Yeah, well, I got it figured out now."

"What else is out there?" asked Dorothy.

Harrison took a long draw of his beer. "Trees, mostly. Some seriously advanced technology." He took another sip. "Occasional monsters."

"I've met talking monster cats," said Dorothy. "And brightly colored rats."

"Monster rats?" asked Mitchell.

"No, just regular rats. But they're all purple and green and mauve and vermillion and things."

"Cool," said the boy.

"I met a dragon."

"A dragon!" exclaimed Dorothy and Mitchell in unison.

Harrison looked up. "Oh, yeah, that was before I found you," he said to Mitchell. "His name was Gustav. Huge wings, German accent. Nice guy, really, apart from the fact he eats people."

"Is this the future?" asked Dorothy. "John—I had a map projector thing that said it was from 2053."

Harrison frowned. "Who—"

"And the software said it was from that time, too," said Dorothy, cutting him off from the question she was not ready to answer. "So I think maybe that means we're in the future?"

He shook his head. "I don't think so. There's a lot of future stuff out there, but there's some stuff from the past, too. I've seen some dead dinosaurs. Plus, you know, dragon."

They all took sips from their respective drinks.

"Where were you the day it happened?" asked Dorothy quietly.

"Massachusetts," said Harrison. "One minute I'm driving to work, the next I'm sitting alone in a forest, surprised and confused. You?"

Dorothy drew in a deep breath and masked her sigh by blowing on her tea. "Confused, yes. Surprised no. By the time it got here, we had already seen it on the news. My mom kept telling us it wouldn't get this far, but she made us stay in the house." She took a sip from her tea. As many times as she had rehearsed this story, no one had ever given her a chance to tell it. "Lorraine was terrified. She was ten. But Fiona was only seven, too young to really understand how bad it was. Mom told us both not to talk about it, so we tried not to. Ever since my father left, Mom counted on me to help take care of my little sisters." She paused and blew on her tea again without sipping it. "Suddenly Fiona just ran for it. For no reason at all. I honestly think she was bored. Mom didn't even see her until she was out the door, and then she started yelling, 'Fiona! Get back here!' I volunteered to bring her back, but Mom just yelled louder and told me to stay in the house and take care of Lorraine."

Dorothy's throat tightened. Her attempt to loosen it with a sip of tea met with little success.

"Then I heard a sound like a big drum beating, and Lorraine just disappeared. I didn't understand what was happening at first. Then the house fell straight down, just like it was made of water. All that was left was grass." She stopped.

"I'm sorry," said Harrison.

Dorothy looked up from her mug. Harrison's eyes held genuine sympathy. "Thank you."

Harrison stood. "We should probably stay here a couple of days. Give Mitchell a chance to heal up."

Dorothy sat up, alarmed. "A couple of days? You're leaving?"

Harrison frowned in apparent confusion. "Oh. Wow. I didn't... We're heading for Chicago. I meant to lead with that, but we had a couple of distractions. Sorry."

"You're just going to leave?" asked Dorothy. "What if those things come back?"

Harrison sat back down. "Shit. I really need to start over here. Dorothy, we are heading for Chicago, and we would like you to come with us."

"To Chicago?"

Harrison nodded.

"On foot?"

He nodded again.

Dorothy laughed, bitterly. "No, I don't think so."

"Dorothy..."

"No!" she said, instantly regretting the emphasis. "Why don't you wait a few days before you decide to leave? Give it a chance. We could fix up the video store for you. We could be neighbors."

Harrison drummed his fingers on the table. "Mitchell, Dorothy and I need to have a grown-up talk. Can I set you up with another movie?"

Mitchell stood. "I know how it works." He left without further encouragement.

Once two partitions separated them from the boy, Dorothy said quietly, "Grown-up talk? What happened to me being a kid?"

"Particle-wave duality of adolescence," said Harrison. "Right now I need you to collapse into a grown-up."

"Here we go again," she muttered.

"Who's John?"

Dorothy froze. "I don't know?"

"Yeah," said Harrison. "Let's try that again. Who's John?"

"Ugh. Fine. John lived here for a few weeks. Now he's gone."

"What happened to him?"

"I didn't kill him, if that's what you're asking."

Harrison stared at her. "Wow... That... really wasn't what I was asking."

"Oh." Dorothy stared down at her hands resting in her lap and wrestled with her bitterness, embarrassment and fear.

"Hey," said Harrison.

She ignored this summons.

"Hey," he said, more gently this time.

She looked up. He had stretched his hand across the table, palm up. He curled his fingers a couple of times and waited. She took his hand. It felt warm, and strong, and he gave a short squeeze that communicated concern and security.

"I am absolutely not running out on you. I promise I am not running out on you. If we accomplish nothing else today, that's the one thing I need you to understand. Can we start there, please?"

She looked into his eyes and narrowed hers. "Pinky swear."

He held out his other hand, pinky extended in a hook. She locked her own pinky with it, squeezed, and released.

"All right," she said.

Still holding her hand, he said, "We found Mitchell in an underground train station. He was all alone there, but he says there was a woman who found him first and left without him. I'm not that guy. For the last three weeks, I have stuck to this kid like glue. He's come a long way, but he still has a long way to go. Whatever happened to him that day, he won't tell me, and I'm not going to push. I know nothing about his history, or his family, other than his mother wouldn't let his father eat breakfast cereal after eleven in the morning. Of all the things he could be telling me about them, that's the one thing I've learned so far. I can also tell you the reason that woman left without him is Mitchell hid from her until she gave up looking. I don't know why he did that. He trusts me, which is a good thing. He also obviously trusts you, which is a very good thing. You with me so far?"

Dorothy nodded.

"Good. The reason we are headed to Chicago is there are people there."

"How many people?" asked Dorothy.

"I have no idea. At least one. There's a DJ named Claudia who broadcasts from Chicago every night, calling for survivors to meet her there. No mention so far of whether she got any takers. I've been traveling there since late July, by car, by train, and on foot. I want to keep going, but not without you. So we need to make a decision together."

Dorothy slowly nodded, and Harrison let go of her hand. "There are monsters out there."

"There are monsters right here," said Harrison, nodding toward the crack in the storefront window.

"But you figured out how to kill those. Right?"

"Yeah, but what I'm saying is that neutralizes your argument about the monsters out there. We have one mark in the stay column and one mark in the go column."

"Okay, fine. Here's a mark in the stay column. I bet this place is a lot nicer than what you're used to isn't it?"

Harrison nodded. "It sure is. I can see you put a lot of work into making this place home. It's very impressive."

"You haven't even seen the bowling alley yet."

Harrison's eyes went one degree wider, and Dorothy smiled at the tiny victory. "For real?"

"Yes. Is that another mark in the stay column?"

"It's definitely another day I want to stay here," said Harrison. "But I'm willing to bet there's bowling in Chicago, too. So no."

Dorothy pouted. "Well, there are other things here. We have a hardware store with all kinds of building materials. That's how I made all these rooms. And there's a grocery store, and a place to get clothes. Plus the drug store."

"Is that what all the ribbons are for?"

"Yes. Yellow is bowling, red is food, blue is clothing, green is medicine. That's got to be another mark in stay, right?"

"What's purple?" asked Harrison.

"Talking monster cats."

"Ah. I think we're even again. Did they really talk? What would cats have to say?"

"Only whatever I said first," said Dorothy. "They kept repeating my words until they understood their meaning."

"So... copycats."

Dorothy stared. "That's terrible."

Harrison grinned. "You're just angry you didn't think of it first."

"You're probably right. Again." Dorothy sighed. "I'm happy here. Does that count for anything?"

"Of course it does. But let me ask you something. What's your long-term plan?"

She frowned. "What do you mean?"

"You've got all these supplies, which is great, but how long can you sustain this life? Have you done the math?"

She had indeed, so she chose to dodge the question. "We can start a garden. Learn to hunt."

"Hunt? Hunt what? Monster bugs? Monster cats? Monster rats?"

"The rats aren't monsters," she said.

"But you see my point. I should warn you, as much as I might seem all big and tough to you, I wouldn't say I'm all that manly. I have never hunted, and I certainly have never had to butcher an animal, let alone a monster. So if we don't count on my hunting skills as a resource, how long can we last?"

"About a year," she said quietly.

"All right, I think we can call that a mark in the go column. Listen, I hate to ask you to leave a place you've put so much time into. And I'm sure life on the road doesn't sound so great, especially with all the roads being pretty much gone. But it hasn't been as hard as you might think." He held up his wrist to show off the compass strapped to it. "This helps us find buildings. Nothing is locked, and everything still works, so we haven't had to rough it too much of the time."

She held out her hand. Harrison unstrapped the compass and handed it to her. She looked at it skeptically. "This is a compass. It helps you find buildings?"

He took it back when she'd finished examining it. "We're not sure why, but it points to man-made objects instead of north."

"Is it magic?"

Harrison took the question without blinking. "I don't know. Maybe. Have you seen a lot of magic?"

"A little, I think. There was a patch of crystals in the forest that tried to eat me. I think that might have been magic. John said he saw a werewolf, and you saw a dragon, so it's out there, isn't it?"

"Yes, it is. And you know what? Speaking of which…" Harrison got up to get his pack, which he brought back to the table. He unzipped a side pouch, and pulled out a small stone, a deck of cards, a ring, and a few other sundry trinkets. He then grabbed a wastebasket and scooped all of those items off the table into the trash.

"What was that about?" asked Dorothy.

"Just belatedly taking some good advice."

"Oh." Dorothy paused. "Who did you lose?"

Harrison's face went blank. "How did you know?"

"You said, 'We found Mitchell.' Who's we?"

Harrison sat back in his chair. His silence drew out, and Dorothy mentally kicked herself for the insensitivity. After a few minutes, he exhaled and looked up. "Glimmer."

Dorothy studied his eyes, looking for meaning in that word. "I don't understand."

"She was a pixie," said Harrison. "Saved our lives, but she had to give herself up to do it."

Dorothy blinked. "A pixie? Like Tinker Bell?"

Harrison laughed softly at that. "Not very much like Tinker Bell. But yes, magical, sparkly, had purple butterfly wings. Incredibly plucky. She would have liked you."

"Oh my God," said Dorothy quietly. "I'm so sorry. And oh my God."

"Yup."

In the moment of silence that followed, they each drained their drinks.

"John showed up here one day," said Dorothy. "He was a mess. I helped clean him up, and he lived in the hardware store for a while. I thought it was going to be great to have someone to help out, but mostly all he did was let me take care of him. A month ago, we went on a long hike to find more technology. That's where we found the monster cats. John ran away and left me there alone. I talked my way out of being eaten, but by then John had taken my backpack. I never saw him again."

"He sounds like a dick."

"Oh, good," said Dorothy. "That means I described him accurately."

"I'm not going to do that to you."

She pointed a finger at him. "You better not."

"I won't."

She sighed heavily. "All right. Give me three days to think about this."

He nodded. "That will give us enough time to watch Mitchell's arm, and for me to beat you at bowling."

"Agreed." She stood. "Now then, if the two of you are going to be in my home for the next three days…" She held her arm out in the direction of the hardware store. "I would very much like to introduce you to my bathtub."

27

SPARE

At the satisfying explosive wooden sound of all ten pins toppling and spinning away, Harrison's upheld fist came crashing down. "Boom!" He spun around with a huge grin. "Boom."

"I heard you," said Dorothy.

"Yeah, but boom."

"My turn!" said Mitchell. He leapt up from his seat and picked up the lightest ball Harrison could find, which still taxed his limits.

"Having fun?" asked Dorothy, her tone pleasant, but neutral.

Harrison flopped onto the bench. "I am indeed."

"You have to admit this is a good argument in favor of staying," she said.

"It sure is. And will be right up until we run out of food, and have to eat Mitchell."

"Not if I eat you first." Holding the ball in both hands, Mitchell walked to the line and scooped it onto the lane. It meandered toward the pins.

"Did you hear that?" said Harrison. "The boy is threatening to eat you."

"I'm pretty sure he just meant you."

"Even so. If he eats me, who's going to do all my chores?"

Mitchell's ball banked to the left, but stayed straight enough to take out four pins.

"Nice!" said Dorothy, applauding.

Mitchell turned around with a grin and ran to the ball return to wait.

"Seriously," said Harrison, lowering his voice. "Where are we with the decision?"

Dorothy shuffled her feet. "I really did hope this place would help change your mind."

"It's awesome. I'll give you that. But it doesn't help with our big problem. If we stay here, we need a long-term plan. The supplies won't last forever."

"What if we just stay here for the winter?" she asked. "The food will last at least that long. We can go to Chicago when it gets warm again."

Harrison took a moment to weigh the idea. "Okay, let's consider that. How many things could go wrong?"

Dorothy frowned. "What do you mean?"

"Let's catastrophize for a minute. Think about all the bad things that could happen if we stay here."

"Bad things can happen anywhere."

"Okay," he said. "I'll go first. What if the heat in the store breaks? I can't fix a furnace. Do we even know where that is? Does it take oil, because there won't be any of that at the grocery store."

"We move to the hardware store. Or one of the other stores."

"What if they're all on the same furnace?"

"We move here," she said.

"In January? How cold are Wisconsin winters?"

"It varies," said Dorothy. "But cold."

"All right, so the three of us move home base to the bowling alley, which will mean dozens of supply runs through the woods in the cold. Not ideal."

"But we could do it. And that's only if the heat breaks anyway."

"I don't think that's as unlikely as you think it is," said Harrison. "If it's about oil, we don't know how much is left."

"Then let's find the tanks and figure it out," said Dorothy. "Maybe we can even find a receipt for the last oil delivery in the paperwork somewhere."

"Wow. That's actually a really good idea."

Mitchell had retrieved his ball by that point and sent it back down the lane, where it clipped and downed three more pins. "Seven!"

"Great work, sport!" said Harrison.

"My turn," said Dorothy, standing. "You were about to explain how good my idea was, so hold that thought."

Harrison laughed.

Mitchell came back and sat with him while Dorothy bowled. "Are we staying here?"

"Do you want to?" said Harrison.

"Kinda. But what about the food?"

"It won't last," Harrison said honestly. "We can't stay here forever, no matter what."

"Oh," said Mitchell.

Dorothy knocked down eight pins with her first ball.

"Does that mean we have to go?" asked Mitchell.

Harrison sighed. "Yeah, that's what it means. Right now we're talking about how soon we should leave."

"Oh," said Mitchell.

"Don't let this worry you. No matter what happens, I'm going to keep you safe. We're just trying to decide which choice is going to be easiest."

Dorothy made the spare. She returned to her seat without fanfare.

"Even if we find the receipt, that won't tell us anything," she said. "If the furnace fails, we will have to move. But the furnace could fail here too. If that happens, we keep the doors shut and pile on the blankets for two months. We might survive that, but it also means no hot water, which will create its own set of problems. If the furnace doesn't fail, we could still lose power in a storm, which would be just as bad. And there is still the possibility those monster bugs will come back. It only took one to crack the window. If more of them come and actually break it, the heat won't matter anyway. But the biggest problem with staying here is if anything unexpected happens, we will have to leave in the cold, and that's not safe. And if there's one thing I know for sure from the last year, something unexpected is going to happen."

After a beat, Harrison said, "Did you work all that out while you were bowling?"

"Yes, and I also got a spare."

"I don't want monster bugs," said Mitchell.

Dorothy put her arm around him and pulled him close to her. "I don't want that either, honey."

"It sounds like you made a decision," said Harrison.

"Not so fast," she said. "I agree staying here poses problems, but so does leaving. We haven't looked at all the things that can go wrong between here and Chicago. For one thing, we can only carry so much food. Sheboygan and Chicago are at least a hundred miles away, maybe two hundred. How many miles have you been able to walk in a day?"

"I'm not sure," said Harrison. "But it's got to be at least thirty."

"I'd be surprised if it's ten, but let's say twenty, to be optimistic. That's a week of walking."

"We won't starve in a week."

"No, we won't," she said. "But if we're burning that many calories without eating, we won't have to starve. We'll be too weak to keep going."

"Mitchell," said Harrison. "Have we ever run out of food?"

Mitchell's eyes went wide with his sudden inclusion in the discussion. "Uh, no."

"That's right," said Harrison. Dragging Mitchell into this was probably a mistake, and Harrison backed away from that strategy. "We never run out of food, because we never run out of sources. The longest we've ever gone without finding a store or a house with something to eat inside is two days. Usually we find at least two buildings a day. There are plenty of calories out there, and we have a tool for finding them." He held up his wrist with the compass strapped to it.

"Okay," said Dorothy, "what if one of us gets hurt? It could be days before we find the right supplies to heal a wound. If you hadn't found me when you did..." She looked at Mitchell. "How's your arm feeling?"

"Better," he said quietly, his usual boyish energy nowhere to be found.

"If we hadn't found you, we would have found the drug store on our own." Harrison again indicated the compass. "Mitchell would have been fine." He placed extra emphasis on that last word to counteract the fear rising in Mitchell's face.

"You're right," said Dorothy.

"Aha," said Harrison. "So... what are the other risks of leaving?"

"Monsters," said Dorothy. "But we've been over that. Getting lost is a possibility, since your compass won't help us with direction. But as long as we stay close enough to the lake, it will take us straight there."

"So, where does that put us?" asked Harrison.

She held out both hands like a balance scale. "Survival odds of staying." She lowered her left hand and raised her right. "Survival odds of going." She switched hands. "There's math for this, isn't there? It seems like it should be math."

"Risk analysis," said Harrison. "It's game theory. I don't think we have enough hard numbers to run it though. But intuitively..."

"It's safer to go."

"I think so, yes."

She nodded. "We can't stay here. I know that. It's just hard. I really made this place home. But we can't stay."

"I'm sorry," said Harrison.

Dorothy stood, and pulled Mitchell to his feet. "You can make it up to me with French fries. There's a fryer in the snack bar, and potatoes in the freezer."

Harrison smiled and stood. "I've never used one of those before."

"You can't be worse than our last chef. Extra crispy, please." She took his hand and led him to the kitchen.

28

MOVING OUT

Dorothy bit into the golden-brown potato. **The crunch** of its outer shell resonated in her mouth as the hot, pulped innards made their way to her tongue, not quite burning it. She closed her eyes, took a deep breath, and chewed with slow deliberation. "You, sir, are my hero."

Harrison took a fry from the pile, dipped it in a gob of ketchup and popped it in his mouth. "Not bad for my first time on the fryolator."

"There's no way that's a word."

"You doubt me after my masterful use of this contraption?" He picked up two more fries.

"I suppose not," said Dorothy. She took another fry, dipping it in the ketchup this time. "So now that you have me set on Chicago, how much do you really know about what we can expect there?"

Harrison shrugged. "I pretty much already told you everything I know."

Dorothy nodded, chewing. "Right. Let me see if I can recap that. There's a woman named Claudia, and she says you should come to Chicago because that's where survivors go. Although, apparently, she has been less than forthcoming about how many have actually done so. Is that about right?"

"All the cool kids are going to Chicago," said Harrison.

"So you say. Has she said anything else? Is the city recovering? What facilities can we expect there? Bowling? French fries?"

"Nope. Nothing specific." He held up his hand. "And before you say it, yes, I am taking an awful lot on faith here."

"What if no one else heard the message?" asked Dorothy. "I mean, I've been here for months, and it never even occurred to me to check the radio. That seems like a long shot approach to get people's attention. What if we get there and there's only one person?"

"Then that still makes us four instead of three, and our survival odds increase."

Dorothy offered a small and bitter smile. "Another survivor is not necessarily an asset. Learned that one the hard way."

Harrison smiled back, less bitterly. "Touché."

"Have you considered the possibility that this is a trap?" She reached for another fry, only then noticing Mitchell's hand hovering over the plate, frozen. She looked at his face, now equally frozen in the wide-eyed gape of youthful terror.

"A trap?" he asked.

Inwardly scolding herself, Dorothy took his hand instead of the food. "Poor choice of words. I meant a prank."

"Yes," said Harrison. "I have definitely considered the possibility that this is a 'prank,' but I think it's worth the risk."

"Oh, I agree," said Dorothy. She released Mitchell's hand and gestured to the plate. He took a handful of fries and stuffed them into his mouth, restoring his outward calm. As she considered his story, her eyes narrowed in thought. "Mitchell, is it okay if I ask you something about when you lived in the train station?" She tensed for a potentially negative reaction. Harrison's account of Mitchell's life before meeting him was uncertain on a few details, but it was obvious even to Dorothy that the ordeal of having his childhood ripped away from him by the world ending had left him with a vague sense of trauma and unease.

"Sure," he said, with no sign of disturbance.

"It's okay if you don't want to talk about this, but there was someone else there for while. Is that right?" Again, she braced for a flinch, and got none.

"Yup."

She pushed forward. "Did she ever say where she was going, or where she wanted to take you?"

Mitchell frowned. "I don't remember. She wanted me to come with her, and I didn't want to go."

Dorothy nodded. "I know. But did she say anything else? About why she wanted to leave? Or what would happen after?"

Mitchell sat back in his plastic seat. "I remember something about a city, I think."

Dorothy looked at Harrison. "So, at least one other person followed the same broadcast. That's encouraging."

"Maybe that guy was heading there, too," said Mitchell.

Dorothy looked at the boy. His face had gone from neutral to cheery in a flash, apparently eager to contribute. From there she turned to Harrison's face, also smiling, but with obvious strain. Ever so slightly, he shook his head no.

"Guy?" said Dorothy, heart pounding.

"It's nothing," said Harrison. "Mitchell and I thought we saw someone, but it turned out to be nothing."

Heat rose to Dorothy's face, threatening to burn away the strands of trust she and Harrison had spent days weaving. Images of this so-called guy sprang to her head, complete with two backpacks. She stared him down. "Don't you dare lie to me."

"Dorothy…"

"Don't you dare!"

A fraught pause followed, and Mitchell broke it unexpectedly. "I'm sorry!"

Dorothy turned to the boy, his face a mess of worry and the beginnings of tears, unclear to whom he meant to direct his apology. She took his hand again. "You didn't do anything wrong, honey." Still rubbing his hand, she turned her face to Harrison and glared. "Don't you dare."

"You're right," he said. "I'm so sorry. You're right. I just wanted to protect you."

"Look around you," she said. "Do you think I need that kind of protection?"

He sighed. "We found a body. Right before we found you. Those bug things had gotten to it. It was awful, and I didn't think there was any reason to scare you with it. But you're right. You deserved to know."

Dorothy's face had gone slack and cold. Harrison's words dimly registered by that point, but one towered over the rest, clear as day. Body.

"Show me."

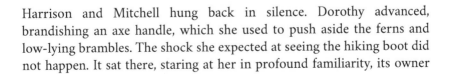

Harrison and Mitchell hung back in silence. Dorothy advanced, brandishing an axe handle, which she used to push aside the ferns and low-lying brambles. The shock she expected at seeing the hiking boot did not happen. It sat there, staring at her in profound familiarity, its owner now nothing more than a pile of bones shrouded in tattered rags. The monster bugs, long departed, had done their work well. No trace of physical features remained to identify the corpse without dental records.

But that was John's shoe.

"I got him those shoes. It was the first thing I did for him. He showed up in sneakers with holes so big I could see his bare feet." She shook her head. "No, that's not even the first thing I did for him. I fed him first. No, wait, the first thing I did was get him away from the sun. He was just sitting there, letting it cook him."

She turned around to face Harrison. He and Mitchell stood quietly, heads bowed. "Did you find two backpacks?"

"No," said Harrison.

Dorothy looked up, and around. "How did he even get here? The cats were in the opposite direction from the store. He must have gotten lost. Blindly stumbled around. Completely missed finding me."

Harrison nodded. After a pause, he said, "Dumbass."

Dorothy bit her lip and nodded. A short laugh escaped from her tightening throat, and she managed to whisper, "Dumbass," before the sobs came crashing down on her.

Harrison walked briskly to her side, and took her in his arms. She cried into his chest as Mitchell came around from her left and completed the group hug.

"I tried so hard," she whimpered.

"I know," said Harrison.

"I tried so hard to fix him, and he wouldn't let me."

"I know."

She pulled away and looked up, her face sore and surely a mess. "This was always going to happen, wasn't it?"

Harrison sighed. "Probably. Maybe not like this, but yeah, probably."

Dorothy took several deep breaths and pulled away. She gave Mitchell one short hug of his own, then walked back to John's final resting place. "I'm sorry," she said to the corpse. "You tried to warn me, and I didn't want to believe you. I know you got scared, and I know why you ran." She took a deep breath through her nose and blew it out through pursed lips. "And I forgive you. Maybe you don't deserve it, but you can have it anyway. Thank you for trying to find me after. Maybe you wanted to make things right. Maybe that's what I'll decide to believe. So, thank you for trying, even though this was the best you were ever going to do. I gave it my best shot, John. And I'm sorry I... I'm sorry we failed." She stood there for nearly a full minute, letting the lingering urge to sob play itself out. Finally, she turned to face her new companions, head held high.

"I'm ready to go now."

═══

Dorothy pulled off her gloves and scratched "bathrooms" off her to-do list. She headed for the pantry area. Mitchell sat in a chair holding a pack of white labels and a Sharpie. Harrison stood by a set of plastic utility shelves, rearranging cans.

"I need one that says dessert," he said to Mitchell. "Two esses."

With great care, Mitchell wrote the word DESSERT on a label, peeled it off and held it out, stuck to his index finger. Harrison took the label and applied it to a shelf of canned fruit and pie filling. He held up a can of chocolate frosting for Dorothy's inspection. "What were you planning to put this on?"

"You would have to ask John." She rolled her eyes. "I'm not sure he got that far in his thinking."

"We should probably take this with us. It's mostly shortening. High calorie to weight ratio. Arctic explorers carry butter for that very reason."

Dorothy raised an eyebrow. "I didn't know that."

He tossed her the can. "Yay! I taught you something! Put that with your pile."

She caught it with both hands, then turned it over to read the nutritional information. "How are you coming along in here?"

"We're almost done. What's next?"

Dorothy tucked the can under her arm and consulted the list. "Laundry. Labeling John's clothes. Sorting the movies."

"Dibs!" said Harrison. "Categories or straight alphabetical?"

"Categories, I think," said Dorothy. "Then alphabetical within each category. I would like it to look as professional as possible. Any traveler who arrives here should feel welcome and cared for." Dorothy's stated reason for all this work was exactly half the story. As an unspoken ulterior motive, if the three of them had to abort their Chicago trip, she wanted her home to be perfect when she came back to it.

She took the can of frosting into the dining room area, where she placed it on the table. Three piles were neatly arranged there, and she put it with the food. The other two piles, clothing and personal items, sat next to an empty knapsack, clearly too small to hold everything there. Culling would be the last stage of the process.

Dorothy pulled up a seat and opened a notebook. On it, she organized her thoughts into a letter for potential guests. It opened with a friendly welcome, introduction, and explanation for why she had arranged the

171

store as she did. She described the ribbon system in detail, as well as listing which resources could still be found at each location, as far as she knew. On a whole sheet of paper, she sketched a floor plan of the strip mall, including all the rooms she had created in the Hallmark store, and every bathroom in every shop. On another sheet, she drew a crude map of the forest, with color-coded trails leading to the different locations she had scouted out, including the black ribbon shortcut from pharmacy to clothing store. She labeled the end of each trail with its destination. For the purple path, she chose the label: DANGER, DO NOT VISIT.

She described both the monster cats and monster bugs in exacting detail. For any encounter with the cats, she suggested it might be advantageous to drop her name as a friend. She provided descriptions of each cat, along with their names.

When she finished with this compendium of helpful information, she took all five pages of it over to the sales counter, and laminated it to the surface with clear packing tape. On her to-do list, she scratched off "Write helpful note."

From there, she went to the hardware store to move the final load of laundry from the washer to the dryer. After letting it dry, she would fold it neatly and leave it in the clearly marked tubs in her bedroom area. While she waited for that, she did a quick inventory of the supplies on the table, with an eye on finding things she could live without. She started with personal items, and set aside all the first aid and medical supplies as essential. As she did this, she turned to the page of her to-do list that included checklists and put a tick next to everything she could account for. When she finished that, one item remained unmarked.

She found Harrison in the living room, on his knees, with several piles of movies on the floor around him. "Do you need anything at the drug store?"

He looked up. "What? Why?"

"I'm out of cough drops."

He frowned in apparent confusion. "Wait. No. Cough drops? What are you talking about?"

"We are coming up on cold season," she said. "We can't go walking in the woods without cough drops. It will be torture."

"You're telling me you want to walk all the way to the drug store to get a pack of Halls?"

"A bag of Ricola, actually. And whatever else you need."

Harrison stood. "Yeah, no. We don't need them that badly."

Dorothy crossed her arms. "What?"

"We don't need them. We're fine with what we have."

"Yes, we do!" said Dorothy. "I'm not going out there unprepared."

"Dorothy, I wanted to be on the road by now. Can we please just finish straightening everything up and get an early start tomorrow? I promise we will find cough drops once we're out there."

"You can't know that." She pulled her arms more tightly across her chest. "Besides, it will only take me a couple of hours. You two can finish up with the list while I'm gone."

"Dorothy, you're not going out there alone," said Harrison. "Maybe you haven't noticed, but I haven't let either of you out of my sight since that bug thing cracked the window."

"Ugh! I'll be fine."

"No, you really won't. If you go, we all go, which basically means the rest of this day is shot. Seriously, they're just cough drops. Don't fret it."

"Augh!" Dorothy's hands came up like claws, pointed at Harrison, and trembled. "You don't understand!" She stormed away, fleeing to her bedroom area, where she tossed her list onto the floor and threw herself onto her makeshift bed of cushions. The sobs came right away, and she lost herself in them.

After some time, once she had cried herself out, a knock came on the store fixture that partitioned her room from the rest of the sales floor. "Can I come in?" asked Harrison gently.

By this time, Dorothy had curled up in a ball. She tried to nod, but couldn't make her head do anything that would be visible without turning over, which she did not want to do.

"Yeah," she said feebly.

Harrison put his hand on her shoulder. She lifted her head. He sat on the floor next to her bed. "Mitchell's worried about you."

"I'm okay," she said, sniffing.

"I know," said Harrison. "You're made of pretty tough stuff. But it's okay to be sad."

She sat up and wiped her eyes. "I'm just so tired of losing things."

"Amen to that," he said.

She laughed. "That's stupid, right? You lost everything. Mitchell lost everything. Why should I be any different?"

"There's nothing stupid about it. You get to be upset about losing everything no matter what happened to anyone else. If you need to cry, cry. If you need us to drop everything and go on a mission to get cough drops, we can do that too."

"It's not about the cough drops."

"I know it's not about the cough drops," he said. "But if getting them helps you work out your stuff, then let's go get them."

She smiled at that. "Did you have any little brothers or sisters? Before everything changed?"

He gave her a puzzled look. "Just an older sister. Why?"

"Because you are remarkably talented at this. I'll be okay. We don't have to get the cough drops."

"I know." He held out his arms. She leaned right into them and put her head on his shoulder. The second her chin made contact with his shirt, the sobs came back. He rocked her.

"I'm sorry," she squeaked.

"Shhh. You're fine."

She let herself cry it out one last time, then pulled herself together. Once she regained her composure, she almost smiled. "I'm just scared."

"I know," said Harrison, still holding her. "I've got you."

"I know." She pulled away from him. "You know, I'm really much braver than this in real life."

"Well, yeah!" said Harrison. "Look around you. Look what you did on your own when a lesser person would have fallen apart. Just because you're amazing doesn't mean you should kick yourself for having feelings. You think I don't cry about this stuff too?"

"Do you cry?"

He shrugged. "Sure."

She pursed her lips. "No, you don't."

"No, I don't. But only because that's not my defense mechanism of choice. Trust me, I have the same feelings you're having right now, all the time, and I'd bet good money you hold it together a lot better than I do, on average."

"Hmm," she said. "You're probably right."

"That's the spirit. Listen, Mitchell and I can take care of the rest of your list. Why don't you take a break?"

"I think I'd rather use this time to figure out what I have to leave behind. It will help me part with this place if get myself completely packed."

"That's a good plan," he said, getting up. "If you need help with anything, give a holler. Otherwise, take care of yourself. We've got all the other stuff."

She nodded, and Harrison headed back to his movie piles.

Dorothy looked around her bedroom, already meticulously organized, and decided most of what was there would stay there. She stood. "All right, you're definitely coming." She picked up her fuzzy bunny slippers and took them to the dining room.

Early the next morning, Dorothy prepared the last breakfast they would ever eat in her home. After cleaning and drying the dishes, she went into the back room to check lights in the bathroom and pantry. She returned to the front of the store and similarly killed all the lights on the sales floor. She left on the outside sign, a beacon of welcome for any traveling survivor who needed the shelter.

Her full pack waited for her at the front door. Before picking it up, she took a moment to review the message taped to the counter, checking it for completeness, spelling and grammar, by the daylight pouring in the front windows. Finding no errors, she pulled on the pack and joined Harrison and Mitchell on the front walk.

"We ready to roll?" asked Harrison.

"Just about." She placed her hand on the glass of the front door and took a final look at her home, and all she had accomplished within. "Goodbye," she whispered before turning to her traveling companions. "Let's go."

They went.

29

SQUABBLES

"**H**arrison."

Sitting upright, uncomfortable and half asleep, Harrison grunted.

"Rise and shine, sir," said Dorothy.

He opened his eyes to the sight of his latest traveling companion holding a steaming mug.

"Time is it?" he asked.

"Almost 7:30. How do you like your coffee?"

He rubbed his eyes. "Lotsa cream. Lotsa sugar."

"We are fresh out of dairy farms. Is powdered creamer acceptable?"

"Sure." He reached for the mug, as the auto parts store in which they had spent the night came into focus. His bed had been a chair in the waiting room. Mitchell lay stretched out in a double-wide seat, his pack under his head, still asleep.

Dorothy handed him a tall container of creamer and a spoon. "How soon can we be ready to go?"

"My head's not there yet. Are we in a hurry?" He blew on his coffee, sipped, and winced. "How is there coffee?"

"I found it in the break room. Is it okay? I followed the instructions on the machine."

"It's fine. Why are we up so early?"

"It's been nine days since we left Sheboygan," she said. "We should be getting close, right? I thought maybe if we got an early start and made a big push today, this could be it."

"Mitchell!" said Harrison. "Looks like we're on the clock! Giddyap!"

"Mmm," said Mitchell, rolling over.

Dorothy crouched down near him. "Hey, buddy. Wanna see Chicago today?"

"Sure," he said.

"Well, you're going to need to get up."

"I am up."

"Clearly you are not up," said Dorothy.

"I am," said Mitchell, eyes closed.

"Let him sleep," said Harrison. "Another hour won't make or break us."

Dorothy stood. "And thus, the tone of the day is set. Again."

Harrison frowned. "What's that supposed to mean?"

"It means if I were traveling alone instead of waiting for the two of you to keep up I'd be there by now."

Harrison took another sip of his coffee.

"Oh," said Dorothy, her face sinking. "I'm sorry. That wasn't…"

"It's fine," said Harrison. "Mitchell, up and at 'em."

"Honestly, I didn't mean that."

"Nah, it's probably true," said Harrison.

"I feel terrible," she said.

"Leave it alone. Mitchell!" Harrison pulled the knapsack out from under the boy's head, which hit the seat with a *thud*.

"Ow!" said Mitchell, followed by tears.

"Aw, shit. I'm sorry." Harrison put his hand on Mitchell's shoulder, only to have it slapped off.

"Is there anything I can do?" asked Dorothy.

"Just pack up," said Harrison shortly. "We're up now. Better not waste daylight."

———

"Stop it!" cried Dorothy.

"Stop what?" asked Mitchell innocently.

"You know very well what, you little snake!"

The three of them marched across rocky terrain through a thick curtain of drizzle, bad enough to make the trip miserable, but not quite bad enough to necessitate shelter. Not that any presented itself. They had gone at least half a mile beyond the last tree they passed, with at least that far to go over quarry-like conditions.

"What the hell is going on back there?" called Harrison over his shoulder.

"Mitchell is being a jerk!" said Dorothy.

"I know you are, but what am I?" said Mitchell.

Harrison stopped short and turned around. "Okay, first of all, Mitchell, never, ever say that again. I know you're a kid, but there are limits. Second, Dorothy, what's the problem?"

"He keeps making faces at me!"

"Seriously? Faces? What are you, five? Ignore him for Christ's sake!"

"He's been doing it all morning!" said Dorothy.

"I have not!" said Mitchell.

"Can't you just leave him alone?" said Harrison.

"Augh!" Dorothy sprinted past both of them and continued on at a brisk pace.

"God damn it," said Harrison under his breath. He and Mitchell resumed walking, but let Dorothy keep an ever widening lead. "Can you guys just not, please?"

Dorothy looked over her shoulder and shouted. "Is that thing pointing forward yet?"

Harrison looked at his compass. The arrow still pointed directly behind him. "Not yet!"

"Ugh!"

The three of them continued in silence right to the tree line. Dorothy stopped there and sat on the rocks to wait for them. When they arrived, she stood and walked with them, but still no one spoke.

A few dozen paces into the woods, they came upon a house, ordinary, two-floor suburban architecture, with a one-car garage, painted dull brown.

Dorothy broke their sulky silence. "I thought you said the compass still pointed backward."

Harrison checked it again. "It's not pointing at this."

"Does that mean it's not working anymore?" she asked.

"I really wouldn't have any way of knowing. If that's the case, we have a big problem." He shook it and whacked it with his palm, to no observable result. "Well, shit. I guess we should probably stop here for the day. Tomorrow morning we'll stock up on whatever provisions we can carry, and look for the next one."

"What?" said Dorothy. "It's barely past three o'clock! You don't think we can find something else before nightfall? There are buildings everywhere."

"Yeah, but now they're going to be a lot harder to find," he said. "I don't think we can afford to take any chances from here out. First place we find on any given day is our home until the next morning."

"Oh my God," said Dorothy, rubbing her face. "This is now going to take twice as long. Isn't it?"

"Probably."

"Okay," she said. "Come on, Mitchell, let's stake out our rooms." The three of them trudged inside.

Harrison surveyed the stark interior. Uncarpeted, walls without paper, and most importantly, unfurnished. The lights worked, as they did everywhere, but in each room that light shone on an empty box. Mitchell and Dorothy headed upstairs to scout out which floors they planned to sleep on. Harrison headed into the kitchen.

He found every cupboard empty, as well as the pantry. The refrigerator probably would have been empty as well, but like every other possible kitchen appliance, there wasn't one. Empty holes sat where a stove and dishwasher should have been. The kitchen did have a sink, but unique to all the spigots they had found in their travels, this one did nothing when turned. Hopefully, that lack of running water did not extend to the showers and the toilets.

Harrison's exploration ended in a downstairs bedroom, or rather an empty rectangular room with one window, one overhead light, and one empty closet. He tried to picture furniture arranged in it, but this exercise backfired, as visions of all the furniture from his own childhood raced past his mind's eye, then vanished, never to return again. This room evoked every bedroom he had ever had and lost, either because his family had moved, or he had grown up and moved out, or the world itself had ended. This place offered nothing but the finality of loss. Home, family, friends, pets, school, work, even toys he had long outgrown waved at him from the back of his consciousness before dropping off a cliff and out of sight.

Harrison sat on the floor, back against a wall, staring into space. Bottomed out in his mourning, he barely noticed the click of the door shutting him inside.

[30]

ALONE

Fiona was gone. **Seven years old, and now never to** grow any older. And not even dead. No service, no marker, no closure. Not even that scrap of memory to cling to. Erased, disappeared, annulled, unhappened. That day she lost her family, Fiona fled out the door, away from Dorothy and into oblivion. The youngest of them, lost in an instant. Last in, first out.

Lorraine was gone. Ten-year-old co-conspirator of Dorothy's best pranks. She stayed while Fiona ran, not that it did her any good. When the house dissolved, wiping away all traces of Dorothy's history and childhood, it took Lorraine with it, with not even a ripple to mark the additional destruction.

Dorothy's mother was gone. Her rock. Her mentor. Her aspirations. Gone like the others, and sacrificed in a futile attempt to rescue Fiona, abandoning the other two girls to their fates. Dorothy's fate turned out to be surviving all of them, to linger on in abject solitude, without family, without anything.

Dorothy's father was gone. Off to California with his pregnant girlfriend, to build a new family and discard his old one. How casually he dismissed three little girls who wanted nothing more than his approval, his joy, and his love. And good riddance to the son of a bitch. The only significant change after his departure was a home with more kindness and less resentment. Dorothy and Lorraine rallied around their mother and the baby. Who leaves a twelve-month old child? Who does that? Someone with zero worth, that's who. Dorothy didn't need him. Other people filled that role in her life with a great deal more skill than he had ever shown. She had a mother and two sisters who all soldiered on brilliantly without him. And when they were taken from her, she had Harrison and Mitchell, a randomly acquired surrogate family. They happily slid into their roles when her first attempt with John failed so miserably. She needed them, and they were there for her, because that's who they were.

Dorothy gasped. Her eyes snapped open. She had curled into a ball in the corner of a closet, the door barely ajar. Slowly unfurling herself, she pushed the door open with caution. It led to a room, empty apart from her own backpack, the door shut.

"This isn't right," she said. Slipping the pack over her shoulders, she made for the door.

It would not open.

She rattled it. The knob was loose, but the latch held, despite no evidence of a lock or deadbolt.

"I know what you are! You think I'm stupid, but I'm not!" She grabbed the doorknob with both hands and strained to turn it, to no avail.

"I'm not staying here!" she said. "I'm not alone! I... have... people!"

On this last word, she threw her entire weight into pulling the door. It popped open.

"Ha!" She strode into the hall. The doors to other rooms were all closed, and configured in a completely different pattern than when she had entered. The hallway terminated at both ends, with no sign of the stairway she had climbed, or any other egress.

"Oh, right," she said bitterly. "This changes nothing! You're not keeping us here!" She walked down the hall, checking doors and calling for her companions. "Harrison! Mitchell! I'm here! It's all right! You're not alone!"

None of the knobs she touched turned. She pounded on the nearest door. "Are you in there? It's all right! You don't have to stay! I know you think you're alone, but I'm right here!" She pounded on the next. "Harrison? Mitchell? I'm here, but you need to help me find you!"

"Dorothy?" came a voice from behind the door, weakly.

"Harrison? You didn't lose everything! You still have us!"

"Hang on." After a few seconds, the doorknob rotated slowly, and the door creaked open. Harrison shambled out, dragging his knapsack behind him.

Dorothy threw her arms around him. "See? Right here."

"I think I know why the compass didn't point here." His words had a numb quality, and he shook his head a bit.

She let go of him. "Me too. We need to find Mitchell."

"I thought I lost you," he said.

"No, you didn't. You just forgot you had me. But I reminded you."

"That's what this place does. It makes you think you're alone."

"Which we are not," she said. "So let's get our boy and show this house who's boss."

Harrison nodded. He turned away from her toward the nearest door. She grabbed his hand tightly, and he turned to give her a quizzical look.

"Together," she said simply.

"Right," said Harrison. He squeezed her hand, and his eyes went one degree more alert. He picked his backpack off the floor and pulled it over his shoulders, clicking the belt into place. "Right! Mitchell!" he shouted down the hall.

"Mitchell!" shouted Dorothy.

"We've got you, pal!" said Harrison.

The first door they tried would not budge, and repeated pleas for a response from Mitchell came up empty. They moved on to the next door, with identical results. The third door opened. Behind it was not another bedroom, but the foyer, leading to an open front door. The forest beyond beckoned them.

"Go," said Harrison. "I'll get Mitchell."

Dorothy looked through the door to freedom. In the silence following Harrison's suggestion—no, sacrifice—birdsongs drifted in cheerily. She grabbed his other hand and held it tightly. "No. We find him together. This thing wants to split us up, and we can't do that."

At those words, the front door slammed shut.

"Shit," said Harrison.

"No," said Dorothy. "We're doing this right. That bait was a good sign. It wants us out because it knows it failed. We're getting close."

They moved into the foyer. From here, the house looked exactly the same as it had when they first entered. Systematically, they checked each room on the ground floor, rattling doorknobs and calling out supportively. At each stage, they met with silence and stuck doors.

"All these doors were open when we came in," said Harrison.

"It's trying to hide him from us," said Dorothy.

"Well, it's working."

She squeezed his hand. "No, it's not. We can't let it. It wants you to give up. It's hiding him because we're made out of better stuff than it expected, and it's scared of us."

Harrison stopped, gazing around the room. "How did you shake it?"

He looked her in the eyes. "I was caught in a loop. Until you pounded on the door, I was completely zoned out. Why didn't it work on you?"

She thought about this. "I don't know. What was your loop?"

"I kept thinking about my family. My old house, my music collection, my schools, all the stuff that's gone now. All I could think about was how much I missed all of it, and I had nothing left."

She squeezed his hand again. His smile, and the squeeze he returned, flooded her with warmth. "But that's not true."

"Obviously," he said. "But I forgot I had you guys until you knocked. Did you go through anything like that? How did you beat it?"

Visions of her sisters and mother being torn from her in an astronomically unfair cataclysm raced back to the surface of her mind. Her throat tightened. "I miss my family. I'll never have them back, and they were all so great." She frowned. "Most of them."

"Run with that," said Harrison.

"My father was a dreadful, dreadful man," she said. "I don't want to talk about him, and I do not miss him."

"Was that what did it? It that what snapped you out of it?"

"Maybe," she said. "That was part of it. I remember thinking I had to get back to the two of you. That you're my…"

"Family. You can say it."

Tears nagged at her eyes. "You're not them."

"We don't have to be them. I don't want to be them. They must have been fantastic, and I can't compete with that. What we have is a totally new thing. Not a replacement. And if you don't want to use the word family, we can call it something else. But I think that's what did it. You remembered us, and I remembered you, and we got out. And your piece of shit dad was probably the catalyst. Some loss is good, Dorothy. I think you figured that out. Loss is a part of who we are. What matters is how we go forward from there."

"Then why can't we find Mitchell?"

Harrison looked around again. "He doesn't have your knack for intellectualizing. Mitchell is a little bundle of complicated emotions. I know he had parents, and I gather they were decent ones, but he won't tell me anything about them. This place is probably tapping into his biggest vulnerability."

"What would that feel like?" asked Dorothy.

Harrison frowned. "What do you mean?"

Ignoring the question, she grabbed the nearest doorknob. It rattled, but the door wouldn't budge. She checked the next. This doorknob felt locked in place. The doorknob after that rattled. "He's in here." She pointed to the middle door. "This one is more stuck than the other ones."

Harrison tried the knob, then threw his shoulder into the door, with zero effect. His second try produced a louder *thump*, but little else. "Ow! Damn it!" He rubbed his arm and looked to Dorothy.

"Hug me," she said.

"What?"

She held out her arms. "He thinks he's alone. The cure is family. We are going to have to kumbaya our way through that door."

Harrison hesitated, then held out his arms. She pulled him into an embrace, looping her hands between his back and his knapsack. "On three?"

He nodded. "One... Two..." On each count they rocked toward the door. "Three!" Dorothy threw her body, linked with his, into the door. The sharp pain in her shoulder coincided with a loud *crack*, and the door slammed inward. Harrison and Dorothy toppled to the floor, and she landed directly on her surely bruised arm, driving a spike of pain into it. Her hand went numb as she cried out. Harrison helped her to her feet.

"Are you okay?"

Dorothy nodded, in silent contradiction of the messages being sent to her brain by every nerve in that side of her body.

Mitchell sat slouched against a wall in the corner of the empty room, eyes wide open, jaw slack.

"Oh, Jesus." Harrison knelt down next to the boy. "Hey, sport! We found you! You ready to go?" Getting no reaction, he put his arm on Mitchell's shoulder. "He's catatonic. We're going to have to carry him out." As Harrison awkwardly positioned himself to put Mitchell over his shoulder, the door slammed shut.

Dorothy whirled at the sound. The doorjamb had splintered from their break-in, and a sizable chunk of it lay on the floor, including the metal latch plate, the latch bolt itself completely exposed. Dorothy tried the knob, frozen as before, and the door would not open, despite the lack of any physical impediment to its doing so.

"We still have a problem," she said.

Harrison gently set Mitchell back down and tried the door himself. "Oh, come on. Really?"

"Do you want to try hugging again?"

"Maybe. Hang on." The room had a single window, and Harrison made for it. He tested the latch, and shook his head. "Because that would be too easy." He looked around the room, then walked to the closet and poked his head in. "Can you come here and keep this door from shutting on me? I have an idea."

Dorothy held the closet door open and braced it with her body. It provided no resistance, but that could change at any second.

Harrison grabbed the rod inside with both hands and pulled, grimacing against the strain. After a few seconds, he let out a big breath, and relaxed his body, dangling from the metal bar. He sucked in another breath and pulled himself up. With a grunt, he rocked himself forward. With another grunt, he rocked himself back. After a half dozen swings or so, the wood holding the bracket screws in place emitted a weakening crackle, followed by the snap of one end coming loose from the wall. Harrison pulled the bar at an angle, further crunching the bracket on the other side, and pulled it loose.

Beneath Dorothy's feet, the floor vibrated, as a low rumbling creak permeated the building.

"Yeah, you felt that!" said Harrison to the closet. "You like that? I got some more for you!" He limped out of the closet carrying the iron bar. "Come here." He waved for Dorothy to follow. They both walked back to Mitchell, whose expression had not changed. Harrison crouched and patted the floor. "I need you to sit with him and cover his face. Keep your eyes closed."

Dorothy sat on the floor, and pulled Mitchell's face to her chest, then closed her eyes tightly. A few seconds later, a loud *whack* rang out, followed shortly by another more productive sounding blow that included the satisfying tinkle of broken glass. The floor rumbled again.

"Can I look?" she said.

"Yeah."

She opened her eyes. Harrison had put the bar through one of the six panes in the bottom half of the window. Several ragged shards of glass remained protruding from the wood. Harrison inspected them, then tapped each with the end of the bar, knocking them outward.

"We'll never fit through there," said Dorothy. The opening looked to be less than a square foot.

"Yeah," said Harrison. "Hide your eyes again."

Dorothy turned back to Mitchell, sheltering them both. Five more crashes followed, the fragmented glass offering death cries somewhere between violent and musical. At each shattering, the house groaned, with progressively increasing volume. "It really doesn't like this."

"Tough shit," said Harrison.

Mitchell stirred against Dorothy, and he looked up at her, his eyes coming into focus.

185

"Mitchell?" said Dorothy. "Are you with me, buddy?"

"It looks like someone is getting distracted," said Harrison to the ceiling, in a sing-song tone. He slipped the bar into one of the empty panes, and attempted to use it as a lever against the wood, but couldn't get a decent enough purchase to break anything. Shifting tactics, he used the weapon as a battering ram, targeting the intersection of two slats. It only took two blows to crack the stress point. As bits of wood splintered away and fell outside, the house quaked. The creaking, settling noises amplified to a roar.

"Dorothy?" said Mitchell.

"Hey there!" she said. "Can you walk?"

The door to the room slammed open, as did the front door, visible from where Dorothy sat.

"That's right!" shouted Harrison. "Suck it!" He turned to Dorothy. "Grab his pack. Do not let go of my hand." He picked Mitchell up of the floor. The boy threw his arms around Harrison's neck. He supported Mitchell's weight with one hand, and grabbed Dorothy's hand with the other. "Run."

The floor wobbled under Dorothy's feet. The three of them made their way to the foyer with unimpressive speed but adequate steadiness. As they got to the door, Dorothy heaved Mitchell's pack out. Harrison similarly heaved her out the door by her hand. She ignored the new knives of pain from her bruised shoulder. The instant she passed through, she pulled him out with her full strength.

All three of them fell gracelessly to the forest floor. Small plants and tree roots dug into Dorothy's torso as she rolled way from the house. She sat up. As she looked back to the front entrance, the door slowly closed itself, with as close to an expression of disgust as a house could manage.

They sat in silence for a while, catching their breaths and rubbing sore patches.

After some time, Mitchell said quietly, "I don't want to stay there."

[31]

NOTHING IS LOCKED

Harrison? How close are we to the next building?" asked Dorothy.

Harrison watched his breath crystallize. The crisp air chewed at his nose and ears, and the thick cover of autumn leaves crunched underfoot. He and the kids had recently stopped at a mall, where they traded in their jackets for heavier coats.

"The compass hasn't flipped yet," he said. "We're still less than halfway."

Mitchell and Dorothy trudged on, both miserable. Now 10:30, they had set out a little after nine, with the plan to keep moving until noon, then stop for lunch. Under the best of circumstances, this regimen usually pushed the kids to their limit. Today, however, they walked through air far colder than they were used to. It had been three weeks since they set out from the Hallmark store, when freshly turned leaves began falling from the trees. Most likely, the mild weather was entirely behind them now. This wouldn't be a cold spell. Autumn had battened down the hatches for winter.

"Okay, people, take five." He opened his pack and removed two small, rod-shaped objects. He whacked one against the heel of his boot and tossed it to the ground a few feet away. It promptly expanded itself into a spindly frame, the approximate shape of a kitchen chair, with a fabric seat. Mitchell flopped into it, without waiting to be asked and without noticing Dorothy had stepped aside to let him do so. With her finely honed, big-sister reflex, she had slipped smoothly into the role.

After popping open a seat for Dorothy, Harrison produced a small can of mango nectar for her and a box of grape juice for Mitchell. He would top them both off with water later, but they would have a little bit of time for a comfort experience first. They drank in silent gratitude.

Harrison checked the compass on his wrist again. He had inspected it, periodically, all morning, but it had not yet given him any useful information. Sometimes, presumably more than a certain distance from any developed oasis, the needle would wobble and spin, lazily and aimlessly. Harrison had not ruled out the possibility they had picked up so much technology along the way, the compass was trying to point back at them now. This time, it pointed in the approximate direction of their travel, twitching only slightly.

"Thank God," he muttered.

He let them sit in peace for the promised five minutes, long enough for them to finish their juice and start complaining (Dorothy was cold, Mitchell, bored). "Okay, kids, let's roll."

Neither of them thought this new idea would improve their situation, as they explained with intense animation. He allowed them to interrupt each other for a few seconds, then held up his wrist for them to see.

"Yes!" they exclaimed simultaneously. They collapsed their chairs with practiced ease.

Another two hours and three breaks later, they came upon the first sign of their objective. They had emerged from forest onto a grassy plain, which in turn bordered a vast expanse of what appeared to be sand, until they stepped onto it. The color of a beach, but the consistency of clay, it compressed under their boots, leaving clear, firm footprints. The compass pointed straight through to the other side. Going around so large an area would likely be untenable. Some plants had taken hold in little clusters, and small animal footprints peppered the surface, indicating some degree of safety. They braved crossing it.

A few yards into the woods on the other side of the curious expanse, they encountered a length of yarn. Someone had strung it from one tree to another, and from that tree to the next, and so on. The trail of yarn wove in both directions through the trees and off into the distance, its end, if it had one, not visible from where they stood.

"Ooookay." Harrison consulted the compass, which pointed toward something beyond the other side of the yarn fence. He shrugged, and reached out to lift the yarn out of the way so the children could pass under it.

An image flashed in his mind. Something hairy, enormous, and swift.

Claws the size of carving knives protruded from more limbs than he could count, and before he could process the image in his mind's eye, those claws tore into his abdomen, spilling entrails to the forest floor. The sight of steam rising from the rope of intestine extending away from him and sliced open everywhere was interrupted as those claws went to work on his eyes.

"Ah! Shit!" Harrison toppled backward, staggering several steps before landing hard, and painfully, on his butt. He threw his hands over his eyes, checking for blood, or empty sockets. The dim realization of no accompanying pain registered, and he pulled his hands away slowly. He scrutinized them, grubby and rough from weeks of travel, but bloodless. "Oh, my God."

"Harrison?" asked Dorothy, wide-eyed and stock still.

As he attempted to form a reply, Mitchell backed away from him in obvious fear, directly toward the yarn.

"Don't touch it!" shouted Harrison.

Mitchell spun at this warning, exactly too late to do anything about it. He fell face first on the strand. Rather than break under his weight, it repelled him backward, landing him soundly on his back. He wheezed for a few seconds, then shrieked.

"Mitchell!" Dorothy dropped to his side and cradled him in her arms, slowly rocking him as he cried it out. She looked at Harrison. "What's happening?"

"I don't know!"

"Are you okay?"

He felt his midriff, detecting no slashes, and no spilled guts. "I think so. Holy shit. We can't go that way."

"You think?"

Harrison stood. Slowly, he approached the yarn again. The closer he got, the fuzzier his head felt. Dorothy and Mitchell were closer still. "Do you feel that?"

"Feel what?"

He tried to shake the disorientation from his head. "I don't know. Something."

"Are you hurt?" she asked.

He checked again. "No. Whatever this thing does, it's not physical."

"Are you okay?" she quietly asked Mitchell.

The boy had stopped crying and nodded. Even from where Harrison stood, Mitchell's trembling was obvious.

"Come here, sport."

Mitchell stood and ran into Harrison's arms.

Dorothy stood as well, and advanced on the yarn barrier.

"What are you doing?" shouted Harrison.

"It's like the house," she said. "It's trying to get into our heads. We beat that. We can beat this."

"Don't!" he shouted, to no avail.

Dorothy reached out and gently lay two fingers on the yarn. Her hand snapped back instantly. "Oh! Oh, that's bad!" She stuck her fingers in her mouth.

"What did you see?" asked Harrison.

"I'm not sure. Something dangerous."

"Amen to that."

She turned to face him. "I take it back. I think this is warning us about real dangers on the other side. So what do we do?"

Harrison looked at the compass again, then down at the still whimpering boy in his arms. They couldn't go forward, but he wouldn't turn back at this point. "We go around." He scanned left and right, chose right, and walked, kids in tow.

As they walked, they glanced at the yarn from time to time, with respect and fear. Every few hundred feet, one color would end in a knot and another color would begin. The different colors did not appear to have different properties. They looked away from it as often as they looked at it, and after some time, Dorothy spotted a building down the line, which she brought to their attention. Harrison could not tell which side of the yarn it occupied, which troubled him. It also did not appear to be the exact target of the compass. Either it didn't count as civilization, per se, or the compass nudged them toward something greater and unseen. As they finally reached the structure, they collectively relaxed. The blocky little edifice sat on their side of the barrier.

Mostly.

The yarn ran straight up to the corner of the building, and ended there, tied to a piton driven into the cinder block of the outer wall.

"Safe?" said Dorothy. "Not safe?"

Harrison shook his head. He experimented with touching the piton, but even holding his finger too close frightened him more than he could endure. The wall itself proved no problem at all. "Oh, thank God." He exhaled. "I was afraid that was going to go on forever."

They walked the length of the wall, which now appeared to be the rear of a small shop. It held a single door, no windows, no ornaments of any sort, with the exception of an unostentatious, three-letter sign above the door, which read CVS.

190

Harrison smiled at the familiarity. He walked past the door to the other end of the wall, where he found another piton, holding a new length of yarn, which trailed off again indefinitely. "Oh, hell," he muttered. He came back to the door. "The yarn keeps going, but the building itself looks safe. Let's check it out."

"What?" said Dorothy. "That makes no sense."

Harrison shook his head again. The yarn effect lingered in the back of his skull and made it difficult for him to focus on explaining his reasoning. "Just... I don't know. The yarn is warning us about something, but not about this store. Maybe it's the beginning of a safe path or something. We should at least see if we can get through it before we commit to walking miles out of our way."

Dorothy closed her eyes, took a deep breath, and blew it out. "With caution. All right?"

"Agreed."

Dorothy hesitantly reached for the door and gave it one visible tug. "Moot. Door's locked. We keep walking."

"Let me try!" said Mitchell.

"You won't be able to open it," she said. "It's locked."

"Nothing is locked." Harrison motioned her out of the way and laid his hand on the door handle. As he pulled, with an audible and tangible *click*, the door swung open freely.

Dorothy frowned. "It was locked."

"Don't worry about it. Let's get in out of the cold." Harrison stuck his head in the door. Seeing nothing but an empty, clean stock room, he motioned the others to follow. "You feel anything wrong?"

"Not yet," said Dorothy.

"Mitchell?"

The boy shook his head.

The back room included two bathrooms, both open, lit, and apparently functional. Harrison walked into one, looked around, and felt no trace of the terror from earlier. The other produced similar results. "Potty break, kids. You can both go, and please make it snappy."

"What about you?" asked Mitchell.

"You guys first. I want to check on provisions. Dorothy, please keep Mitchell here until I give the all-clear." Not a lie, but a diversion. With the store appearing more and more secure and safe, and with them out of the way, he would load up his pack with a broad assortment of candy. When they emerged, he would then make a show of telling them they couldn't take any sweets, that candy wasn't good for them. Well, okay, he'd say, maybe one, just this time. Once out of the store, and out of whatever danger that yarn presented, he would have a secret stash of goodies to ration out. They would resent him for a little while, but the tactic would pay many dividends on the road.

He emerged from the back, into a familiar scene. The shelves, however, looked oddly under stocked, conveying the appearance of a store in its clearance phase, about to go under. All the brand-name candy was gone. Instead of the desired Hershey bars or Skittles, they would be forced to settle for store brand mints and circus peanuts. He grabbed a few packages and hastily loaded them into his pack.

His primary objective met, he made for the cough and cold section. Dorothy's concern about a cough drop shortage had been prophetic. While he browsed through flavors of lozenges, the sound of something falling—a cellophane bag, perhaps—came from behind him. He spun around, the unwelcome image of a clawed monster returning to him in the beginnings of a panic.

Rather than a monster, he found a girl. Older than Dorothy. A teenager, certainly, but difficult to tell exactly how old. Anywhere from sixteen to nineteen would be his uselessly wide guess. She wore an insulated denim jacket and blue jeans. Her complexion was medium brown, and she had a thick mane of dark curly hair with one bold white stripe running down the front, not quite in the center. Thin, but not undernourished, the way Mitchell had looked back in the Worm station. Unlike Mitchell and Dorothy, when he met them, this girl was petrified.

He spoke softly, smiling. "Hi. I'm Harrison."

No response.

"Are you okay?"

Still nothing. The residual fuzziness in his head made itself known again, and the possibility this girl represented the danger they hoped to avoid did not seem out of the question. It would not be the first time an apparent human proved to be something much worse.

"Are you alone?" he asked clumsily.

She nodded, ever so slightly, then caught herself and shook her head vigorously. No. An absurd bluff. Possibly a sign she was human, and safe, but a bad move on his part. Her first communication with him, and he had cornered her into lying. Great. He tried again.

"I have two other kids with me. They're in the back." He pointed behind him.

This appeared to elicit the exact opposite effect than intended. Her eyes got wider, no doubt imagining horrible things about him. He looked down to the bag of cough drops in his hand, and it inspired him. Using it as an anchor, he started over, holding it up for her to see.

"I wanted to pick up some cough drops for them," he said calmly. "Cold season and all."

This took her off guard, and she looked at him, puzzled. As they attempted to reach a new equilibrium, another person entered the store through the front door.

Harrison could see the new arrival from where he stood, but the girl had to turn. Harrison held still for the second she had her back to him, trying to generate integrity rays. She turned back swiftly and frowned at him, eyes locked. The man walked briskly to her.

Glaring at Harrison, he asked, "Who's this, then?"

The words emerged in an English accent. This man stood several inches shorter than Harrison, carried a slighter build, and looked much tidier. Under an expensive-looking, tan wool overcoat he wore a pressed shirt and a tie, looking for all the world like he was on his way to the office.

The girl turned on this tidy man. "Alec! What the *fuck?*" She punctuated the last word by slamming her palms into his chest. He wobbled, frowned, and held his ground. "You said the store was secure!"

At these words, the man's eyes went wide. Shoving the girl out of the way, he charged Harrison, and threw him to the ground, pinning both arms behind his back, swiftly and painfully. With his knee digging into Harrison's spine, he said, "Security breach. Two agents to the north border CVS, right away." More assertively, he said to Harrison, "How did you get past the inhibitor?"

At that moment, the children emerged from the back room. "What's going on?" asked Dorothy, panic in her voice.

A plastic zip-tie bit into Harrison's wrist, and the man—Alec, the girl had called him—stood. Harrison rolled over to face Dorothy and Mitchell. They had a clear shot at the door.

"Run," he said to them.

Dorothy grabbed Mitchell's wrist and bolted for the door. Alec moved to intercept them so swiftly Harrison could barely see him. The largest knife Harrison had ever seen appeared in Alec's hand, and he held it out at arm's length, at an angle to the children.

Dorothy screamed.

"They're clean!" said Alec. "Get them."

The girl ran to Dorothy's side and took her hand. "It's okay. I've got you. Come with me."

"What?" cried Dorothy.

Alec dropped his knee to Harrison's back again, and the weapon flashed in front of his face, clearly not a knife, but a small sword. Harrison caught a glimpse of his reflection in the flat of the blade. It gave off a slight green aura.

"He's got magic on him," said Alec, "but it looks residual. Possible human."

"Let go of him!" shouted Dorothy. The new girl had her arm on Mitchell's shoulder, and Dorothy pulled on it.

"It's okay!" the girl said again. "You're safe now! But we have to get out of here!"

Two more men entered the store and silently reported to Alec. They wore no uniforms, no black jackets, no sunglasses, no coiled wire behind the ear, but ordinary coats over ordinary clothing. Alec spoke to them, curtly. "We have a guest. I would like to see he is interviewed before we consider his application to immigrate." He gestured to the children. "His companions will need a temporary foster home. Special Agent de Queiroz and I will take them down to Adoption and get the paperwork started."

The men nodded. One of them pulled Harrison to his feet.

"You know," said the girl, "this is the shit I'm talking about. You boys play your little spy games and pretend we're all snug as a bug, and it's all bullshit."

"This isn't the time," hissed Alec.

"How did you get in here?" she asked Harrison.

"Through the back door," he said.

The girl glared at Alec.

"That's impossible," he said evenly.

"Look," Harrison offered, "this is obviously a misunderstanding. Why don't I take my kids and go? I'm sorry to intrude."

"Shut up!" said the girl. She turned on Alec again. "I've been saying this for weeks, and I get no support from you. You can't patrol a border by proxy. I can't fucking believe we've got somebody coming right in the back door, thank you very much." With that much to work with, Harrison finally recognized her voice.

"Claudia?"

Her eyes narrowed, taking in Harrison anew. "Oh. A fan."

"Is it really you?"

Her dark eyes became narrower still, riveted on Harrison. "What, you expected a white girl? I get that a lot, asshole."

He shook his head. "I expected an adult."

"Yeah," she said. "That's my second favorite."

"Children," said Alec. "Come this way, please."

Before Harrison had a chance to object, one of the two agents holding him pulled a cloth bag over his head, and they hauled him roughly out the door.

ORPHANS

Mitchell had gone catatonic, his grip on Dorothy's hand tight enough to affect her circulation. He stared straight ahead, eyes wide, in silence.

In the wake of Harrison being forcibly removed from their presence, Dorothy had no readily available words of comfort for him. She turned to the one person in the room she feared the least. "Claudia?"

The girl stood at Dorothy's height, probably of the same build, though difficult to tell through her jacket. Definitely older than Dorothy, but still young. Dark-skinned, of African or Latina descent, or possibly both, with wild and unique hair—dark, wiry, splayed out at random, and accented with a white stripe. Whether the coloring was an affectation or a condition Dorothy could not tell. Her expression still held the rage she showed Harrison moments before, but it softened as she turned to respond to Dorothy. "It's okay. We're gonna take you somewhere safe."

"It is *not* okay," said Dorothy. "What are they doing to Harrison?"

"Not your concern," said Alec, short, overdressed, British, and easy to despise. "Come on, let's get you out of here." He reached for Mitchell, who flinched and whimpered.

Dorothy pulled Mitchell into her arms and held on tight. "Not happening."

Claudia put her hand on Dorothy's shoulder, with a tenderness that belied everything about the current situation. "What's your name?"

Dorothy responded with silence, looking away.

"I'm Claudia."

"Obviously," muttered Dorothy.

"Okay," said Claudia. "That's fair. You're scared. That's fair too. That guy you were with? How much do you know about him?"

"Nothing I'm going to share with you," snapped Dorothy.

Alec spoke into his hand. "CVS secure. Two children here. Please send two more agents and a social worker."

"Listen," said Claudia to Dorothy. "I know you're pissed, and scared, and I probably made a bad first impression, but all we want right now is what's best for you. There's good reasons to think the guy with you isn't what he seemed to be, and we need to check that out before we can let him get near you again. Do you understand what I'm saying?"

"Of course I understand you," said Dorothy. "You're just wrong."

"Maybe. But better safe than sorry." She looked at Alec. "I've got this. Why don't you go do whatever it is you do?"

Alec nodded, then took up a position by the door to the back room, blocking their egress.

"Our packs are back there," said Dorothy.

"Leave them," said Alec.

Given they contained nothing but supplies they would surely not need anymore, Dorothy let it drop.

Claudia held out her hand. "Come on. I think there's still some ice cream in here somewhere."

Mitchell still clung to Dorothy, but at the mention of ice cream he loosened his grip.

Dorothy refused Claudia's offered hand, but did follow her into the store to the freezer, where they found a handful of ice cream bars and sandwiches still available. Mitchell picked out a Snickers ice cream bar. Dorothy resisted the temptation until she conceded not eating ice cream would not constitute punishing Claudia, and chose a Mrs. Field's Chipwich. They retired to the chairs in the prescription waiting area with their snacks. Claudia sat with them, eating Ben & Jerry's directly from the container with a plastic spoon.

After a few minutes of waiting in a silence she strived to make as awkward as possible, Dorothy stood to stretch her legs. Claudia stood as well, assuming a guarded stance.

Dorothy sighed. "I'm not going anywhere."

Claudia relaxed. "Sorry about that."

Dorothy did not acknowledge the apology.

Sounds came from the front door.

"We're back here!" said Claudia.

Three new adults made their way back to the prescription waiting area, a man and two women. One of the women, dressed in a tan skirt and matching jacket over a white blouse, and heels, came all the way to where the children sat, and crouched down in front of them, presenting a huge and professionally cultivated smile. The other two new arrivals were dressed identically to the two agents who had abducted Harrison. They held back, standing in positions that effectively blocked any direction Dorothy might attempt to flee.

"Hi there!" said the woman. She wore her hair in a bob, dyed the same red as her lipstick, both dark against her exceptionally pale skin. "I'm Melissa. Heard we had some excitement today. Everyone okay?"

"Excitement?" shouted Dorothy. "You arrested my friend!"

Melissa put her hand over her heart, and the smile faded. "I didn't arrest anybody. Has anyone mistreated you?"

The taste of vanilla ice cream and chocolate chip cookies still on her tongue, Dorothy said, "No. Not us."

The smile came back. "Well, that's a start. I know this has been a tough day for you, and I'm sorry. I'm here to see how we can make it better for you. Has anyone told you where you are yet?"

Mitchell shook his head.

Dorothy put her hand on his knee. "This is Chicago."

"This is New Chicago," said Melissa. "And let me be the first to welcome you here."

"What happens to us now?" asked Dorothy bluntly.

"Well, assuming you plan to stay, we have temporary housing for you, until you're placed with a family."

"We already have a family, and you arrested part of it."

Melissa sighed, and the professionally cheery façade slipped away. "Look, I can see you're upset. But whatever happened with your friend isn't something you and I are going to fix right now. I am offering you a place to call your own for a while. A little safe haven where you can get cleaned up, fed, new clothes, whatever you need. Once you get settled, we can figure out where to go from there. But right now you two are cold, dirty, and probably hungry."

"We had ice cream," said Mitchell.

"That's not much of a lunch," said Melissa without missing a beat. "What would you say to a sandwich, or a piece of fried chicken, or some lasagna?"

This got Mitchell's attention in a big way. They had been subsisting on nothing but canned goods. It had been months since either of them had tasted bread or freshly cooked food. "You have all that?"

"Yes, we do."

Dorothy pretended to ignore the temptation, but the thought of lasagna had her mouth watering. "And what if we say no thank you to your kind offer of food and shelter?"

"Then I'm afraid it will become something more than an offer," said Melissa.

"The Adoption Center is a good place," said Claudia. "All our intakes start there if they're minors. She's not lying about the food. They eat better there than most of us do."

"Is that where you live?" asked Mitchell.

She shook her head. "No, my situation is a little different. But I've been there. You'll like it."

"And we don't have a choice," said Dorothy.

Claudia nodded. "And you don't have a choice."

"Fine." Dorothy held her wrists out. "Cuff me and take me away."

"Wait here a sec, can you?" Claudia asked Melissa, before heading into the store, and down an aisle. Less than a minute later, she came back with a pack of two pens and a memo pad. She tore the blister pack open, removed a pen, and left the remains on the pharmacy counter. "Listen, I know we got off on the wrong foot here, but I want to help out." She opened the memo pad and scribbled in it. "This is my phone number. If you need anything, call me." She ripped the page out and held it out for Dorothy. "Please take it."

"This is a very good friend for you to have," said Melissa.

"I'm kind of a big deal around here," said Claudia.

"Harrison?" asked Dorothy.

Claudia shook her head. "Out of my hands. Sorry. Anything else though."

Hesitantly, Dorothy took the slip of paper and stuffed it in her pocket. "My name is Dorothy."

Claudia beamed. "Dorothy. Got it."

"I'm Mitchell," said Mitchell.

"Hi Mitchell!" said Claudia cheerfully. "You two get settled in. We'll catch up later." She squeezed Dorothy's shoulder. "Seriously, call me. Okay?"

Dorothy gave a non-committal half smile. Claudia let go of her arm.

"All right, then!" said Melissa, broad smile back in place. She led them away from the pharmacy toward the front door. The two agents brought up the rear. Claudia stayed behind. As Dorothy turned down an aisle, she glanced backward one last time. Claudia stood next to Alec, still watching them. She waved.

And then they were through the front door and in a city.

The CVS turned out to be near the edge of the forest, and they emerged into a vast, cleared plain. New Chicago was a scattered collection of surviving buildings and new construction, linked by dirt roads. The original buildings were widely spaced, like much of what Dorothy and Harrison had discovered in their own travels. Unlike those discoveries, the deforestation zone allowed for multiple buildings to be visible. Between them, log cabins lined the roads, most still unfinished.

Melissa led Dorothy and Mitchell to a ground vehicle, the approximate size of a car, but otherwise bearing little resemblance to any make or model from Dorothy's memory. It sat low to the ground, on at least eight tiny wheels, positioned to be barely visible. One of the agents held the door open. Melissa, Dorothy and Mitchell stepped inside. The interior was more spacious than apparent from the outside, owing partly to the fact none of the space appeared to hold an engine of any sort, and partly because the two rows of seats faced each other, with no obvious driver's seat.

Melissa pulled the door shut. "Fido, Adoption Center." The vehicle accelerated to a moderate speed.

"Fido?" asked Dorothy.

"It's a trigger word, imprinted to my voice," said Melissa. "Lets the car know a command is coming."

"I worked out that much on my own," said Dorothy. "I just thought it odd you would name it Fido. Is this yours?"

"Company car. But essentially, yes."

"It's cool," said Mitchell, his eyes fixed out the window on the nascent city drifting by them outside.

"Thank you," said Melissa with her standard smile.

It took about fifteen minutes to reach the Adoption Center. They passed several buildings under construction, some of which were being assembled by machines completely alien to Dorothy's experience. One of the buildings had no construction equipment in evidence whatsoever, but glowed dimly, and sprouted a small wooden projection as Dorothy watched.

They arrived at the Adoption Center, located in a repurposed high school building. As they entered through the main office, Melissa stopped to speak to the receptionist, a man who appeared to be in his forties. "Hello, Derek. Two new intakes today. This is Mitchell." She placed both her hands on Mitchell's shoulders. "And this is Dorothy." She gestured to where Dorothy stood.

"Welcome aboard," said Derek to the children before looking back to Melissa. "You can go ahead and take her down. Mitchell can wait here until I get someone up here to take care of him."

"You're deliberately separating us!" shouted Dorothy. This startled Derek, and evoked rolled eyes from Melissa.

"First stop is the locker room. We measure you for clothes and give you a chance to clean up. Girls go the girls' locker room, and boys go to the boys'. We're not trying to split you up, and if we were, at this point I would just tell you, and save you the trouble of being paranoid." The smile had gone, this time perhaps for good.

"He'll be fine here," said Derek.

Mitchell gave her his best brave look. "It's okay. See you soon?"

"Count on it," said Dorothy. Then she pulled him into a tight hug and kissed his forehead.

The girls' locker room included an office, where a young woman measured Dorothy with a tape before giving her a towel and pointing her in the direction of the shower. The adults gave her privacy, or at least as much as she could feel in a shower room with eight heads and no door. She stripped and dropped her clothes in a hamper outside the shower, as instructed. Having sustained her hygiene in a bathtub for half a year, Dorothy devoured the shower experience, despite her multitude of misgivings. She lingered far past the point of cleanliness, and no one came by to put a limit on her. Only when her fingers pruned did she relent and shut off the water.

When she emerged in her towel, she found the hamper empty, and a set of fresh, clean clothes waited for her, folded neatly and resting on a bench. Nothing ostentatious; a white button down shirt, blue jeans, underwear, bra, socks and white sneakers. Everything fit, with the crispness of brand new clothing in need of a breaking in. She hung the towel on a hook and made her way back to the office.

"Oh, you look nice." Melissa stood. "Next stop on the tour is the nurse's office."

A woman in a lab coat gave Dorothy a brief exam. Nothing invasive, but notably thorough otherwise. From there, Melissa led her to a former classroom, now housing a row of bunk beds, with trunks at their feet. Several girls about her age sat in their beds or the handful of lounge chairs near the window. Most had homework to do, or worked on puzzle books. A few talked quietly among themselves. The two girls in the lounge chairs watched her come in and whispered something to each other.

Dorothy took in her surroundings with glum realization. "I'm in an orphanage."

"We don't use that word," said Melissa. "This is the Adoption Center. There are no orphans in New Chicago, only children waiting for families. And everyone gets placed."

"I already *have* a damn family." Dorothy turned around and looked Melissa straight in the eye. "What's happening to Harrison right now?"

Melissa opened her mouth to speak, but nothing came out. She looked away.

[33]

QUITE A TALENT

The two men escorted Harrison out of the CVS in silence, blindness and fear. A short walk away from the door, one of the agents pushed his head down. "Step." He felt with his toe and found a step up, ducking as he went forward. They deposited him in a cushioned seat, and a door hissed shut.

"Foxtrot, holding facility," said the agent.

A sense of motion ensued. No one spoke to him or near him.

Some time later, the motion stopped. Someone pulled Harrison out of the seat, into the cold November air, and further into a heated building. Down a hallway. Around a bend. Stand still. Into an elevator. Sensation of dropping, swiftly. Out. More walking. Stop. Turn around.

His handlers removed the bag from his head.

Harrison stood in a sparse room, furnished with a cot, a table and two chairs, and equipped with a sink and a toilet. Bare walls held a single door, opposite a broad mirror, and no windows. Interrogation room, then, though the toilet implied his stay here would not be brief. The drain in the floor implied it would not be pleasant.

By the door stood the two agents who had taken him from the CVS, each man armed with a sword at his hip, both considerably larger than the one Alec had used to detect magic on him. A third man, taller than the others, also wearing a sword, entered the room, holding a pair of wire cutters and a clear plastic bag. He advanced on Harrison. The other two drew their swords.

"Keep your hands clasped behind your back," said the newcomer as he walked around Harrison. "Eyes front. Make no moves until instructed. Clear?"

"Clear," said Harrison.

An agent removed Harrison's compass and watch from his wrists. The man behind him probed each one of his fingers, and tugged his collar down in the back. The chain holding Glimmer's medal pinched him as the agent undid its clasp and took even that from him.

The zip tie holding his wrists together tightened briefly in the man's grip, then with the *click* of the wire cutters biting into it, came off. Harrison kept his hands behind his back, as directed, his eyes on the drawn swords.

The taller agent came back around to Harrison's front. The plastic bag now held his few effects. "Strip. Clothes go in the bag." He pointed to a spot near Harrison's feet. An open black duffle bag sat there. He exited the room without any follow-up. The other two agents held their ground and their swords, with no indication this process would involve any privacy.

Harrison took off his coat and dropped it in the bag. He kicked off his shoes and pulled off his socks, and tossed them in as well. Shirt. Pants. Boxers. Harrison stood naked before two strangers for an indeterminate amount of time before the taller agent returned. With him entered a woman wearing green scrubs and blue latex gloves, holding a black bag. She did not make eye contact with Harrison.

"Sit."

Harrison sat on the cold, metal chair as the tall agent cuffed his hands to the table. The woman pulled a blood pressure cuff from her bag, wrapped it around Harrison's arm, and pumped. Once his arm reached a suitable level of pain, she held his wrist, released the valve, and let the air slowly hiss out. She removed the cuff and put it back in the bag, from which she produced a tongue depressor and a long swab.

"Say ah."

Harrison complied, and she pressed his tongue down while swabbing his throat roughly. The swab went into a sealed container. She took his temperature, shined a penlight into his eyes, examined his ears, and used a lancet to draw blood from his index finger. She drew it into four tiny tubes, sealed them with wax, and stowed them in the bag.

Her final act before leaving the room was to place three small plastic containers with lids on the table across from Harrison. Once she had gone, and the door closed behind her, an agent uncuffed him and pointed to the containers. "Fill those."

Harrison reached across and picked up the smallest one, labeled SEMEN. "Oh, come on."

The other two said URINE and STOOL. All three agents left the room for as much time as he needed to complete the task, though given the inescapable mirror, the privacy was an illusion.

Without windows and daylight, it became impossible to tell the time of day. Meals were delivered from time to time, but all identical, a protein bar and a glass of water, and the intervals between them did not feel consistent.

Out of boredom more than anything else, he tested the door once. Like every other door in the world, it opened for him. Two men stood outside the room, looking neither surprised nor amused. Harrison closed the door again.

Five meals after his arrival, an armed agent entered the room alone and placed a folded pile of cloth objects on the table. He did not draw his sword.

"I take it you figured out I'm not dangerous?" said Harrison from his cot, his voice ragged from disuse. The question got no response, and the man left.

The stack included a pair of cotton pants with an elastic waistband, and a cotton tunic, both solid beige. It also included two white towels and two white washcloths. Harrison soaked one of the washcloths in the tepid water from the sink, stood over the floor drain, and wiped himself down. He did this several times before putting on his clothes, in full view of whoever was behind that mirror. The shirt and pants felt like pajamas, significantly more comfortable than his previous nudity.

A small man with glasses and a mustache, dressed smartly in a jacket and tie, visited Harrison several meals after the clothing delivery. He entered with a clipboard full of papers, and two armed guards. A guard beckoned Harrison to sit at the table, but did not cuff him to it this time. The man sat across from him.

"I need to get some standard information," said his interviewer.

"Where are my kids?" Harrison asked.

The man across the table scanned some forms and did not look up. "You'll have to take that up with someone else. Last name."

Harrison said nothing.

"You'll find cooperation works exceedingly well in this environment," said the man with the clipboard.

"Are you threatening me?" asked Harrison.

"I don't need to threaten you. You're already in this room, and you're probably the only person who cares how long you stay here. Should we continue?"

Harrison rubbed his eyes. The events of the past however-many-days caught up with him in the form of huge yawn. "Yeah. Sure."

"Last name."

"Cody."

The interviewer wrote that down in ink. "First name."

"Harrison."

"Middle?"

"Wallace."

"Date of birth?"

"July 4, 1976," he said without emotion.

For the first time, the interviewer looked up at Harrison's face, possibly to gauge his truthfulness. The topic of Harrison's birth date had always been a source of novelty in his life and a fun fact that usually amused new friends. But this reaction carried something other than amusement. The man had a strange, awestruck expression, and he turned to look at his cohorts standing at the door. They, too, wore expressions of amazement.

After a moment's pause, the questions continued, with no further discussion of his birthday.

"Were you a US citizen?"

"Still am, as far as I know."

"Yes or no, please," said the interviewer. "Did you ever serve in the US armed forces?"

"No."

"Have you ever been convicted of a felony?"

"No."

"What was your last occupation, prior to May 30 of this year?"

"I was a bookseller," he said.

The man looked up again, less awed this time. "Bookseller?"

"I managed a Borders," said Harrison.

"I see." The interviewer checked a box on his form. He flipped the paper over the back of the clipboard. "How did you come to be in Chicago?" He asked this with no change of inflection, but the choppy segue indicated a whole new category of question.

"I walked," said Harrison.

The man made a note. "From where?"

"Massachusetts."

The man looked up, surprise in his face again. "Massachusetts?"

"Northampton," said Harrison.

"That's a long way," said the interviewer. "And east of here."

"Yes, it is."

"How did you get inside the border?"

"I'm not sure where the border is," said Harrison truthfully. "The first I knew I was in Chicago was when I was in the CVS."

The man wrote that down. "How did you get into the CVS?"

"I came in through the back door."

"Was it locked?"

"No."

"You're quite sure," He persisted in a flat tone, perhaps to give Harrison a chance to contradict himself, or confirm something they already knew.

"When I pulled on it," he said, "it opened. I do not believe it was locked."

The interviewer made another note. "Please describe any magic or magical artifacts you have employed since May 30."

Harrison's heart accelerated. He had certainly seen magic, and had in fact employed it against the bug monster with his wind-stone. That stone currently rested at the bottom of a wastebasket in Dorothy's Hallmark store, along with every other magical item he had picked up along the way. He doubted revealing this to his captors would serve his best interest at that moment.

"Mr. Cody? Did you hear the question?"

"Yes," he answered quickly. "It just surprised me. I haven't used anything like that." His heart pounded more heavily in the wake of his lie.

"Right." The man clicked his pen and tucked it in his pocket. "Thank you for your time," he said with absurd courtesy, got up, and left.

Shortly after that, another meal arrived. He ate, slept for a while, woke up on his own, and had another meal.

The second visit had a different tone. The same man (with a different pair of door loiterers) entered, unannounced. This time, he carried a briefcase. He put the case flat on the table, spun it so the handle faced Harrison, and said, "Open it."

Harrison inspected the case. It had two latches, one on each side of the handle, each activated by a thumb trigger, and each trigger mounted above a four-digit combination lock. Every digit on both locks had been set to zero. He pushed the triggers outward with his thumbs. The latches popped obediently, and he pushed the case open.

It contained nothing.

The man closed it, turned it around, fiddled with it, and turned it back to Harrison, having set the combinations to different, seemingly random, values. "Again."

Harrison glared. Without breaking eye contact, he pressed the triggers again. The latches popped. The man snatched the case away from him, and took it straight out the door.

A few meals and a few naps later, the man returned. This time, in addition to the two door guards, Alec, the agent who subdued him in the CVS, accompanied him. The interviewer held a cardboard box heavy enough for the strain of carrying it to show on his face. He placed it on the table and remained standing. Alec sat down and motioned for Harrison, still on the cot, to come take the other seat.

Alec reached into the box, pulled out a combination padlock, spun the dial once, pulled on it to check it was secure, and slid it across the table.

Harrison reached for it, pausing to give Alec a questioning look. Alec nodded. Harrison picked up the lock and pulled on the bar. It opened without resistance. Alec produced another lock, this time a keyed padlock. He tested it and handed it over. When it touched Harrison's hand, the spring-loaded mechanism snapped open. Alec took out another keyed lock and set it on the table in front of Harrison. He slowly reached out and touched it with one finger. As soon as he made contact, it popped.

"That's quite a talent you have, Mr. Cody," Alec said, appearing neither surprised nor impressed.

Harrison's adrenalin surged. Was this magic? Had he been using magic without realizing it, while claiming under interrogation he had not? His lie about the wind-stone might in fact have been only the surface of his deception. "I swear I didn't do that on purpose!"

"Yes. We know. The ability is innate, not deliberate." Alec paused. "We've even considered the possibility you were unaware of this ability until now. The problem...," He paused again. "The problem is the matter of your curious and transparent lie."

"I don't know what you mean," he said, keeping his voice as even as possible.

"The one where you march out of Wisconsin and then tell us you're from Massachusetts. The three of you arrived at the north border. We have three sets of perfect footprints in the putty strip that match the shoes we took from you and the children."

"Putty?" Harrison asked, trying to keep up. His lie about magic went unchallenged, but somehow his entirely true statement about his place of origin had him in hot water?

"That's right. So," Alec said, bringing the diatribe back to a question, "why would you lie about that?"

"We came the long way," he said.

Alec said nothing.

"We found an underground train in New York, and it went to Chicago, but we had to go by way of Canada."

Alec's face, which until then had been the picture of smugness, took on its first shade of surprise. He waved Harrison on.

"We had an accident in Milwaukee."

Alec's jaw dropped. "That was you? You bloody, stupid son of a bitch! Do you have any idea how far you set that project back?"

"It was an accident," Harrison repeated. At last, after all his non-deliberate untruths, half-truths and misconstrued truths, he finally gave forth a profound lie. The tunnel had been sabotaged, booby-trapped for the sole purpose of killing him. It had not been an accident; it had been a deliberate attack.

Alec turned to the other man. "Pick up the locks!" He stormed out, leaving Harrison alone again.

Some time later, Alec returned. This time, he brought no assistant, no guards. He stood in the door without entering.

"Come," he said.

Harrison followed him to an elevator. They ascended. Harrison's dim hope of imminent release faded to black after they passed the ground floor. They continued for two more floors, and stopped.

The door opened onto a hallway. A man sitting at a desk stationed there looked up, nodded, and made a note in a log book.

Alec escorted Harrison down the hall and into a spacious office. Floor-to-ceiling windows presented a glorious view. Harrison had seen none of the city on the way in, but he saw it now. Hundreds of log cabins stretched across the city, most of them putting out smoke. Interspersed among them were various buildings, such as the one he currently occupied, and a quirky mixture of paved and unpaved roads. Civilization was certainly denser here than anywhere he had been yet, but the city was still, by any previous standard, a backwater.

Chicago's most striking feature by far, though, was its populace. Harrison had no way of telling how many people lived there, but from this window at least a hundred people visibly braved the cold, some running errands, perhaps, or simply going for a walk outdoors. Some of them looked purposeful, some looked miserable, some laughed as they shivered. People, the sight he had traveled a thousand miles to see.

Alec pointed to a side door, leading to a full bathroom. "In here. Get yourself cleaned up."

Harrison closed the door behind him. A shirt, a tie, and slacks hung behind it, all of which appeared brand new. Argyle socks and paisley boxer shorts still in the wrapper sat on top of slick black shoes. All these clothes were the same sizes as the garments they had confiscated from him when they arrested him.

He took a long, hot shower, luxuriating in the process of shampooing and conditioning his hair. A toothbrush, still in its box, rested on the counter, along with a generous assortment of personal hygiene products. He swiped himself with deodorant, gargled, brushed, flossed, and decadently applied an adhesive patch to his nose, designed to remove any lingering blackheads. While he waited for it to do its job, he went to work on his toenails.

He emerged squeaky clean and well-dressed. Alec gave him a once-over. "We're getting there." He motioned for Harrison to follow again.

Several doors down on the same hall, Alec brought him to a barber. The simple comfort of sitting in a barber's chair with a cloth draped over him hypnotized him.

"How do you want it?" asked the barber.

While he pondered choices, Alec said, "Short. Neat. And lose the beard."

From there, Alec took him, clean-shaven and tidy, to another room one floor up. "Wait here." Alec left. Harrison waited.

He took a seat in an antique armchair, running his fingers along the velvet upholstery. Alec had left him in a room with a gorgeous view of the lake, magnificent furnishings, and a fascinating library. The beautiful, luxurious space felt like old money, and like an obvious attempt to draw out Harrison's good nature.

He stayed there for the better part of an hour, inspecting the books, gazing out on the lake, and generally looking for courage in whatever random game they wanted him to play. When they finally came for him, they interrupted him reading a forty-year-old copy of The New York Times (which evidenced no sign of age or wear). A soft courtesy knock sounded on the door right before it opened, as though Harrison were somehow in the position to grant or deny anyone entrance.

Alec came one step into the room, hand still on the doorknob. "Mr. Cody? The president will see you now."

In his mind, Harrison raced to reevaluate his position. Somehow, they had given him an upper hand. He could not guess why, but he did not want to squander it. He counted to five before looking up from the paper, then waited a beat before standing.

"Right, then," said Alec. "Shall we?"

"Do let's," said Harrison.

Full of himself, he went to meet the president.

34

SHADOW

Back at her home in Wisconsin, Dorothy spent her day picking up the endless supply of her sisters' toys. Though in no way clear where they came from, or where exactly she put them after picking them off the floor, she carried on. This was her task, after all. Her sisters were nowhere to be found, though she did manage to interrupt her parents having lunch. The two of them sat at a homemade table, sharing a single can of chocolate frosting, which they ate with two spoons. Her mother seemed happier than any time she could recall, laughing at all her father's lame jokes, although, wait, that didn't look like her father. It looked like Harrison. But that was fine. Better, even.

Dorothy decided to join them, so she rapped against the glass wall separating them from her. They didn't hear, so she rapped louder, which put a single loud crack in the glass.

"We can't stay here," said Mitchell, who had evidently been standing next to her this whole time.

"Can't we just stay until winter?" she asked him.

"We just want what's best for you," said Harrison, or her mother, or possibly both.

At their feet sat two knapsacks, open and empty, with a pile of gadgets scattered all around them. Dorothy was about to accuse them of stealing the packs from her when Dorothy's mother reached out and gently shook her shoulder.

"Dorothy?" she said. "It's time to get up."

Dorothy slowly opened her eyes. She was in a bed. Not her pile of cushions from the store, or any of the real beds she had slept in traveling with Harrison and Mitchell, but a cot. Thin mattress, one pillow. It took her a moment to remember why.

She rolled over, and looked straight up at the bottom of someone else's bed. Not a cot, then. A bunk bed. One of at least half a dozen. Bleary-eyed girls milled around the room, stretching and yawning. None of their names came readily to her, though one of them waved and smiled.

She sat up. A woman, salt-and-pepper hair pulled back in a bun, crouched next to her bed. "Hey, there. Good morning."

"I'm still in the orphanage," said Dorothy, a touch groggy.

The woman smiled. "Adoption Center. My name is Rachel, and I'm the dorm mother." She extended her hand. "I'm sorry I missed meeting you last night."

Dorothy took her hand, on reflexive manners. "Where's Mitchell?"

"You'll see him at breakfast," said Rachel. "It's time to get your day started."

Dorothy pulled off her covers and planted her bare feet on the cold tile floor. "Bathroom?"

"Right next door. On your left as you exit the room. There are fresh clothes in your trunk if you want to change."

In the trunk at the foot of her bed, she found a set of clothes identical to those she had been issued the day before. One of the other girls wore this standard attire of white shirt and blue jeans. Two others still wore their pajamas, also identical to the ones she currently wore. Only one of her roommates violated the apparent dress code, wearing an orange shirt and black shoes in place of the whites.

Dorothy collected her clothes and headed for the bathroom. Inside she met another girl, washing her hands, a bit shorter than Dorothy, darker skin, and dressed in a Nirvana T-shirt and ripped black jeans.

"Hey," she said on making eye contact with Dorothy.

"Hey," said Dorothy.

The interaction apparently having reached its logical conclusion, the girl pulled several paper towels from the wall dispenser and dried her hands on the way out the door.

On the sinks sat a cup of toothbrushes, a tube of toothpaste, several toothbrushes still in their packages, and a Sharpie. Dorothy opened a toothbrush, wrote her name on the handle, and dropped it in the cup. She changed into her clothes in a tiny stall before brushing her teeth and heading back to her room.

Another girl in pajamas, and carrying a bag, passed her on the way to bathroom with a polite nod and smile. In the room, yet another changed into her clothes in full view, chatting with Rachel, leaving Dorothy one of only two girls now dressed in the standard issue.

"Are you ready for breakfast?" Rachel asked.

"Sure," said Dorothy.

Rachel smiled. "Heather, would you take Dorothy to the cafeteria?"

The girl dressed like Dorothy nodded, at least two inches shorter than her and thirty pounds heavier. Dorothy tried to place her from the day before, but she did not look familiar.

"C'mon," she said, heading out the door. Dorothy followed.

"Did you just get here, too?" she asked once they were in the hall.

"Two days ago," said Heather. "But I don't think anyone has been here more than a week or two. That's what they say, anyway."

They arrived at the cafeteria. At least three dozen children and teens sat at tables or stood in line for food, including one she recognized. "Excuse me." She hastily pulled away from Heather. "Mitchell!"

Mitchell sat at a table with three other boys of various ages. Hearing his name, he looked up, then jumped out of his seat and charged across the room. He and Dorothy collided in a hug.

"Are you okay?" she asked.

Like Dorothy, he wore a white button-down shirt and blue jeans. "I'm fine. Will you sit with us?"

Dorothy looked over to his table. She now had the attention of all three boys there. One looked to be about Mitchell's age. The other two were indeterminately older, and scrutinizing her with noticeably different expressions on their faces than the little boy.

"Sure," she said. "Let me get some food first."

"Okay. I'll save you a seat!" He ran back to his table with purpose and joy in his step.

Dorothy waited in line with a plastic, partitioned tray, which a server eventually filled with two small pancakes, one sausage patty, and a scoop of fried potatoes. She pulled a tiny can of orange juice from a chest refrigerator, and made her way to the condiment station, where she found syrup, but no butter.

When she arrived at Mitchell's table, the two older boys identified themselves to her as boy-with-inflated-ego and boy-terrified-of-girls.

"I'm Danny!" said ego-boy. "Are you new?"

"I am!" Dorothy shifted her attention to Mitchell. "Everything is fine? Is everyone being nice to you?"

He nodded.

"Are these guys watching out for you?" She indicated Danny and frightened-boy. Danny sat a bit straighter. The other boy demonstrated remarkable focus on his pancakes.

"It's fine," said Mitchell through a mouthful of sausage. "I got the top bunk!"

"That sounds like a victory."

"Yeah! And I get to meet my teacher today!"

"What grade are you in?" asked Danny before Dorothy had a chance to process this.

"I... don't know." She filled her mouth with pancakes to buy herself a few more seconds.

"I'm in tenth," said Danny. "Should be in eleventh though. I'm trying to get that fixed."

Dorothy nodded and chewed.

<hr />

On her way back to her room, Dorothy passed a great deal more hallway traffic than she had on the way to breakfast. Mitchell had to catch a bus to school, which gave Dorothy an excuse to bid farewell to her new admirer.

Melissa waited for her at her bunk. An impeccably dressed girl stood with her, exhibiting approximately the same smile. At their feet sat Dorothy's confiscated knapsack.

"Hello, Dorothy. Settling in?"

"I guess. Do all those kids live here?" She indicated the dense hall traffic.

"Oh, my, no," said Melissa. "They're here because the school day is about to start. These two wings are the only part of the building we use for adoption. The rest is still a high school."

"Ah." Dorothy pointed to her pack. "Do I get that back now?"

"Yes," said Melissa.

Dorothy picked it up and plunked it on her bed. The contents appeared to be complete, and all her clothes looked freshly laundered.

"This is Ashley," said Melissa. "You'll be shadowing her for your first day."

Ashley held out her hand. "Hello."

"Hi." Dorothy kicked off her white sneakers and replaced them with the bunny slippers from her pack. She faced Ashley and took her hand.

"Um," said Ashley, with a newly confused aspect to her smile. "So, I hear you're in tenth grade. Me too."

"I haven't been told anything about this," said Dorothy. "But tenth grade sounds right."

"Great!" said Ashley.

"The first day you'll follow Ashley's schedule," said Melissa. "There are some placement tests you'll be taking tomorrow, so we can figure out what classes you should take. Today is about getting to know the place. Try to have fun, okay?"

"Can you get a message to Harrison for me?" asked Dorothy.

"I don't think so," said Melissa, her tone neither reassuring nor scolding, simply a businesslike statement of fact.

"Yeah, okay." She looked at Ashley. "Lead on."

First period Ashley had algebra. Dorothy sat through a lesson on quadratic functions, a topic she had not seen in class before, but she had taught it to herself from the ACT prep book. While the teacher walked through the first example, Dorothy found the roots of the function by factoring, by completing the square, by using the quadratic formula and by finding the values of the x-intercepts of the graph she drew in her head. It turned out of those methods he only taught graphing that day, and she spent the next forty-five minutes watching fifteen students her age grapple with varying degrees of understanding, and experience varying degrees of success with the mechanics. She offered to help one boy, obviously struggling. This act of charity resulted in six students relying on her help exclusively for the rest of the class, some of whom quietly explained how bad the teacher was. Dorothy felt he explained the principles clearly enough, but kept her opinions to herself.

Period two they went to biology, in which she saw a lesson in photosynthesis. This briefly excited her, until she discovered the teacher devoted the whole period to only the simplest aspects of the overall concept, and nearly none of the specifics of the process.

In period three English, she watched what few students had done the reading in *Of Mice and Men* stumble their way through a painfully superficial analysis.

Period four Ashley had a study hall.

"If you have any questions, this would be a good time for us to talk," she said.

Dorothy thought for a moment. "Is there somewhere I can make a phone call?"

Ashley laughed politely.

Dorothy did not return the mirth.

"Wait, you're serious?" asked Ashley, confusion and surprise in her voice.

"Yes," said Dorothy.

"There are phones in the main office, but you're not going to be able to call anyone from there. There's only a few working phones in the whole city. Who do you want to call?"

Dorothy hesitated, her hand in her pocket clutching the note she had been given the day before. Lying to Ashley might be the best strategy, but she had no plausible lie to tell. "Claudia."

Ashley's eyes bugged. "Claudia? *Claudia* Claudia?" She laughed lightly. "Good luck with that."

Partly to earn Ashley's trust, and partly to impress her, Dorothy produced the note and unfolded it for her to see. "I guess Melissa didn't tell you."

"Wow." Ashley's face had gone pale. "Wow. Okay, yeah. Main office. I have lunch after this, so if you don't make it back here before the bell, meet me in the cafeteria."

"Will do," said Dorothy.

"Wow," said Ashley.

Dorothy got a pass to the office and permission to use a phone, along with privacy to make the call. At each stage, these things were granted to her only after she presented the note.

Receiver in hand, heart pounding, she dialed. Claudia picked up on the fourth ring.

"Hello?"

Dorothy's throat constricted around whatever words she intended to form. This was Claudia, whom Harrison had traveled a thousand miles to meet, only to be shunned by her and led away in shackles. Meanwhile, Dorothy was no one. What possible favor could she ask from this powerful icon that would be anything other than pathetic?

"Is someone there?" asked Claudia.

"I... I'm sorry," said Dorothy. "Never mind."

"Wait!" was all she let herself hear before hanging up.

Thirty minutes left of study hall, and about that much time for lunch, bought her a good hour before anyone expected her to be anywhere.

She politely thanked the receptionist for letting her use the phone, and requested a pass back to her class. With this permission in hand, she slipped into the hall, found a side exit, and went out onto the streets of New Chicago.

35

THE PRESIDENT

Alec took Harrison to another room in the same building. Several people he had not met yet all rose as he came in the door. Two of them were older men, one dressed in a jacket and tie, the other in an army uniform. An Asian woman older than Harrison also wore a uniform, this one dark blue. Navy, perhaps. Next to her a thin man with glasses and long hair smiled and fidgeted a lot. The remaining two women wore civilian clothes. One looked to be in her late forties or older, dark hair with gray streaks and cut about as short as his. She wore a charcoal gray jacket over a white blouse. The other looked extremely young, perhaps in her teens. She had a distant look to her, and her long, dark hair appeared to have faint green and blue highlights.

One of these people would be the President of the Republic of New Chicago. Preferably not one of the ones in uniform, as political leaders in military garb were not, in Harrison's understanding of world history, usually icons of freedom. In any case, Harrison did not consider the notion the only survivors of the end of the world had already felt the need to reinvent politics ideal. He had not answered to a government in a long time, and although he did not consider himself an anarchist by nature, he had developed a taste for the lifestyle.

"Madam President," said Alec, "this is Harrison Cody."

The older civilian woman held her hand out to Harrison. "I'm Louise Hatfield." The name sounded familiar, and Harrison tried to recall if Alec had mentioned it already. "It's a pleasure to meet you." Friendly, though unsmiling.

He shook her hand. "Madam President."

She gestured to the cluster of chairs arranged around a coffee table at which she and the others had been sitting. "Please make yourself comfortable."

He took a seat, not quite as comfy as the chair in the waiting room.

"When can I see my children?" He asked.

"I suppose that depends on this interview," the president answered, and Harrison bit his tongue. That bungle would cost him rhetoric points he couldn't afford to lose. He would have to hold that topic in reserve now, despite being his foremost—possibly only—concern. "Would you care for something to drink?" Arranged on the table were several glasses of water, a coffee mug, and a rocks glass with whiskey over ice.

"I'd love a glass of water," he said, playing it safe, and seeing a pitcher and several empty glasses already set out. She poured him one. He sipped at it politely, then put it down on the table.

"Mr. Cody," the president said, "I'd like you to meet some of my staff. This is Steven Reuben, Secretary of Esoteric Affairs."

The man in the suit and tie nodded. "Mr. Cody."

"Mr. Secretary," said Harrison. "Ah, is that right?"

Reuben laughed quietly. "Yes, quite so. Well done."

"This is General Thomas Berry, Chairman of the Joint Chiefs of Staff."

The uniformed man nodded. "Mr. Cody."

"General," said Harrison.

"This is Doctor Hadley Tucker." President Hatfield gestured to the man with long hair and glasses. "You will be getting to know him very well I expect." She gave a wry smile, not quite easy to interpret.

Doctor Tucker stood and extended his hand. "It is a pleasure, Mr. Cody. May I call you Harrison? Harry?"

"Harrison is fine," said Harrison, taking his hand, which Tucker shook vigorously.

"This is Doctor Jeanette Lee, the Surgeon General of New Chicago." The president indicated the woman in the naval uniform.

"Mr. Cody," she said, smiling warmly.

"Dr. Lee."

"This is Susan." The president indicated the young woman across from Harrison.

She nodded in silence and gave a subtle smile, borderline seductive.

"Ah," said Harrison. "Hi."

"And you already know Director Baker." The president indicated Alec, still standing.

Harrison pulled his gaze away from Susan and shook off whatever

219

was happening in his head. "Of course." He grinned. "Always a pleasure, Alec."

"Yes," the director replied coldly. "Madam President, unless you have further need of me?"

"Not at all," she said. "Will you be in your office?"

"No, ma'am. There are some cases down at immigration that require my attention. They've been a bit of a back burner of late." He glanced at Harrison and continued. "I'll be at the Welcome Center if you need to reach me."

"Thank you, Director." After he nodded and left, President Hatfield turned to Harrison, and said, "I imagine you have quite a few questions."

"Why don't you anticipate some of them?"

"All right. You are currently a guest of the Republic of New Chicago. The nation was founded on July 4, 2004, and, yes, the symbolism was intentional. Our Constitution was ratified the same day, general elections were held July 8, and the government installed on July 14. We are a democratic republic, modeled closely after the United States Constitution, but with some necessary modifications for matters of geography and population." She spoke like a politician, reciting a stock answer fluidly and expertly.

Harrison put up his hand to cut short the civics lesson. "Am I still under arrest?"

She looked at Secretary Reuben.

"Your call," he said bluntly.

"No," she said, turning back to Harrison. "Your detention was unfortunate. Once this meeting is over, you will be released. You will also be encouraged to apply for citizenship."

"That's not an apology," said Harrison.

"No," she said. "It is not. I said it was unfortunate, not that it was the wrong decision."

"Really? Not the wrong decision? To keep me naked in a cell? Was that you on the other side of that mirror? Did you get to see me poop into a cup?"

Hatfield's composure slipped by a degree.

Secretary Reuben held up his hand. "Before you take that any further, son, the decision to detain you was mine. Director Baker reported detecting magic on you. I agreed with his risk assessment, and I stand by the call. So, if you want to give any more lip on that subject, direct your sass to me."

"Noted," said Harrison coldly.

"On that topic…" Reuben picked up a stapled packet of papers from the table and flipped several pages over. "You claimed in your questioning to have no experience with magic. That is obviously untrue. Since you still represent a risk, you're not quite in a position to grouse about your treatment."

"Then why did you let me out at all?" asked Harrison.

"It wasn't my call," said Reuben. "But make no mistake, putting you back in would be simple enough."

"Really? You want to play alpha male? I would whip out my dick, but I'm pretty sure you've already seen it."

"Gentlemen!" shouted the president. "Decorum!"

Flustered, Reuben cleared his throat and sat back in his chair, dropping the papers on the table with a soft *slap*.

"Let's try this again, Mr. Cody," said Hatfield. "I won't threaten you with imprisonment, but I do ask that you keep a civil tongue in this company. To answer your question, you have been released because your story checks out, and because the children traveling with you have both vouched for you. The girl in particular has been quite vocal about it."

"That's nice to know," said Harrison.

"She has a remarkable natural resistance to magical mind control," said Dr. Tucker. "That allowed us to rule out brainwashing."

"You can test for that?" asked Harrison.

"Yes," said Dr. Tucker. "It's a simple test. I requested it to be added to her medical checkup when she was taken to the Adoption Center. She likely didn't even notice it. I thought it would expedite establishing your bona fides."

Harrison frowned. "Thank you?"

"You're welcome. If you're curious, the boy's test came back normal."

"That's still far short of giving us a reason to trust you," said the president. "It would have gone a long way toward putting us all at ease if you had come in the front door like every other immigrant." She leaned back, steepling her fingers. "In point of fact, Mr. Cody, you're a special case. The reality is we have no solid reason not to trust you, and, if I may cut to the chase, we need you on board. The sooner the better."

"On board? Meaning?"

General Berry coughed.

"Are you at all curious," Hatfield asked slowly, "about your gift with locks?"

Harrison willed every muscle in his face to relax. "Not really." It had to have been Glimmer. She did something to him, and now he had some weird, and highly specialized, power. But he wouldn't be giving her up in this conversation.

She smiled. "Be careful, Mr. Cody. We'd still like to trust you, remember?"

"It's not magic," said Dr. Tucker.

"What? What do you mean?" asked Harrison.

"Your ability to open locks," Tucker said. "It's not a magical phenomenon. It's a hyper-specific application of telekinesis, for lack of a better term. Your unconscious mind identifies a lock and activates a trigger, which projects a field that moves whatever physical components are necessary to open it." He moved his hands as he spoke, and looked from person to person around the table. "We think it's a new particle, but we haven't detected it yet. The effects are quite measurable and predictable, though."

"You've seen this before?" he asked.

Tucker shook his head. "Not specifically with locks, no, but the effect is almost identical to some other manifestations of this field we have observed. For each subject, the focus appears to be unique, but the mechanism is always the same."

"How many people have this... this field thing?" asked Harrison.

Tucker looked at Secretary Reuben. "This is your purview. Entirely up to you."

Reuben nodded. The bitterness had not quite drained from his face. "Four. Including you. That's just here in Chicago. There's no way to know how many cases exist worldwide. One thing we do know, the other three all claim they did not have these abilities before May 30. We assume this ability was created by whatever force altered the world."

"The only other thing the four of you have in common is something that really shouldn't be a factor in any way," said Tucker.

"And that is what?"

"It's fascinating, actually." Tucker grinned. "All four of you have historically significant birth dates."

"Like Bicentennial Day."

"For example, yes."

"Four," said Harrison. "Out of how many people here?" He looked at the president.

"About ten thousand," she said.

Harrison became momentarily dizzy in the face of this number, so much greater than expected or hoped.

Tucker continued. "I should stress there may be more cases we haven't observed. Of the four known cases, apart from you, only one other person shows the ability with any dramatic effect, so there may be many subtle manifestations of the field we simply haven't caught yet. We can test for it, but the tests are time-consuming and vary from manifestation to manifestation, so it would be impossible to test everyone. The best we can do is test an already unexplained observation. We have to find those first."

"Are you saying I'm a superhero?" asked Harrison.

Dr. Tucker raised an eyebrow at this. "I suppose, after a fashion, that's what I'm saying. I hadn't thought of it in those terms before. Actually, in your case, the specific manifestation would be less suited for fighting crime than for committing—"

"Yes, well," General Berry interrupted. "We have other matters to discuss."

"Agreed," said the president. "Here's the bottom line, Mr. Cody. We live in a world in which everything we know is now horribly wrong. This nation was formed, in part, to create an opportunity for the people who remain to combine our resources. Ultimately, our goal is to create the safest possible environment for the human race. We are also devoting a tremendous amount of manpower to research. To determine what happened in the first place. And find out if it might be reversible."

"May I ask," said Harrison, "why none of this was mentioned in Claudia's broadcasts?"

The president frowned. "Security considerations. It was felt the safest way to build a community of this sort from scratch would be to draw people in with no preconceived notions." She looked away. "It was a controversial decision."

Harrison laughed bitterly. "I'll bet."

She looked back at him. "Needless to say, your rare talent makes you an invaluable resource. There may be broader applications beyond what you can do to locks, and we would be willing to help you explore them. We would like you to stay on. Become a part of what we're trying to accomplish here."

Of all the things that could be happening to him in this insane, scrambled, perilous world, they were offering him a job. "So I'm a resource. Do you consider magic a resource, too? You've got a border of yarn that has a spell on it to keep people out, don't you?"

"It was an expedient," she said unapologetically.

So, they had been using magic. The idea stirred anger and fear in Harrison. Magic was no simple tool. It belonged in the hands of beings like Glimmer, not himself, and certainly not these people. They were playing a dangerous game. And here he had been worried what would happen if he told them about one little pixie. An expedient, she called it. What a cold description. A politician's euphemism. And then he connected the dots, and mentally kicked himself for not picking up on it sooner. "You're *that* Louise Hatfield. Senator Hatfield. Aren't you?"

"I prefer to be called President Hatfield these days," she said humorlessly, "but, yes, I am that person."

"God, this must all be so exciting for you! What a grand opportunity to start up your very own pretend government!"

"You will find, Mr. Cody, the government of New Chicago, and the laws herein, are quite real. I'd be happy to arrange a tour of the capitol if you'd like. Or the prison."

"It's a perfectly harmless spell," said Reuben. "The inhibitor. It's not to keep them out, it's to herd them to the Welcome Center. It projects an anxiety aura so anyone who comes too close to it feels too nervous to touch it or cross it. The same effect causes the target to feel an obligation to find a breach in the line. It's quite effective. And efficient."

"If you had followed it far enough," Hatfield added smugly, "you would have found that front door I was talking about earlier."

"You just used the word 'target' to describe a nine-year-old boy, who sobbed uncontrollably when he got near your 'harmless' spell."

Hatfield's smugness diminished by a degree.

"Are you people insane? Do you really think you can control this stuff? Do you have any idea what's out there?"

Reuben spoke up. "We have every idea what's out there, Mr. Cody, which is why it is so urgent for us to take every precaution."

"But magic?" Harrison blurted. "What the hell do any of you know about magic?"

Reuben sighed. "Not every citizen of New Chicago is human." The secretary managed to keep the statement generalized and subtle. Tucker apparently had a substantially less developed sense of subterfuge, however, and as soon as Reuben said it, he looked, blatantly, at Susan.

Harrison looked, too. Susan gave him a sly smile and nodded toward his glass of water. The water began swirling. It picked up speed until a little bit splashed out the top of the glass, and he looked down into the eye of the whirlpool. At the bottom of the glass was a dry circle.

"She's a naiad," said Reuben, with obvious annoyance her cover had been blown. "Her name's not really Susan. At least, we don't think it is. She tends to communicate nonverbally." As he said these things about her, Susan batted her eyes at Harrison, deep, briny green, and rippling as she fluttered her lashes.

This woman who appeared to be a teenager was probably the oldest living being at the table. This community, at least in part, consisted of humans and magical creatures working together for a common good.

Harrison had been part of a team like that, once. The prospect of doing it again held some appeal.

"I want my kids back," he said.

"That may be possible," President Hatfield replied. At that moment, the discussion became a negotiation.

"Have they been placed in homes yet? Alec said something about adoption."

Dr. Lee spoke up for the first time. "If I may?"

Hatfield nodded.

Lee looked at Harrison. "Under New Chicago law, Dorothy and Mitchell are already legally adopted."

The blood drained from Harrison's head. He tried to count the number of days since the CVS. Too short a time to wreck a family. "Is there some sort of appeal?"

Lee frowned for a moment, then offered him a wide-eyed smile. "I think you have the wrong idea. Adoption law grants parental presumption to a child's first adult human contact, post-May 30. In a dispute, the onus is on the State to demonstrate unfitness. As soon as you crossed the barrier, the three of you were granted automatic probationary citizenship, so your claim was immediately recognized by default. Congratulations, Harrison." She winked. "You're a father."

His heart pounded. "I think I owe you all cigars."

A round of polite, tension-breaking laughter passed over the room.

Before the final terms of his employment could be agreed upon, an object the size of a ballpoint pen in the president's pocket buzzed quietly and flashed a green light.

"I need to take this." She took the object out and held it to her mouth. "Yes?"

"Sorry to interrupt," said the small object in Alec's voice.

"No trouble," she said. "Do we need a secure line?"

"No. I just arrived at the Welcome Center," he said, "and there's a fairy down here asking for Mr. Cody and swearing like a sailor."

Eyebrows raised, the president looked at Harrison. "Is there something you'd like to share at this point?"

Harrison's entire body had gone rigid. "What... is she wearing?"

"Did you catch that?" she asked the object.

"Affirmative. The fairy is wearing a white sweater with a capital B on it. And a pink poodle skirt. No shoes."

Harrison refrained from screaming long enough to say, "Take me to the Welcome Center. Right now."

36

ESCAPE

With respect to urban hiking, in terms of both practicality and inconspicuousness, the least valuable footwear imaginable turned out to be fuzzy bunny slippers. Dorothy made it less than two blocks from the school before attracting enough attention to warrant stealth. Unfortunately, as the city was almost entirely still under construction, she had to pass through several entirely vacant lots, and many others had frames of buildings incapable of hiding her on the go. She assessed which direction held the densest-looking part of the city, and made her way there.

For the first time in her memory, Dorothy lacked a plan. Her objectives were clear: Find Mitchell's school. Find Harrison. Negotiate his release. Once she met those, the three of them could return to their home in Wisconsin, or perhaps head south toward milder climates to wait out the winter. Surely other settlements had formed by now, communities who would receive them kindly and meet their needs instead of arresting people and consigning children to Dickensian boarding houses.

Dorothy found her way into an alley behind one of the partially constructed buildings, and took a moment to regroup. At the edge of the lot stood a supply shed, next to three pieces of advanced-looking construction equipment, lined up in a neat row. There were no workers nearby, lending an abandoned look to the place, though Dorothy had already passed several other such un-peopled sites. No doubt with resources spread thin, projects were in a constant state of reprioritization. She sat on the dirt against the shed, between it and the heavy machinery. Well out of sight, she picked up a piece of rebar lying on the ground and used it to start digging pebbles out of the dirt.

The sun shone brightly, but the temperature felt like low forties. Dorothy would need to organize her thoughts in a timely manner in order to get herself back inside a heated building soon. The ground had not yet frozen, but excavating pebbles from it proved challenging enough a task to distract her from her woes, if not actually help her concentrate on how to fix them.

"Hey," said Claudia.

Dorothy looked up, slowly. Claudia stood before her, holding two paper cups with tendrils of steam rising from sip-holes in their plastic lids. She wore a black bomber jacket, with an identical jacket draped over one shoulder.

"Oh my God," said Dorothy. "Seriously?"

"Hold this, will you?" said Claudia, extending one of the drinks.

Dorothy took it. The warm cup soothed her hand, and the aroma of chocolate drifted into her nostrils, daring her to stay upset.

With her free hand, Claudia pulled the second jacket off her shoulder. "Trade."

Dorothy stood, handed the hot chocolate back and took the coat. Printed across its back were the letters NCSA in large white capitals. She pulled it on, and flipped up the collar. Claudia handed the cup back to her, which she took in both hands. She put her mouth over the lid and inhaled the gloriously warm chocolate steam. "What does NCSA stand for?"

"New Chicago Security Agency."

"Security Agency?" Dorothy inspected the jacket more closely for hidden pockets or any other special paraphernalia, but found none. "Whose is this?"

"Mine. Long story."

"How did you find me?" asked Dorothy before taking a sip of her hot chocolate. It was mediocre, obviously from a powder, and absolutely delicious.

"How do you think?"

"Fuzzy bunnies?"

"Got it in one," said Claudia. "I called the school back when you hung up on me. It took them five minutes to figure out you left."

Dorothy pouted. "It was supposed to take them an hour."

"Well, it didn't. Once I knew you were out and about, it was easy to track you. We have surveillance tech you wouldn't believe."

"I'll be sneakier next time."

Claudia sat on the ground next to Dorothy's small pile of excavated pebbles and poked them with her finger. "Is this what you came out here to do? We can set you up with some rocks, if that's what you need."

"I need Harrison back," said Dorothy bitterly. "And I need to leave this place."

Claudia patted the dirt next to her. Dorothy stood her ground. "Your guy's out of lockup." She patted again.

Dorothy took a seat. "Does that mean we can leave?"

Claudia shrugged. "If that's what you want. I don't think he's going anywhere though."

"I thought you said you let him go."

Claudia took a sip of her drink. "We did. It's complicated. You'll have to talk to him about it."

"Why did you arrest him in the first place?"

Claudia hesitated, and took another sip. "Thought he was a demon. Turns out, he was just an asshole. Listen, I really didn't come out here to talk about that guy. If you want to stick with him, that's up to you. Honestly, I think you can do better, but that's not my call. But like I said, that's not what I'm here for."

"You're here to take me back the orphanage," said Dorothy. "I won't go."

Claudia waved away the defiance. "Nah. You don't have to go back there. They're gonna let you live with that guy. You and the kid. Adoption happens like wildfire around here. And if that doesn't suit your fancy, I have a couple other ideas to float past you. But we'll get you out of that dorm by tomorrow. Maybe later today."

"Okay, then why are you here?"

Claudia stood up and offered her hand. "C'mon."

"Where are we going?"

"Someplace that's not sitting in the dirt at a construction site."

Dorothy took Claudia's hand and stood. "We're not going back to the orphanage?"

"Nope."

"Then can we stop there on the way to wherever? I need to change my shoes."

Back in her room, Dorothy changed into her hiking boots and donned a fake fur hat from her knapsack. She found her coat there as well, newly laundered, but she chose to keep Claudia's jacket for the time being.

Their destination took about half an hour to reach from the high school on foot. Along the way, Claudia made various attempts at small talk, which Dorothy largely deflected. At last, they arrived at a small office building, clearly a structure from the original Chicago, complete with graffiti. Up one flight of stairs, Claudia knocked at the second door down the hall, already open. Behind a desk within, a man with a short gray beard in a brown cardigan stood to greet them. "Hello, Claudia. Is this Dorothy?"

"Hey, Doc," said Claudia. "Dorothy, this is Dr. Banks, my shrink. Doc, Dorothy, Dorothy, Doc."

"Hello, Dorothy," said Dr. Banks.

"Hang on," said Dorothy. "You dragged me across town to see a psychiatrist? You think I'm crazy?"

"Dotty, the world just came to a screeching halt, and now everything is magic and future tech and superpowers and shit. You'd have to be crazy *not* to be in therapy. But that's not why we're here, anyway."

"If I may?" said Dr. Banks. "Dorothy, why don't you have a seat?" He gestured to a pair of facing comfy chairs.

"You two have fun!" said Claudia, grinning. "Gotta head back to work. Call me when you get settled in, will you?"

Dorothy nodded. "Thanks... for everything. I think?"

"Trust me, kid. You've got this."

As Claudia walked out the door, Dorothy took a seat in one of the two chairs. Dr. Banks took the other. A notepad sat on his lap, as yet unopened.

"What did she mean that's not why I'm here?" asked Dorothy.

"She meant you're not here for therapy. If you want that, we can do an intake, but that's not on the agenda."

"What, then? Why do I need a psychiatrist?"

"Well," said Dr. Banks, "I'm not a psychiatrist. I'm a psychologist. I do some counseling, but I have other jobs too. You can call me Will, by the way. Or Dr. Banks if that floats your boat, but I don't stand on ceremony around here."

"Claudia calls you Doc."

He grimaced. "Not my first choice. Makes me feel like a Disney Dwarf. But, it helps her feel in control, so there we are."

"Why am I here?" asked Dorothy.

"All right, let's get down to it. Claudia says you're very bright."

"That's kind of her. We only just met."

He shook his head. "I don't think you follow me. She says you're *very* bright. Genius level. She's afraid you're getting lost in the system already, and it's exacerbating some problems that started with the welcome you got when you arrived."

"I wouldn't call it a welcome," she said. "How could Claudia possibly know how smart I am?"

"Claudia has an IQ of 154," said Dr. Banks.

Dorothy's eyebrows went up. "That's only a few points…"

"Below yours, you were about to say, right?"

She nodded.

"Claudia is used to being the smartest person in the room. Has been her whole life. She has developed an uncanny sensitivity to being outmatched. Says she spotted your intellect when she first met you in the CVS."

Dorothy shook her head. "I… how?"

"Beats me. Vocabulary? Bearing? Confidence? I'm not even sure she knows. So, let me ask you a question. You're fourteen, right?"

"Yes."

"And prior to May 30, you were in ninth grade?"

"Also yes."

"Why?"

Dorothy frowned. "I don't understand. Because I was in eighth grade the year before that?"

"Hmm. Your school had a gifted program, right?"

She nodded.

"I assume you were in it?"

"Yes, but it wasn't very…"

"That's what I thought." Dr. Banks leaned forward. "What would you say if I told you that you could start school here tomorrow in twelfth grade, and have a chance to take some college level courses at the same time?"

She sat up straight, eyes wide. "I can do that?"

"Let's find out," he said. "I'd like you to take a few tests. One is a survey of multiple intelligences, one is personality inventory, and three of them are college placement exams in different subjects. Do you think we can get started on that today?"

"Oh my God, yes."

37

TIANANMEN

They got to the Welcome Center on foot in less than ten minutes. From the outside, the building looked nondescript, short and broader than the building where Harrison had been held, and no signs identifying it, nor any official government looking symbols or logos visible.

Inside, the structure and activity resembled a typical bureaucracy. The front door opened into a narrow hallway, which led to an enormous room filled with people sitting in rows of hard plastic chairs, waiting. Many read paperbacks or magazines (all of which either hopelessly out of date or anachronistic). On the wall inside the door hung a rack of pamphlets describing various attractions in New Chicago, and a variety of advantages to becoming a citizen. A row of desks ran along the back wall, each with a person seated on either side, filling out paperwork. Alec Baker stood near one desk, looking disgruntled and probably taking it out on the hapless caseworker sitting behind it. A pixie paced across the top of the desk, gesticulating.

"Excuse me," Harrison said to the doctor. He made straight for the desk, ignoring several people who complained about his inability to identify the end of a line. His heart raced. Theoretically, this could still be some other pixie.

"Glimmer!" he shouted over the din.

The pixie looked up, straight at him, and instantly became a streak of light that smacked him in the face. The background murmur of voices grew briefly quieter. Still in mid-air, she held his face, one arm under his chin, the other around the back of his ear. Her face nuzzled his cheek. That whole side of his head felt like pins and needles. He closed his eyes and soaked it up.

"I thought you were dead," he whispered.

"Shh," she whispered back.

Alec and Dr. Lee reached them, from opposite directions, at the same time. "Is this making anyone else uncomfortable?" Alec asked. One onlooker raised his hand. "Right, then. Mr. Cody? If you're quite through snogging Tinker Bell—"

Glimmer looked up. "Hey! That's one crack too many out of you, mister! I can put up with you being a total prick if you say it's your job, but I will not have you dragging Tinker Bell into this!" She flew toward him, stopped an inch from his face, and hovered there, wagging her finger threateningly. Her other hand, covered in bandages, hung at her side.

"I knew Tinker Bell!" she shouted, and Baker's face went one shade paler. "Tinker Bell was a friend of mine!" She paused there, glaring, until abruptly snorting. "I was sure I could do that with a straight face." She rubbed her eyes, giggling, then flew back to Harrison, lighted on his shoulder, and sat, resting her head against his cheek.

"Did you really know Tinker Bell?" asked Alec.

Glimmer stared at him. "No. Tinker Bell is made up." She leaned closer to Harrison's ear, and asked, apparently seriously, "Is this guy retarded?"

"Yes," said Harrison.

Glimmer nodded.

Baker turned to Lee. She maintained her professional composure, but with smiling eyes. "We're through with the fairy here. If you still need Mr. Cody?"

"We do," she said.

"She's a pixie," Harrison said to Alec.

"You forgot to say asshole," said Glimmer.

"Fine," said Alec shortly. He produced a small, red plastic card from his pocket, and scanned it with something small that buzzed. "This will get you in the door at NCSA headquarters." He handed the card to Harrison. "You are to report to Assistant Director Denisov at 7:30 tomorrow morning for briefing and assignment. At 8:00 you are to attend a meeting with the other telekinetics and myself."

"NCSA?" asked Harrison.

"Correct. Your first assignment, Special Agent Cody, is to find that building." He turned back to Dr. Lee. "Why don't you take them both back upstairs. Barring any more unforeseens, I'll be here the rest of the afternoon."

The doctor nodded.

"Wait," said Harrison to Alec. "How long was I locked up?"

"Locked up?" said Glimmer. She growled at Alec.

Alec glanced at his watch. "Just shy of twenty-six hours."

"What?" cried Harrison. "One day? It felt a lot longer than that!"

"Solitary confinement renders a subject's sense of time remarkably manipulable," said Alec in an even tone.

"Hey!" Glimmer looked around, frowning. "Where's the kid? You didn't lose him, did you?" She pointed an accusing finger at Harrison.

"No," he said calmly. "Mitchell's in school right now. I get to pick him up in a few hours. I think?" He glanced at Dr. Lee. She nodded. "He'll be thrilled to see you. You'll get to meet his sister, too."

"Sister?" Glimmer repeated. "That sounds like a story!"

"It is. It turns out I'm a father now."

"Wow." Glimmer cupped her chin in thought. "What does that make me?"

"Hmm," said Harrison. "Good question. Um… crazy aunt, I guess."

She nodded. "That sounds about right."

Dr. Lee raised her hand. "Excuse me. Sorry to interrupt. My name is Jeannette Lee. Harrison was in the middle of a very important meeting when we heard you were here. If you don't mind, I'd like to introduce you to the Secretary of Esoteric Affairs, Miss…?"

"Glimmer," she replied. "I'd like that, too. We need to talk about your inhibitor. It'll work on the rubes, but it won't keep the beasties out."

"I don't think that will be necessary," said Alec, only a few steps away. "That spell was put through some rigorous field tests before we used it. We have a panel of experts in that department."

Glimmer glared at him. "Your sword is showing."

Alec glanced down to his right side, lifting his hand slightly.

"Made you look," said Glimmer. She did not smile.

Baker scowled and walked away.

"What was that about?" Harrison asked.

"He's wearing a short sword," she said. "It's got at least two charms on it. You'd probably see it if you looked at his crotch and blurred your eyes."

As Alec walked away, Harrison unfocused his eyes. The sword came into view, hanging from his belt on the right-hand side, a bit like looking at a magic-eye image. Once he knew to look for it, he spotted it easily.

"Where's the NCSA building I'm supposed to find tomorrow?" Harrison asked Dr. Lee.

"We just left there," she said. "And we're headed right back to finish that meeting."

Harrison rolled his eyes. "Cute. Well, I managed not to fuck up my first assignment, so I guess there's that."

"Shall we?" asked Dr. Lee. They did.

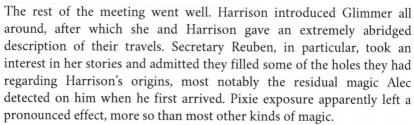

The rest of the meeting went well. Harrison introduced Glimmer all around, after which she and Harrison gave an extremely abridged description of their travels. Secretary Reuben, in particular, took an interest in her stories and admitted they filled some of the holes they had regarding Harrison's origins, most notably the residual magic Alec detected on him when he first arrived. Pixie exposure apparently left a pronounced effect, more so than most other kinds of magic.

An hour later, Harrison had a job and a place to live. Three large hotels still stood within the environs of the city, and Harrison got two adjoining rooms in one of these. It would be a little bit tight to house one adult, two children, and one pixie, but it would suffice.

Late in the meeting, he met a woman named Melissa, who introduced herself as Mitchell and Dorothy's caseworker. She told him they were staying in the Adoption Center. Dorothy was shadowing at the high school, and Mitchell had been bused to an elementary school a few miles away. Mitchell was also being treated for post-traumatic stress disorder, though he had not yet been informed of the diagnosis. She gave Harrison a summary of the support Mitchell would need and made an appointment for him to talk with Mitchell's therapist. He would have a chance to spend some time with both his children after school that day, at which point they could move into their new rooms.

From the meeting, he and Glimmer walked to the hotel, where they found a sizeable crowd in the lobby.

"Let's check out the room," he said.

"Why don't you grab something to eat first?" she asked. "You must be famished."

Harrison glanced at her right hand again, covered in bandages. She moved it behind her back. "Yeah, sure. I could eat."

The hotel restaurant had been converted to something akin to a cafeteria, and Harrison received his first introduction to what most of the people of New Chicago ate most of the time. Early on, someone had discovered several processing machines that converted the raw molecules from practically any organic matter into an edible, highly nutritious substance. The machines appeared to be military in design (and, indeed, the most logical explanation anyone had offered so far for their existence was they had been used to create field rations) and were efficient and portable. Stations had been set up around the city where anyone could come by and be fed at virtually any time of day. The machines created food primarily from waste vegetation, collected from the process of clearing and developing the land. In theory, they could be loaded with animal tissue, but the government had been extremely careful about not allowing that to happen, to keep the *Soylent Green* jokes to a minimum. By spring, the farmland currently being cleared would start growing real food again. Until then, they would have to subsist on whatever canned goods the salvage parties brought back, and on the products of these machines.

The substance was served in the form of a small rectangular solid the approximate size, texture, and flavor of a kitchen sponge.

"Ew," Glimmer opined examining two of these on Harrison's tray.

"Yeah, well…" He casually inspected one of them, embossed with a symbol comprising a straight line and a wave. "I wonder why I wasn't served these during my stay in the basement."

"They probably thought you wouldn't identify it as food."

"That's a fair point. At least the kids don't have to eat these." Melissa had shown Harrison a copy of the Adoption Center menu in their meeting. For now, New Chicago reserved its best cuisine for its most vulnerable citizens. Harrison couldn't argue with that, despite having to eat this substance as a consequence.

It was late afternoon, and many people trickled in to get their share. The tables were mostly full, and since Harrison only knew upper echelon government types (probably off somewhere eating the world's last duck or something), he tried to find a table that looked as empty as possible. As he scanned the room, a shock of white caught his eye.

"Hey," he said, recognizing it, "I need to take care of something."

"Okay," said the pixie, following him.

At a round table, with several people Harrison did not recognize, sat Claudia. The streak of white in her otherwise dark hair contrasted with her dark skin and made her stand out like a lighthouse on the rocks. The table had a wide array of condiments on it, all hopefully to make the sponge things at all palatable. A bottle of ketchup, some pancake syrup, vinegar, salt, honey, and a variety of other things not readily identifiable adorned the area. Claudia applied a generous amount of vanilla frosting to her sponge and took a bite.

"Is this seat taken?" he asked timidly, indicating the seat next to her.

She looked up and, mouth full, shook her head. She waved him into it.

He sat. Glimmer lighted on the table, stuck her left hand into the frosting, and licked it clean.

Claudia smiled. "Wow! What are you?"

"I'm a pixie," she said cheerfully.

"You're beautiful!" said Claudia. "I love the wings!"

Glimmer beamed. "Thank you for noticing." She whispered to Harrison, "I like this one."

He smirked. "Hey, I just want to say I'm sorry about the other day. I know I didn't come off too well, but I think I'm settling in here."

Claudia gave him a quizzical look, as if seeing him for the first time. Then the light went out of her face.

"Oh, Christ," she said through a mouthful of sponge. "Cody?"

Harrison experienced a wave of mild queasiness, and he looked down to his own clean, neatly dressed appearance. Before that moment, Claudia had only seen him long-haired, bearded and filthy.

"Um, yeah," he said.

The other people at the table stopped talking.

"So," said Claudia before Harrison could regain his bearings, "I hear you're the fourth."

"That's what they tell me," he said.

Glimmer had taken on a confused, indecisive expression as she looked rapidly back and forth between them.

"I didn't realize they'd let you out already," Claudia said. "Things must be more desperate than I thought. But, then, I guess there was no point trying to keep you locked up, anyway."

"Yeah," said Harrison. "I mean, no." A bead of sweat formed on his temple, and he wiped it away.

"Your daughter ran away from school today. Did they tell you that?" Claudia took another bite of her sponge, chewing dramatically.

"What?" said Harrison. "No! Is she...?"

Claudia held up her hand while she swallowed. "It's cool. I took care of it." A second later, she muttered, "Someone had to."

"Oh. Thanks."

She looked at her watch, and stood. "I have to get to work. See you at tomorrow's meeting." She turned her back on him and carried her tray to the bussing station.

"Well," said Glimmer. "She was nice."

"That was Claudia."

Glimmer's jaw dropped. "That was Claudia?"

It was the first time Harrison had successfully shocked her. Unfortunately, he was not in a mood to fully enjoy it. As she pulled herself back together, the remaining few people at the table all conveniently finished their meals and left in a group. He had come in looking for an empty table and had managed to create one.

"I don't think you're quite her type," said Glimmer.

"That's really not the issue, and I seriously don't want to talk about it."

"What the hell happened?" she asked.

"I said I don't want to talk about it."

"Hey, I didn't mean..." She faltered. "Listen, I, uh... I hear there's a camp of centaurs close to the lake, and I wanted to, you know, check it out? Mingle?"

"What happened to your hand?" he blurted.

She looked away. After a few seconds, she said, "I hurt it, and I'm not ready to talk about it."

Harrison sighed. "I'm sorry. You were just gone for so long."

"Harry, you need to let this go. You made it here okay, and I caught up with you. That's just going to have to be enough for now."

"Are you ever going to tell me?" He got no response to this. The moment drew out. "Go ahead and meet your centaurs. I think I might crash early, anyway. It'll be nice to sleep on a real bed."

She smiled. It was a polite smile, an awkward smile.

"Glimmer?" he said. "I missed you."

Her smile warmed up, but it retained a trace of sadness. "Right back at you, sweetie," she said, and then she zipped off. He watched the trail of sparks until every one of them had completely dissolved.

A man sat next to him, older, a little overweight, and with about two days' worth of beard on his face. Harrison merely nodded a greeting.

"You're Independence," said the man, smiling nervously. "Aren't you?"

"I'm not sure I understand," said Harrison.

"You know, Bicentennial Boy?" He spoke in a hushed tone, almost conspiratorial.

Harrison gritted his teeth. "Does everybody in the whole city know who I am?"

"Naw, it's cool." The man held out his hand for Harrison to shake. "I'm Dallas."

"I'm Harrison," said Harrison, reluctantly taking Dallas's hand.

Dallas shook his head. "Naw, Dallas. You know, November twenty-second? Nineteen sixty-three?"

"Oh," said Harrison, his eyebrows rising. "Right. The Kennedy assassination. You're one of the four."

"Yeah, man! Hey, it's good to meet you. Have they told you much?"

"They told me a bunch of stuff, but it all came pretty quickly, and I don't remember all of it. There's a team meeting tomorrow, and I'm going to take some notes."

"Those meetings suck," Dallas said. "You should expect to be bored off your ass for two hours. Mostly, it's a lot of 'what if' stuff." His eyes brightened for a moment. "Except maybe now that you're here, they'll let us go do something. You're the first one with a decent spy power, if you ask me."

"What can you do?"

"Check this out." He pulled a pair of dice out of a pocket. "Give 'em a roll." He handed them to Harrison. Harrison rolled a three and a five. "Again." He rolled double fours. "Again." He rolled a five and a one.

"I don't get it," he said.

"Gimme." Dallas took them from Harrison and rolled. Snake eyes. He rolled again. Snake eyes. He rolled five more times, and every single time he got double ones.

"Wow," said Harrison, more confused than impressed. "Can you control that?"

"Nope. Always comes up snake eyes. Coins always come up tails, too. Damnedest thing."

"What about the other two?"

"Well," said Dallas, "There's Eagle."

Harrison stared, waiting for the explanation.

"You know? July twentieth? Nineteen sixty-nine?" He held his hand over his mouth and spoke slowly. "That's one giant leap for mankind!" He put his hand down and grinned. "Heh-heh. Anyway, she has a really dumb power. She stops clocks. That's it. Funny thing is, she's really good-looking, but, you know, 'the face that can stop a clock.'" He laughed. "And you've already met Tiananmen."

Harrison waited for him to go on, but he didn't. "Tiananmen?"

"You know. June fourth? Nineteen eighty-nine? You were just talking to her."

Claudia. He meant Claudia. She possessed some unique mind power, but it hadn't come up in conversation. She already hated him, and now they would be working together, closely. And the birth date! Tiananmen Square. Harrison was old enough to remember that day. It had been a Sunday. His sister had wept while she told him about the student uprising in China. "They killed them all," she said over and over. The day before, she had been explaining the beauty of China on the verge of a peaceful revolution, and that the Chinese would soon be free, like him. It became his first memory of true political awareness, swiftly followed by his first memory of true political disillusionment. What a burden for Claudia to

238

carry! Had she even been aware, growing up, what an infamous day her birthday had been? All of these thoughts raced through Harrison's mind in a fraction of a second, but one overwhelming realization beat them all up to the surface.

"She's fifteen? My God! She's just a kid!"

"I know!" said Dallas. "Sucks, don't it? The youngest one gets the biggest power. Is that fair?"

"What can she do?" asked Harrison.

"They didn't tell you? She does that thing with her voice. It's like, super-ventriloquism or whatever. Works with radio waves, too. That's why they gave her the station, so they could broadcast all across the country. She throws even farther when it's dark out. At night, we got people from all the way out in California heard it! Where are you from?"

"Massachusetts."

"Exactly!"

Harrison reeled. They had given the most important job in the country to a child because she had a superpower they could exploit. What kind of a life could she have? And the first thing he did on meeting her was to terrify her and make her an enemy. There had to be a way to make this right.

"Excuse me." Harrison stood. "It was nice meeting you. I'll see you at the meeting tomorrow. We'll talk."

He fled to find the radio station.

SCHOOL

"**M**iss Hill?"

Seated behind a desk in an empty classroom, behind a pile of papers, a woman looked up. Likely in her thirties, brown complexion, closely cropped black hair, and glasses nearly as large as Dorothy's. "Yes?"

Dorothy cautiously entered the room. All the other students had long since gone home, as had most of the other teachers. "My name is Dorothy O'Neill? I was added your roster today?"

Miss Hill picked up a grade book. "Which class?"

"Calculus."

The woman flipped to a page in her book. "O'Neill?"

Dorothy nodded. "Two ells."

"O'Neill... comma... Dorothy," she said aloud as she added the name. "Welcome aboard." She looked up, smiling. After a second, the smile faded. "How old are you?"

"Fourteen," said Dorothy.

"Huh," said Miss Hill. "What was the last math class you took?"

"Geometry," said Dorothy, "but—"

Miss Hill held up a hand. "Stop." She picked up her phone and dialed. "Come on... Pick up."

Dorothy approached her desk, pulled up a chair, and waited.

"Ugh," said Miss Hill, hanging up. "You're brand new, right?"

Dorothy nodded.

"What happened is this: The schools have only been up and running since mid-October. Every day, a hundred or so new refugees come into the city, and we do the best we can setting up all the children where they need to be. And every day I get to explain to at least three kids they are in the wrong class."

"I can see we've gotten off on the wrong foot," said Dorothy.

"Honey, I'm sure you're very bright, and someone thought jumping you to calculus would be a great challenge, and I'm *sure* that worked out wonderfully for scheduling purposes, but this is big kid math. I teach adults in here. It's basically college level content. You're just not going to have the background..."

Dorothy wordlessly placed a booklet on Miss Hill's desk.

"What's this?" She opened it, looked over the first page, and turned to the next. Her eyebrows rose briefly, but she otherwise maintained a steady facial expression. On the third page, she said, "You're weak in trigonometry."

"I'm aware," said Dorothy.

Miss Hill smiled without looking up. "But you are unusually strong in functions. Did you learn all of this in geometry?"

"No, ma'am," said Dorothy. "I figured most of that out while I was taking the test."

Miss Hill looked up at this. "You 'figured out' how to predict end behaviors? You 'figured out' how to generalize function compositions? While you were taking this test?"

Dorothy nodded again. "Once you get past the clunky notation, a lot of that stuff is pretty obvious."

Miss Hill dug through a stack of papers on her desk and pulled one out. "This is our syllabus. Come." She stood, and walked to a bookcase. Dorothy followed. She pulled a large, hardbound book off the shelf and handed it to Dorothy. "This is our textbook."

Dorothy took the book, feeling its heft in both hands.

"You will need to be caught up through the second unit by the end of the week. We are starting differentiation tomorrow, and I need you to understand what limits are."

"Got it," said Dorothy.

"And this," said Miss Hill, pulling another, slightly smaller book from the shelf, "is your pre-calculus textbook. You can skip most of it, but chapters five through seven hit most of the trig you are going to need. You'll want to be caught up with that by about two weeks from now. Just do the chapter tests and hand those in to me. If you have questions, please find me after school."

She handed over this book as well. Dorothy clutched the heavy books to her chest. "Got it. Anything else?"

Miss Hill laughed. "No, that should do it." She shook her head. "Girl, you are heaven sent."

"No ma'am," said Dorothy, beaming. "I'm in heaven right now."

<hr/>

When Dorothy returned to her room, her caseworker, Melissa, waited for her there. "There you are! Heard we had some more excitement today!"

"Oh, you." Dorothy dropped her books on her bed. "Yes, very exciting."

Melissa smiled. "I heard all about it. Everything is good now, I understand?"

"Hmm." Dorothy tapped her chin. "Let's say it's good for now."

"I assume you heard your adoption was approved today?"

Dorothy lit up. "Harrison? Is he here?"

"Not at the moment, I'm afraid. Should be soon, though. I hear you're moving out tonight."

"Oh." Dorothy pouted. "Well, I have plenty to do until he gets here. Is Mitchell here? Does he know?"

"Yes, he is, and no, I don't think so. I thought it would be best for him to hear it from you. I also need to make you aware as of now, both of you are off my docket."

"Thank you. I'm sure we'll be fine," said Dorothy. She put out her hand. "Thanks for everything. Sorry if I was a grouch about it."

"I've seen worse." She shook Dorothy's hand. "If you still need anything, you can always contact me through Youth Services."

"All I need right now is to find my brother."

"Do you know your way around the building?"

"I think so," said Dorothy.

"Then I guess my work here is done," said Melissa. "Take care."

Dorothy headed over to the boys' wing of the Adoption Center, dragging her finger along the lockers on the wall the whole way there, with a satisfying, metallic *clack-clack-clack*. She knocked at Mitchell's room before opening the door.

"Mitchell?" she said, poking her head in. A handful of boys about his age turned to look at her.

"He's not here," said one of them.

"Any idea where he went?" she asked.

"Nope," he said, and went back to whatever little boy thing he was doing. Two others giggled.

"Well, that was helpful!" said Dorothy. Irresistibly, she giggled herself.

These children, like her, like everyone, had lost their entire worlds, and had doubtless endured hardships on their way to safety here, yet still took joy in teasing a girl.

She found him in a lounge. Like every other room in the Adoption Center, this was an adapted classroom. The desks had been removed in favor of several couches, card tables, and other assorted furniture of leisure activity. Mitchell stood at a pool table with two boys slightly older than he, holding a cue.

"Mitchell?"

He looked over to Dorothy and waved. She sat down on a couch and patted the spot next to her. Mitchell consulted briefly with the two older boys, who promptly checked Dorothy out, took his cue and patted him on the back. Time would tell if that scored them any points with her.

"Hope springs eternal," she whispered to no one in particular.

"Hey," said Mitchell, sitting down.

"Hi there. How was your day?"

"Good," he said. The simple certainty and succinctness of childhood.

"That's good," she said.

"How was yours?"

She thought about this for a moment. "Complicated. But good. I think very good."

"When is dinner?" he asked.

"I haven't the foggiest. My plan was just to follow these people, or listen for a bell." She took his hand, earning her a look of caution. "Hey, I need to let you know, we're not staying here."

The look of caution turned to one of apprehension. "Why?"

She shook her head gently. "It's nothing bad. Harrison is coming to pick us up soon. We're going to live with him."

"He's not in trouble?"

"Not as far as I know," said Dorothy. "In fact, he has adopted both of us."

"Whoa! Does that mean he's our father now?"

"Oh, Mitchell!" she said, laughing. "He's been our father this whole time."

HOME

Finding the radio station proved too ambitious an objective. By the time Harrison made it to the street, Claudia was obviously long gone, so he could not follow her. Worse, he had only been in New Chicago for one day, nowhere near enough time to understand the random layout of the reborn city. What little remained of the original infrastructure was scattered and widely spaced, with a vast array of log cabins and occasional futuristic towers mixed in, the roads so far nothing more than paths of beaten dirt. Given the arbitrary state of current technology, he could not be sure the radio station would even have an antenna tower or any other feature he would recognize. Even if he knew where to look, he might not see it right in front of him.

Fifteen minutes into following a trail that apparently led everywhere, he gave in to his emotional and physical exhaustion and collapsed on a nearby wooden bench. Claudia would simply have to hate him for the time being.

The late autumn weather had grown milder this day. Alone, and unable to complete his self-imposed mission, Harrison took the moment to enjoy the fresh air. From his vantage point, hundreds of people went about their new lives, wrapped up in the business of rebuilding human civilization nearly from scratch. Odd vehicles passed by sporadically, but most of the people trekked from one part of the makeshift city to another on foot.

A woman came along the path, pushing an umbrella stroller with a sleeping toddler in it. She pulled the stroller up to the edge of the bench and parked it. "Do you mind if I sit down?"

She appeared to be in her early twenties, with remarkably fair skin. Hair so blonde as to be nearly white peeked out from a wool cap.

"Not at all." Harrison scooted aside to give her ample room on the bench. As she sat, he leaned forward to look at the child. Layers of protection from the cold concealed the toddler's gender. Dramatically dark skin peeked out between scarf and hat. He grinned. "And who is this?"

She smiled and adjusted the child's clothing, though to no obvious effect. "This is Celia."

"Is she yours?" he asked.

"She sure is."

"How old is she?"

The woman turned to look at him. "I'm guessing two, but we'll never really know. Are you new here?"

"Just got in this week. My name's Harrison." He extended a hand. She took it.

"Thought so," she said. "Elaine. You're going to meet a lot of children like Celia here. Every one adopted. The youngest ones don't have much in the way of history, unfortunately. Celia was lucky. She at least knew her name."

"I've got two kids," he said.

"Two!" Elaine exclaimed. "Then I guess you don't need the tutorial." She laughed. "Sorry about that. Celia and I were two of the earliest settlers here. I feel like I've had to do so much explaining about her it's reflex now. How far did you come?"

"Well," said Harrison, "Massachusetts, first. I picked up my... uh, son in New York, my daughter, in Wisconsin."

Elaine offered him a quizzical look. "That's pretty roundabout."

"Yeah, that's a very long story." For a moment, neither of them spoke, then he added, "Someone tried to kill me on the way here."

Elaine gasped. "What?"

"No lie." He stared off in the distance. "Sabotaged a train to do it. Damn near killed my best friend in the process. For a while there, I thought she was dead."

Elaine absorbed this in silence. "Why?" she finally asked, with awe in her eyes.

"I have no idea," he said.

She stared at him curiously, but said nothing.

He let the silence linger for a moment. "Can I ask you a question?"

"Sure."

He cleared his throat. "Back in May, when everything went... well, when everything went. Did you wonder what happened?"

"Of course," she said. "Didn't you?"

"Honestly?" He gave his head a shake. "Not really. Not at first, anyway. At the time, it seemed like one more damn thing. I got to quit my job, so that was an upside."

He waited a moment for her to react, but she said, "Go on."

"It's different now," he said. "It's not just me anymore. It all matters now. I have to know. Someday." He shook his head again. "Maybe not today. But at some point, I'm going to have to know." He frowned. "Am I making any sense at all?"

"Probably more than you think," she said.

He sighed and looked away. "Meanwhile, I have another albatross. Do you know where the radio station is?"

She rolled her eyes. "If you're looking to meet Claudia, you're in for a surprise."

He gave a half-smile. "It's not like that. We've already met. I think I owe her an apology."

"For what?" Elaine asked, raising an eyebrow.

Harrison thought about it. "I'm not sure, actually. Probably not whatever you're thinking, though."

"I'll take your word for it. So, what do you plan to tell her, to apologize for not-whatever-I'm-thinking?"

He threw his arms up in defeat. "I don't know. It just... it turns out we're going to be working together. She and I are like mutant freaks or something."

She gave him a new, appraising look. "Are you that guy they arrested at the CVS?"

He closed his eyes and pinched the bridge of his nose. "Yeah." Pause. "Anyway, we didn't exactly hit it off. I just... Uh, I want to apologize for not thanking her the moment I first saw her. I want to explain to her this whole trip out here for me, it was all about her." Another pause. "And everything I keep running through my head to tell her sounds fake, even to me."

"I bet I know why," Elaine said, and when Harrison looked up from his wallowing, she offered him a sympathetic smile.

"What? Everybody went through this?" he said. "She's probably so sick of hearing it, it won't mean a damn thing, coming from me. Right? I mean, you had the same experience, didn't you? You came all this way for her, didn't you?"

"Actually, my journey was about someone else entirely."

Harrison waited for her to drop the other shoe. In the silence, Celia yawned and opened her intense brown eyes. He shook his head with a soft, tired laugh. "I'm completely stupid, aren't I?"

"I don't know," said Elaine. "I just met you."

"First impression?"

She thought for a moment. "I think you're confused."

He shook his head again, this time with certainty and confidence. "Not anymore, I'm not. Forget the radio station. Can you point me to the lake?"

The centaur camp was surprisingly vast. They had staked out a stretch of lakefront property that amounted to a hamlet, at least. Rather than an exclusive centaur club, the area included a number of humans wandering there, taking in the sights, swimming, and generally interacting with the half-horses. A large, bearded centaur unselfconsciously defecated in the middle of a discussion with two teenage boys. Living in this community would be an entirely new level of culture shock.

He waved down a passing centaur. "Excuse me!" he called to a small group (or perhaps herd). They all turned to look at him, and a female galloped right up to him. She showed no concern toward her state of undress. Naturally, centaurs would be a top-free people. Or rather, as she also clearly wore no pants, not top-free, stark naked.

"What can I do for you?" she asked.

"Have you seen a pixie come through here?" he asked.

"Glimmer? Sure. Need me to take you to her?"

"That would be great. Thanks!"

She bent all four knees and lowered herself to the ground. Harrison hesitated as the nature of her offer became clear. "I've... never ridden a horse before."

"Well, I'm no horse," she shot back, "so hop on."

Harrison put his hand on her back, then shied away. "I don't know. It feels like I should buy you dinner first or something."

"Ha!" She laughed and stood up. "All right, little boy. Keep up." With that, she made a show of trotting off. Harrison had to jog the whole way. By the time they reached Glimmer, his heart pounded.

"Harry?" Glimmer sat perched on the back of a male centaur, nude, and apparently quite comfortable. "I thought you wanted to be alone."

"I thought so too," he said. "Turns out I was wrong. Put your poodle skirt back on. We're going to get the kids."

School had let out by the time they got back to the city, so they went straight to the Adoption Center. Neither of the children were in their rooms. It took a few minutes to locate them in the lounge. Mitchell was watching a DVD with a dozen other kids. Dorothy, sitting by a window and reading a novel, looked up to see Harrison walk in the door.

"Harrison!" She took a moment to carefully mark her place with an index card, then jumped up and ran into his arms.

"Glimmer!" Mitchell shouted. He jumped up from his movie and ran to the pixie.

Dorothy looked up from hugging Harrison. "Glimmer? This is Glimmer? You're not dead!"

"I'm not dead."

From that point, the children stumbled over each other piling questions on Harrison.

"Listen," he said. "I have a job now, and we all have a place to live together. They gave us two connected hotel rooms with a little kitchen. It's going to be a tight squeeze, but it's a nice building."

"Are we moving right now?" Dorothy asked.

"If you want. How quickly can you pack?"

"We're packed already." She grinned.

Harrison took in the sight of his family. Early the next morning, he would start a new career as a super-powered secret agent. He would be working with an organization with a mission to learn what had actually happened to the world, and whether it could be reversed. Somewhere in there, he hoped to use his new position and resources to learn who had tried to kill him, and why. But even in the face of all those grand developments and questions, all that mattered to him in this moment were two children and a pixie.

"Are we supposed to call you Dad now?" asked Mitchell.

Harrison laughed. "You can call me whatever you want, sport."

[40]

GOODBYE

Dorothy stood in the bitter cold in a barren dirt lot. In the center of the city, an entire block had been set aside for a special construction project, to be a memorial to the fallen. Survivors had been submitting names for inclusion, and the number had already grown to the hundreds of thousands. Though it would still be months until they broke ground, the city encouraged residents to visit the site. Lacking graves for their loved ones, hundreds of mourners toured the grounds every day, willing it to suffice.

In a crude rectangle she had drawn with her toe in the dirt, Dorothy laid a single piece of paper with three names written on it: Theresa O'Neill, Lorraine O'Neill, and Fiona O'Neill. She weighted the corners down with loose pebbles and crouched to take in her makeshift headstone.

"Mom," she said, "Lorraine, Fiona, I made it. I'm okay. I don't know where your names are going to end up here, but I promise I will visit once they are." She looked around her at other visitors having similar conversations with similar temporary grave markers. "I wish you could see the place. It doesn't look like much yet, but it's going to be amazing. It's people, doing that thing people do. Surviving, fixing the bad."

Dorothy sat on the ground, easily ignoring its coldness. "This is the first time we've really talked, isn't it? There's so much that's happened. I lived in a mall for a while. Hallmark store. Lorraine, you would have loved what I did with it."

She paused there, allowing herself a smile.

"You know, I really didn't want to have to grow up this fast. But I guess that's always who I was, right? Big sister? Second mom?" She sighed. "I miss having an actual mom."

Dorothy reached down and brushed her mother's name with her fingertips. "The thing is, somehow, I managed to pull a dad out of all this. That's new, right? Whoa, what's a dad?" She pictured her mother laughing, and joined in briefly and lightly. "No, but really, he's great. I've hardly had to train him at all. Oh, and I have a brother now. What's that about?"

She held for more imaginary laughter, but got none.

"You can't be replaced. None of you can. I love you all, so much. But I want you to know I'm okay. I have someone to take care of me. And honestly? I'm doing an okay job of taking care of myself. So don't worry about me, all right?"

Dorothy looked away for a moment to collect herself. Harrison and Mitchell approached, having wrapped up their visits with lost ones. Harrison sat next to her, while Mitchell stood, gazing around. Glimmer fluttered in and landed on Harrison's shoulder. Dorothy found the pixie delightful, but that would still take some getting used to.

"How are we doing?" asked Harrison.

"Hey, Mom," said Dorothy smiling. "This is the guy. Harrison, Mom. Mom, Harrison."

"Ma'am," said Harrison, tipping an imaginary hat. "You've raised quite the remarkable lady here. You should be very proud."

"Why, thank you," said Dorothy. "See, Mom? A little rough around the edges, but I think he'll polish up just right."

Glimmer cupped her hands around her mouth, and whispered into Harrison's ear, loudly enough for Dorothy to hear. "Who are we talking to?"

Harrison put his finger over his lips. Glimmer pouted, then sat down on his shoulder with her arms crossed. Dorothy laughed lightly.

"Do you need more time?" Harrison asked. "I think the boy might have reached his threshold."

"Give me half a minute, and then we can go get something to eat," she said.

"You got it." He stood, and walked off with Mitchell toward the edge of the lot.

Dorothy sighed. "I guess that's all I have for now. I have to go spend some time with my new family. They're not the same, but they're pretty great."

She kissed her fingertips, and touched the names on the list, lingering for a few seconds on each.

After a longing stare at the paper fluttering in the breeze, she stood and raced off.

ACKNOWLEDGMENTS

As always, I must first pay my gratitude to Guinevere Crescenzi, who brought me into her writers group twelve years ago and catalyzed my transformation from hobbyist to author. That group critiqued and nudged along the first draft of *Static Mayhem*, elements of which formed the core of this very book. To that end, I owe additional thanks to Steve Carabello, Paul Murray, and Kate McGourty for their contributions, reaching across more than a decade now.

Similarly, my thanks go out to Lori Bentley-Law, Mitch Geller, and Michelle Montgomery for their contributions and observations as I workshopped an early draft on TheNextBigWriter.com of what would eventually become this novel.

Special thanks to Sol Nasisi, who took a chance on the original version of *Static Mayhem* by publishing it through WorldMaker Media. So many factors have contributed to my progress and momentum as a writer, but signing that first publishing contract must count as one of the most significant. I must doubly thank Sol for working with the good people of Curiosity Quills to help bring the newly revised and expanded *Prelude to Mayhem* and *Static Mayhem* to a greater audience.

My continuing gratitude goes out to my mother, Rosemary Morgan, who passed away only a few months before my first novel was published. So much of who I am, and how that translates into the pages of my books, springs from her encouragement, wisdom and humor. Having been a big fan of the original *Static Mayhem*, she surely would have been delighted to see how it has grown. The Mayhem Wave is very much her grandchild.

Lastly, I would like to extend my deepest thanks to my daughters Thessaly, Delphi and Aenea, and their beautiful mother Annelisa Aubry-Walton. They have paid the dearest price for my success as a novelist, the time I have stolen from all of them to pursue my crazy stories. I hope the results of my obsession come close to making up for that sacrifice, and I thank them for forgiving my indulgence of loosely basing some of my characters on their delightful selves. I can honestly say they are the only people from my real life who have found homes in my imaginary playgrounds. But really, why would I ever want to go into those worlds without them?

ABOUT THE AUTHOR

Edward Aubry is a graduate of Wesleyan University, with a degree in music composition. Improbably, this preceded a career as a teacher of high school mathematics and creative writing.

He now lives in rural Pennsylvania with his wife and three spectacular daughters, where he fills his non-teaching hours spinning tales of time-travel, wise-cracking pixies, and an assortment of other impossible things.

ALSO BY EDWARD AUBRY

Unhappenings

When Nigel is visited by two people from his future,
he hopes they can explain why his past keeps
rewriting itself. His search for answers takes him
fifty-two years forward in time, where he meets
Helen, brilliant, hilarious and beautiful.
Unfortunately, that meeting has triggered events that
will cause millions to die. Desperate to find a
solution, he discovers the role his future self has
played all along.

The Mayhem Wave Series

On May 30, 2004, the world suddenly transformed into a bizarre landscape
populated with advanced technology, dragons, magic and destruction. Now what
few humans remain must start over, braving wilderness, dangerous beasts, and
new and powerful enemies.

Prelude to Mayhem

Static Mayhem

Mayhem's Children

Balance of Mayhem

Made in the
USA
Middletown, DE